Tales From The Creek: 2025

SCMS 8th grade

Contents

Foreword

Anklestone

> I travel that path no longer, but sometimes I wonder
>
> as I watch children enter the tangled, interwoven trails
>
> which only they can navigate with the arcane knowledge of youth
>
> I wonder whether they are plagued by the same stone
>
> that once snapped at my ankles
>
> as a wolf might bite at it's mother's tail.
>
> I wonder whether they are caught unexpectedly
>
> by the slight, gradual curve on the trail
>
> onto which this jagged edge protrudes
>
> an adamantine serpent penetrating young flesh
>
> Sometimes... I can't help...
>
> wondering about Anklestone.

There is nothing profound about the poem above, except that it was written. It was written because an English teacher named Dr. Lanza pulled me aside and told me to write. Then he encouraged me, corrected me, pushed me, and showed me I could do it. There are few joys greater in a teacher's life than watching a student learn "I can do this."

I am proud of my students. They took time each week to write a 500 word or more story. For most, writing became a normal rhythm of life. They were given prompts in fiction, nonfiction, and even poetry. At the end of the third quarter students had an opportunity to edit and submit their favorite work. This is the collection of those submissions. In addition, we have included here several pieces of art for our students who participated in that Related Art course.

It is my hope you will enjoy reading these as I did. As I would tell my students, perhaps they will generate for you thoughts, questions, ponderances, percolations, ruminations, or... (dramatic pause)... palavers.

Mr. Harwood

This year's anthology is dedicated to Jayley Shadrick.

6/23/2011 – 10/16/2024

The 'Real' World

by Trinity Shipley

"This is boring!" Charlie whined as the sound of the car tires running along the road hummed in the background. She was around fourteen with short brown hair that matched her eyes, she was wearing a large hoodie and jeans. She always preferred a more ambiguous look.

"C'mon Char..." her mother groaned as she had heard that phrase so many times she was close to snapping. Her mother had thick dark brown hair that contrasted with her grayish-blue eyes. She always wore church dresses and eyeshadow that matched her winter color palette.

"But it's so booooring." Charlie fussed once more. She wished this car ride would end. They had been in the car for what seemed like eternity (thirty minutes) and even then there was more to go. "How much longerrr?"

Their mother sighed, "About three more hours." She braced herself for Charlie's reaction.

"*THREE HOURS!?*" Charlie yelped as she leaned forward in her seat, shocked by the amount of time it would take to go from New York to Maryland. She let out an exaggerated groan and slumped back in her seat, ever since her mom and dad divorced things never went her way. She leaned heavily on the car door, the seatbelt pressing uncomfortably onto her neck, "I hate this."

"I know but once we get there it will all be worth it, I promise." Her mom chirped, trying to keep a positive attitude. She gripped the steering wheel tightly as she tried to keep herself from scolding her daughter. She kept her voice high and proud despite it all. Charlie groaned once more but nearly lept out of her seat when she looked out of the window. The sky was cloudy and gray, it looked like it was about to storm. She had always hated storms.

"Mom, can we speed up? I don't wanna get caught in the rain." She groaned at her mom, who was still trying to stay positive. Her mom sighed as her knuckles turned white on the steering wheel and she glanced at her lap for a swift moment before looking back out towards the road.

"No Charlie, I'm not speeding up." Her mother groaned as she kept her usual pace. But her daughter continued to groan and whine about the rain, Charlie slumped back further into her seat. "Sit up." Her mother hissed, "If we got into an accident you'd get really injured sitting like that."

A few minutes later the rain finally catches up to them; within moments it begins pounding down onto the car, filling their ears with the sound. As the minutes go on the mother's line of vision out of the front windshield starts to close in, even with the windshield wipers on their highest speed. Her mother looked back at Charlie, who had her headphones in and was still slouched back in her seat with her head resting on her seatbelt.

Charlie looked up to meet her mother's gaze, her bored expression quickly turned to one of terror as she saw through the rain on the windshield that while her mother was distracted they were starting to slide out of control. "Mom, eyes on the road!" Charlie yelped as her heart was nearly beating out of her chest. Her mom quickly turned around and gripped the steering wheel tighter.

"It's ok, Char." Her mother mumbled as she yanked the steering wheel in the opposite direction of where they were sliding. She instantly regretted their decision as the car spun around on the slippery road. She tried to put the car back on course but they were going too fast. Charlie squeezed her eyes shut and curled into a ball as the car slid into a tree.

"Wh...what happened..?"

Charlie gently opened her eyes and saw... her *bedroom?!* She examined her walls, the same faded posters and baby blue walls. Her beige bedspread was as bleak as she remembered, **Was it all a dream?**

She sat up in bed and rubbed her eyes, for a split second she got a flash of what looks like a hospital. She immediately opened her eyes and got out of bed, walking to her window. **What is that?** She thought as she gazed out of her window, seeing a gaping hole in the backyard with nothing but an inky abyss at the bottom. She quickly backed away from her window and tried to remove that image from her mind, but it was almost like it was calling out to her.

Charlie nearly jumped out of her skin when she heard a loud knock on her bedroom door, with cautious steps she tiptoed closer. The knocking got louder and she heard a voice from the other side of the door, "Charlie, are you awake?" It was her father's voice.

"Yes" Charlie called back towards her father's voice, her mind racing with questions. **Was it all a dream? What happened to mom? It felt so real...** she quickly pushed the thoughts away as she creaked open her door and saw her father standing outside, happy as ever.

"Good morning Char, your mom made pancakes!" Her dad singsonged, his blonde wavy hair bouncing along with him. Charlie couldn't help but smile as she looked into her father's brown eyes, he didn't seem to show any distress.

A subtle memory flashed across Charlie's mind, "Dad?" Her voice was quiet, almost hesitant to ask.

"Yes, sweetheart?" Her father hummed with his usual energetic tone.

Charlie's voice trembled slightly as she reluctantly piped up, "What about the divorce? I thought me and mom were meant to be leaving today."

Her father's face flashed with confusion and worry, "What divorce, sweetie? It must have been just a bad dream, your mother and I are as happy as ever."

Yeah... it must have been just a bad dream. Charlie reassured herself as she followed her father downstairs. The aroma of pancakes and syrup filled the air as they trotted closer to the kitchen. She peeked inside and saw her mother next to the stove cooking pancakes, not noticing her yet.

Charlie walked closer and her mom perked up, swiftly turning around. "Hey, sweetheart, are you hungry?" She hummed as she ruffled Charlie's hair.

"You bet I am!" Charlie sang, she took a deep breath. But she couldn't help but remember the pit in the backyard, it felt like it was trying to pull her closer. Charlie shoved the feeling of dread into the back of her mind, but it still lingered there.

The rest of the day goes on like usual: Charlie eats breakfast, gets dressed, goes to school and talks with her friends, gets back home and does her homework, eats dinner, and gets into her pajamas for bed. But she can't shake the feeling that something is off, everyone seems too happy... too unchanging... too *normal*. She brushed her hair and looked back out the window, staring into the abyss inside of the hole.

Suddenly, a voice rang in her ears, "Charlie... can you hear us?" She couldn't recognize this voice. She stared further into the pit, backing away from her window. **This isn't right... something's off.** She walked to her parent's room and peeked in.

"Mom?" She called out, and within seconds her mother appeared before her. Wearing her usual nightgown and her hair in a low ponytail.

"Yes honey" her mother yawned, rubbing her eyes. She cocked her head to the side, curious for what Charlie had to say.

"Is all of this...." she hesitated before finishing her sentence, "real?"

It was almost as if the life was drained out of her mother's face, the silence more deafening than a jet engine. "Yes" her mom mumbled, "This is real. The 'real' world." Charlie felt uneasy from the way her mother mumbled the word "real" and turned to walk away.

"Ok... I'm gonna go to bed now... goodnight, mom." She quickly walked back to her room, not even looking back at her mother. She layed on her bed and tried to push the feeling of dread away, but it kept creeping back. Charlie took a deep breath and made a plan, she was going to see what was in that pit.

She waited until her parents were sure to be asleep before she snuck downstairs and opened the back door, walking closer to the pit. The closer she got, the more it seemed like it was calling out to her. More and more voices rang in her head, all telling her to wake up and that everything would be ok. She took a deep breath and jumped into the pit, a warm feeling spreading throughout her body as she quickly sat up, her eyelids shooting open.

She looked around and saw... a hospital room? It was the same one from when she woke up at home... or was that her home? She looked to her right and saw her dad, his face laced with tears; he quickly hugged her and held her tight.

"Oh thank God" he mumbled, "I was so worried about you." He kissed her forehead and sat beside her on the hospital bed. Just as Charlie was about to speak, she quickly remembered her *"dream"* from earlier, her eyes widened.

"Where's mom!?" Her voice was shaky with worry.

Her father's face turned pale as he looked towards the floor. "I'm sorry, Char... she didn't make it out of the crash." The words dripped from his mouth like tears, laced with sorrow. Charlie's breath caught in her throat as he uttered those words, she tried to choke back her tears.

A nurse peeked into the room, "Oh, she's awake?" She spoke with grace. The nurse stepped closer to Charlie and began checking her vitals, noticing her distress. "I'm sorry for your loss, but at least now you're back in the real world."

Jayley Aleeh Shadrick: The Events Leading Up to Her Passing, My Side of the Story.

by Lex Hixson

This all started on Monday, October 14th 2024. I had just got home from Louisiana because my great grandma passed away and we went to her funeral. I found out Jayley was in a really bad accident and she was badly injured. That night, along with the next day, I just prayed and prayed and hoped she would be ok. That way, we could all have our sweet Jayley back.

Then October 16th comes... I found out that morning that they were going to do the last test on Jaybug. If she had no brain activity, they were going to take her off life support. If she had brain activity and survived she would have been paralyzed from the neck down. Through the day I was so worried she wasn't going to make it but based on her injuries I had doubts that she would make it. I kept getting updates from her family throughout the day. Then 11pm rolls around... Jocelyn called me crying and I knew as soon as I heard her voice I knew that Jayley had passed away then she told me the news. I laid in bed for two hours and cried.

The next few days (October seventeenth and eighteenth) nothing felt real. I just lied in bed and didn't go anywhere until October 18th. That night I went to Jayley's visitation, it still didn't feel real even though I saw her in the casket and touched her, I still couldn't believe it. The next day it was her funeral and it still didn't feel real but then they played *Pink Skies* by Zach Bryan (that is the song she wanted played at her funeral if she ever died young, which is something she shouldn't have had to think about) and I completely lost it, that's when it hit me that she was actually gone and it wasn't just a dream. Her pastor from her church preached her entire service beautifully. It was just the way she would've wanted it. Her casket was pink and she was wearing a grey hoodie with *Hello Kitty* and the Chevy logo and all of her flowers were pink. At the end of her service before we went to the cemetery, I walked up to her to touch her hair one last time because I used to play with it all the time.

Jayley was such a kind and caring young lady. She has so many people who love and miss her so much. I feel like I know so much about her but I don't at the same time, I only had a short two months to get to know her. In those short two months we made so many memories together. She was so funny and her laugh was contagious. Her and Caiden went so well together, they were my favorite couple.

All of this has taught me to deal with loss and never to take someone for granted because you never know what is going to happen. Everything can change in the blink of an eye. I think I have definitely matured mentally since this has all happened even though it's been really hard. I just hope Jayley has strong wings and I know she is walking those streets of gold up in Heaven.

"Your funeral was beautiful I bet God heard you coming" -Zach Bryan

"when I talked to you this morning I said I'll see you soon would have said so much more if I knew that you'd be in heaven by noon" -Megan Moroney

Time

by Layla Brooks

Time

    Ticking

Fast

You're in kindergarten

First day of school

I'm so excited to be in 6th grade

I'll be so old

Time

Ticking

Fast

You're in middle school

First day of school

I'm so excited to be in 9th grade

I'll be so old

Time
    Ticking
    Fast
    You're in high school
    I'm so excited to graduate
    I'll be so old

Time
    Ticking
    Fast
    You've graduated
    I'm so excited to get married
    I'll be so old

Time
    Ticking
    Fast
    You're married
    I'm so excited to be a mom
    I'll be so old

Time
    Ticking
    Fast
    It's your child's first day of kindergarten
    She comes home
    She says
    "I'm so excited to be in 6th grade"
    "I'll be so old."

Fishing

by Derrick Turner

My hobby is fishing. To be a great fisherman, there are certain terms you need to know. Knowing these terms will help you have a conversation with other fishermen and not get made fun of. The most important terms are live scope, reels, and bag limit.

The live scope, also known as a forward-facing sonar, is a type of sonar that is new to fishermen. A live scope allows fishermen to see the fish under the water. If you learn how to properly use the live scope, then it can tell all types of things that would be helpful to catch fish. If you learn the live scope, you can watch your bait in real time; you may even see your bait falling through the water on the screen. You can see the fish hit the bait on the screen before you even feel it. On the graph screen, you can adjust the depth to however deep the water is. This will be helpful so that you know how deep the fish are. You can also make adjustments on how far out the graph can be viewed, similar to the graphs in math classes. Depending on how clear or murky the water is, you can adjust your graph screen to see better in the water. Now that we can view the water, we need to choose what kind of reel should be used.

There is an appropriate type and size of reel to use for every species of fish. For beginners, a spin-cast reel is probably the best option. To use it, all you have to do is hold the button in, and when you cast, let go of it. The button, not the rod. Time to move on to bass fishing. This is where it gets tricky. There is a type of reel and gear ratio or speed of reel for every bait. For a slower, more finesse bait, you would want a slower gear ratio reel. For a faster bait, you would want a medium to fast gear ratio reel. When it comes to ultra-light bass fishing, using lightweight baits and fishing line, you would want a 1,500 size to a 2,500 size reel. The size of the reel increases as the bait size increases. Now that we know what size reel to use, we need to discuss bag limits.

A bag limit is how many fish you can keep in a tournament. In big bass tournaments (when the biggest bass wins), you can keep up to five fish. In small dog-fight tournaments, tournaments with less than fifty people, sometimes the limit is only three fish. No matter what the limit, if you catch all your fish and then you catch one bigger than one of the fish you already have, you can cull the smaller one. Cull means to throw out or get rid of the smaller fish. Anyway.

All of these terms are important for you to learn before you start fishing. Knowing the terms will help your fishing game when other, more experienced fishermen help you. This may be just my hobby right now, but I would like to turn it into my career.

Jayley Aleeh Shadrick 6.23.11 – 10.16.24

by Abigaile Hanley

The saddest part of my whole life was losing my best friend, Jayley. I've lost many people but I was really young so I didn't really understand. The day before she passed away we were on the phone and the last thing she said to me was "byeee I love you and I will see you after fall break" and just knowing that I would never see her alive after that. Dealing with the loss of a girl that was like a sister to you is going to be very hard on you mentally, I haven't been the same since I found out she was gone and there was no saving her. I wish I could've stopped her from going but when I think of her I always think of the quote "God doesn't put you through things you can't handle". It's always going to be hard on me and I probably won't ever heal from losing her and actually I know I won't but I will get better at handling it.

How I found out

I didn't know about how she passed until Aspen told me about it**(not saying how she passed because of privacy reasons)**. Aspen texted me and said "Jayley is in the hospital and they don't know if she will make it" . Right when I got that text my whole body went numb it was like I couldn't speak at all. I remember bursting out tears because I was hoping she would be okay, but that never happened. I found out she passed away right when everyone else found out because her uncles texted me since I was one of her best friends and told me that she was no longer with us. I have never felt the same after I got the news that my best friend wasn't here anymore. She already entered the gates of Heaven and is with God. After she passed away, I didn't eat for a while besides when Aspen told me I needed to eat and everything will be okay.

Her Funeral and Visitation

The day of her visitation, which is when you can go see her with her casket open, I broke down in front of the casket because it was hard to see my best friend like that and then I touched her hand and it was stone cold and her hands were always warm. I was crying so much to the point that it was getting hard to breathe so I had to step outside for a minute. I went back in and saw her again and I played with her hair for the last time. Her visitation was on October 18th and her funeral was on October 19th, her funeral was probably the hardest part for me because I didn't know it was also open-casket so I wasn't prepared to see her like that and knowing my Jayley would never wake up. They played "Pink Skies" by Zach Bryan and i was crying a lot because that was the song she told me she wanted to play at her funeral if she ever died young, she was only thirteen.

Her Burial

After her funeral all of her family and friends lined up behind the hearse which is the car that carried her casket to her final resting place. Once we got to the cemetery our friend group and her friends from her hometown got to go near her casket so we could say our final goodbyes and her grandpa Mike told us to get a rose off her casket and we could also put it on top of the casket before they put dirt over her. I put a pink rose on her casket because her favorite color was pink.

Going to Her Grave after

Me and our friend group try to go to her grave on special holidays like New years eve and around Christmas time. We also got to see one of her friends from her hometown named Journey, she is very sweet. We plan to go the weekend after Valentine's day and bring Caiden, Jayley's boyfriend. Last time we went, Lex got her a Hello Kitty planter and we put pink flowers in it and a Hello Kitty bow onto the front flower.

Summary

I'm so thankful that I have my friends to help me get through this and I'm happy that I don't have to do it alone. I will forever cherish the moments me and Jayley had together. I only have videos and pictures of her now but that is okay because she may not be here physically but she is still going to always be there in our hearts.

Mysterious Hole in My Backyard

by Brooklyn Speller

I've all of a sudden woke up in the middle of the night. I have straight panic and fear with a slice of trembling throughout my body. It's maybe two thirty in the morning. I get up, and all I hear is a drill-like sound. I know that nobody's drilling through my yard, right? Gosh, that sound it's deeply agonising and harrowing. This noise is strange, but mainly because I haven't even gotten the chance to think, stretch, or yawn. All I know right now is that the sound is coming from the backyard, right outside my window.

I'm not going to dare to look though. I'm racing down the stairway to my parents bedroom. I forgot that they are on their sixth trip of the year up north. At this point, they left maybe three hours before I woke up. Wow. Now it really sinks in, I'm alone. I'm used to it but also not really. Usually I like to be alone, I just hate to feel lonely.

I know I have to do something. I think that this could be anything, but in the back of my head, I'm thinking the worst. It could be aliens, dinosaurs coming back, ultimately anything. I'm not thinking of the good at the moment. I blame fear. I'm finally gonna just take some deep breaths, try to relax. I'm hoping I will be okay. I know my mom and dad's car would be in the driveway in maybe five days or so.

As I open the drapes in the living room I see the stars highlighting a massive hole. I carefully and slowly walk up the steps to grab my phone and call authorities but then I think to myself "Wait. I want to explore." Deep down I know that curiosity always kills the cat. Either way I put the phone down.

I really want to see what happened in my backyard, I should be a courageous gal and go for it. So I do. I'm trying to put some pep in my step but I'm still pretty nervous. The door lets out a loud creak… almost as if it were just as scared as I was. My heart is pounding in my head. Like after you wake up in fear from a nightmare. I'm kind of hoping it is one. I pinch myself, it's not a nightmare.

I make it to the hole, taking a deep breath, and I look beneath me. The stars aren't beaming it up this time. Carefully, I climb back in. It feels like dirt and grass. Literally nothing is really weird at all, other than the fact there is a hole in my yard in the middle of the night. I start to climb back out, then I suddenly feel something furry touch my foot. This took me by surprise and it sent shivers down my spine. That freaked me out.

But I peek back down, and I'm seeing nothing. I quickly climb back in, I felt around for whatever it was that just touched me. I surprisingly hear a "meow." I know exactly what's happening to me, I'm just tired and hearing things and nothing actually touched me. I'm getting up from the dirt as I dust myself off and climb back up to normal ground. I walk back into my house then I hear a "meow" again. I'm following the sound and suddenly, the destruction in my yard wasn't just a hole.

It's best to say I was more than just shocked to my core. The best way to describe this thing is as a portal to an alternate dimension. This cat is dust particles. It gave me little to no guidance. The best way to describe it is that it is a void of darkness. Uh, what a way to make me panic!

I want to ask the cat if it would go away, so I do. "Hey, buddy. Do you mind leaving?" Weirdly enough, it happily says, "I'm not real, pal." Oh? So a talking cat is with me I guess? I'm just gonna leave the cat. I kind of feel bad, but it's literally a group of dust particles that talk. I wanted to explore around for a little bit, but there was nothing to explore. But for some reason I kept on going, until I can't see the opening of the hole anymore.

At this rate, there's no signs of life. I'm searching and searching for a way home but I have nothing; no clues, no signals. I miss my family; my parents, but I doubt they miss me. I'm getting desperate for some type of company. I don't even know how long I've been here. My family always takes "business trips". My dad works for Wall Street and for my mom... I have no clue. They always fight with me. They usually get mad when I stay in my room too long but can they even blame me? I don't wanna be upset at the moment, but I've been drastically depressed lately. If I'm being honest, part of me wants to stay stuck in this hole. I was digging myself deeper.

I think I'm going to keep going on optimistically, which will be hard. Hopefully I'll spot differences in anything, like the air. I'm pretty much just floating now. How fun. As I go further, the chillier and more humid it felt. Was this normal? Obviously, it wasn't. I feel so drained and tired at this point. I am floating in what feels like an endless black room. Instead of going forward with this, I'm gonna go backwards.

From where I'm beginning, I can't see much light, but I knew I wasn't blind. I'm squinting and hoping to find any light at all. After making no progress, I start to backfloat, except I'm not in water. I'm with my own thoughts before I manage to find a little glimpse of light, but still have no idea where I am. I am drowning in so much regret at the moment. Why would I do this to myself and why in the world would I leave the cat?

"Please someone help me!"But, I'm assuming no one heard a thing. I'm kind of scared of myself because I just screamed into a void of nothing-ness. This fear I'm feeling is encouraging me to keep going back. So I do.

While I'm on my side quest back, I'm just trying to look for any-thing, but I'm in a void of emptiness, but I know somewhere there has to be a way out. At this rate, since I'm so bored, It seems as if it's been a month since I've seen my bed, got sleep, ate, or had any entertainment. No wonder I'm so miserable. I'm thinking with my eyes shut. I'm thinking of everything I know and have experienced. I'm looking through my eyelids as if they're a pair of drapes over a window when I see some brightness. Like a street light type of brightness.

I'm putting my hands together as I pray to God that I've found my way home. Before my eyes open I say "amen" and take a deep breath. My eyes opened. I drew the drapes open. And all I see is my house.

"I have so much to look forward to." I think to myself before I exit whatever I've gotten myself into. I have a camping trip with my friends and I have cheerleading, I have school, and my parents, even though I'm not too excited for them. I started to see my way out of this void. All I'm capable of is laughing. I'm really pondering how I managed to get in that situation.

I slowly place a light step on the soft grass of my backyard. I exhale as I sluggishly walk. I make my way into my backyard door to my house and I close it after me. After I shut it behind me, I slide myself down and thoughts start pouring. I think to myself for a few minutes. Then I decided that I want to start sleeping. I yawn as I lock the doors. Then, I climb up the stairs slowly. I see my bed and I let out a joyful scream, I leap into it and rub my feet together as I get bundled up. Even though by this time it was almost four in the morning, I hope I sleep better knowing I found the light at the end of the tunnel.

Their Impact

by Charlotte Hayes

If I could write a book about anything in the world, I would write a memoir about the people and backstories of the relationship's between the people I love and care or cared about the most. I care and love a lot of people, so I would choose to write about the people who had made the biggest impact on me, good or bad. I would organize the book into chapters for every person I choose to write about. I would tell the reader how this person made me feel, what and how they did the thing they did, and their overall story.

The first person I would tell about first in my book is my mom. She died fairly young but she lived life to the fullest. My mom showed me what real love feels like. She was smart and she had the largest heart ever. She was kind to almost anyone. She was also very funny and was the light of a dark room. She was my best friend and my favorite person. Even though she was my role model she did have her downs, I wouldn't even try to realize them until many months after she died. My mom was an addict. I was around her when she wasn't sober all of the time and just being around that really impacted me. Her toxic boyfriend encouraged her through all of the drinking. He created so much anxiety in her life, and she had to get through it all alone and still stayed strong. The theme of this section of the story would be that some people may be going through alot and you wouldn't even know, but it is good to stay strong and always show love and kindness.

The next person I would write about in my book would most definitely be Avery Bates.

She is the type of person to act happy and fun to be around, but deep down is not really ever perfectly okay. Avery and I have both been through our ups and downs but even through it all we are still there for each other. She is always honest with me and has supported my decisions whether she thinks they are the best or not. But in closed doors we pour it all out to each other, and when we do it's almost like a magical moment. We both get what we each have going on, and we both listen to each other, then we comfort each other. The theme of this section of the book would be without question, that even though friends have a lot going on it's important to be there for each other, and to choose your friends wisely because if you do you may end up with an amazing friend like Avery Bates.

The third person I would write about would be about this guy. I loved him, and I still do. He was there for me when my mother died and he was also an example of someone who showed me love. He might seem like a jerk but I saw him when he wasn't. I saw how he acted towards my family and how he used to care for me. We are broken up now, for the third time. I would do anything to get him back but he is almost like a book, Because I have a feeling that each ending we have will be the same. I do know that he is not good for me but I still love him for when he was good to me. And it is hard to believe I was never enough, judging that there was always at least one other girl. The love he had for me was fake, but the love I had for him was not. I think I am attached to him because of my moms death, and he was the person that was there for me. I believe the theme of this section of the book would be, just because you love somebody does not always mean they are the best for you, or that you need them.

In conclusion I would say these are the three people who made a very large impact on me as a person, even if it was for the good or bad. I would dedicate this book to them for making me the person I am now. I love them all (maybe some more than others). The book would be called " Their Impact". There would obviously be more people in this book but these are the definite top three impacts on me.

The Three Billy Goats Gruff

by Carr Holzhauer

Once upon a time there were three billy goats, who were all named Gruff. They all wanted to cross the escalator to get to the movie theater to watch Inside Out 2™. The billy goats wanted to cross the elevator, but Trevor, the goat eating security guard, was defending it. He was a mean old security guard who didn't let any animals pass.

"Look! He is sleeping, we might be able to cross now!" said the oldest Billy Goat Gruff.

"Hurry along and we might get past before he notices!" said the middle Billy Goat Gruff.

"Ok," replied the youngest Billy Goat Gruff nervously. He trotted along to the elevator, "Trip trap, trip trap," he went.

"Zuhhh Zzzzz" the officer snored loudly. He couldn't hear the small goat over his snoring, so the first Billy Goat Gruff passed by without any problems.

Next came the middle Billy Goat Gruff, "Trip trap, trip trap," he went.

"Who's that trotting on my elevator?" the security guard said scarily.

"I am the second of the Billy Goats Gruff," he trembled. This talking to the man made his hooves clack on the ground. He barely made it up the elevator without falling.

"I'm gonna gobble you up!" the security guard roared,

"No, please, don't do that!"

"Why not?" the security guard sat up with an evil grin.

"The third Billy Goat Gruff is *way* fatter than I am," he answered.

"Alright, go on," the security guard answered.

Finally came the last of the Billy Goats Gruff, "Trip trap, trip trap," he went. He wasn't as foolish or scared as the other two. He knew he was able to get past the guard with a secret trick he had.

"Who's that trotting on my elevator?" the security guard roared.

"It is I! The third of the Billy Goats Gruff!" he answered, with a loud voice of his own.

"I'm gonna gobble you up!" the security guard roared.

"You can try as you'd like," he said, far braver than the others. "I've got two large buckets of popcorn and I'm ready to use them! Nothing you could do is going to stop me from seeing how Riley's teenage years are gonna play out!"

"I'd like to see you try to stop me!" the security guard challenged.

The third of the Billy Goats Gruff jumped off the elevator and landed right on top of the security guard. "Take this you old piece of junk," he poured both buckets of popcorn on the security guard. The security guard happened to be buried under a mountain of popcorn, and couldn't move.

The three Billy Goats Gruff then went on with their day, trotting past the elevator to the movie theater. There they bought more popcorn, and binge watched all the best movies for days. They became paunchy and plump after eating and watching movies to the point where they almost couldn't stand up.

There Is No Reason...

by Claire Freeman

There is no reason that schools need to meet five days a week. We already give them seven hours a day. If you play a sport or if you have something to do on Saturdays and if you go to church on Sundays like me then you most likely do not have any time to rest on the weekends. If we had only four days of school in a week then we could have at least one day of a break. Which could benefit everyone from parents to kids to even admin.

One way that I know that we do not need to go five days a week is in the text, "Green Light" studies say, " Increased Attendance: with longer weekends students will be less likely to miss school." This means that if we had four day weeks then the attendance rate would be so much better. This could benefit schools a lot, if we miss school and there is a better attendance rate then kids will miss less work and won't be behind in work.

"Journalists Studies", by Denise-Marie Ordway says, "Parents mention that they would like their children to have four day weeks because it would give them more family time together." This makes it even more beneficial for everyone more than just kids. People get to have more time with their family than they might normally get to. Some families might not even get to see their children at all so this would be helpful.

The last way that I know we do not need to go to school all five dyas is,"Linq Blogs" states, "According to a study conducted in 2018 by the Office of National Statistics in Great Britain, teachers do twenty percent of their work (ten hours or more) before school, after school and on weekends." This helps my case because studies say that this could even help teachers play an important role in the fact that schools should only meet four times a week. Also if the teachers are happy then everyone else is happy.Ha ha! If schools only met four times a week then teachers would also be able to spend time with their families and friends or do their hobbies.

The other side of this argument would disagree with me because kids might forget what the teachers would tell them or teach them. Green Light studies states, " There can be child care issues as families may struggle with finding childcare arrangements on the extra day off from school." They might say this because I do get that it could be hard for families to be able to find childcare arrangements.

Schools do not need to meet five days a week if we already give them seven hours a day. As you can tell by my evidence you know what side of this I am on. I do not like meeting g five times a week for many reasons and these are just a few of the reasons why I know that schools only need to meet four times a week. No hate to people who do think that schools should meet five times a week, but why?

Tommy

by Bo Howard

Fourteen-year-old Tommy looked extremely distraught as his mother drove away from his eccentric uncle's house in Muscle Shoals, Alabama. She assured him she would return as soon as the family emergency in Chattanooga allowed her to. He slowly turned around and entered the house. His Uncle Frank saw Tommy and his eyes started to water. It wasn't that Tommy didn't like his Uncle Frank. It was that Tommy was upset when he had to miss his football games.

As Tommy wipes the tears from his eyes, Uncle Frank suggests a tour of the old creepy house that has been in the family for years. At first glance, Tommy notices an exotic bird collection made up of different parrots that his uncle owns. Tommy enjoyed seeing the family history and birds, but the old art studio caught his attention the most. Tommy had always wanted and tried his hand at painting. Uncle Frank told Tommy he was welcome to use the art studio whenever he wished. Tommy was ecstatic about the endless possibilities in this art studio.

As the sun creeps through the window, Tommy rolls over to hear Uncle Frank enter his new room. Tommy's eyes pop open to see his uncle displaying a big smile while holding a kiss on the art teacher's coffee cup. I'm off to school this morning, "Tommy, so make yourself at home and remember to feed the birds, please". "I will be home around 4:00 p.m." I reply.

Tommy prepares a bowl of Cinnamon Toast Crunch as he hears his uncle's car drive away. The house is silent with the expectation of the parrots talking to each other. He decides to explore the Arts Studio and all it offers. The art studio is a bit spooky and creepy, especially when you're all alone. Tommy stumbles over a box with the words: "do not open under any circumstances" painted on the top. Of course, this piece interests the fourteen-year-old boy to explore the Box. Tommy Sully opens the box and observes what appears to be a neon green paint. This will be perfect for my first art project, Tommy thinks to himself. Tommy gathered all the supplies he needed for his first Masterpiece painting in Alabama. Tommy loves the cartoon that shows The Simpsons, so it makes perfect sense to paint the new car plant and use the fake neon green paint to access the radioactive waste barrel in the painting. Tommy hangs his newly painted picture in the studio with pride, to allow it to draw. Tommy cleans up the studio and proceeds to complete his chores of feeding the birds from his uncle.

The next morning, Tommy awoke as he heard his uncle drive away from the house. Tommy proceeded downstairs to enjoy breakfast when he heard a strange noise from the art studio. As Tommy's hands begin to sweat from the fear, he slowly enters the studio. To Tommy's surprise, they sat on the barrel of green ooze just like his painting. As he approached the barrel, he noticed a bird print in the ooze. As he looked up he noticed his uncle's parrot preached on the curtain rod and had crawled into a mutant from contacting the ooze. Tommy ran outside of the art studio through the front door, but in his startled state he forgot to close the door, which allowed the mutant parent to escape outside to the world. Tommy scrambled to his room and hid underneath the bed to await his uncle's return.

Sometime later that day, Tommy heard a firm knock at the front door. Tommy slowly descends the stairs to see who the visitor is. Tommy glances out at the people and notices clean-cut men dressed in all-black suits and radios standing on the front porch. Stay tuned for the Ooze Part 2 to see how Tommy navigates this mutant Ooze predicament.

My Faith Journey

by Kierra LaFerry

When I was younger I was saved at Vbs in 2016 when I was six years old. The theme was shipwrecked and we had an altar call. And I confessed that I was a sinner and prayed the sinner's prayer. Ever since then my faith journey has grown and flourished. My parents had struggled with addictions so when I was six years old my aunt got custody over me ,my brother and sister. After my aunt got custody over me and my siblings I started going to church more. We have been since I was six years old!

When I was twelve years old I went to my first youth camp on signal mountain.Youth camp is a Church of God camp where you stay one week, hang out ,have fun, and go to two worship services each day. At one of those services I had felt moved by the testimony of a girl who struggled with mental health so I fell to the altar and started praying about what I had been going through and after a few minutes my jaw started shaking. In my mind I kept saying "what's happening". I was so scared because I really never experienced anything crazy with my faith. People at church had spoken in tongues and danced but I had always stood off to the side and watched. But this time was different. At this point my jaw was shaking like crazy and my face felt hot and I had this tingle feeling all over my body. This lady came to me, I didn't even know her and she never told me her name. She said

"I can see the lord all over you dont stop asking God don't give up".

All of the sudden I was saying weird sounds, sounds that sounded like another language. This had been the first time I had a big encounter with the Lord and after that I felt so much peace.

After a while I sort of just lost my ability to speak in tongues. I had continued praying about it and I haven't received it but I never gave up on it. This last year I went to a church event that my church takes us to called winterfest in Pigeon forge. We go in March and stay Three days or the whole weekend (including friday) in Pigeon forge.The first worship service I didn't feel anything. At the time before I had gone I felt really disconnected from God but on the second night I felt his presence everywhere. A lady who goes to my church named Michelle said

"Kierra come here" during the worship part of the service.

I felt Confused on why she needed me but I went anyway. I walked over to her and she pulls me close and says

"Kierra,Gods still listening and still loves you even when you can't feel him,don't let the enemy try to tell you otherwise".

When she said that tears instantly fall from my face, so much so I couldn't get any words out. The next thing I know I was speaking in tongues like crazy. I was so proud that I had done that because every time I speak in tongues I feel so at peace and so close to God. I encourage everyone to not give up and always keep praying!

Proud of an Accomplishment

by Madeline Lowman

In one of my previous essays I wrote about all my struggles last year and how I finally got some help. I will show you how getting some help has led me to this moment. So in this summary I will tell you about my biggest and proudest accomplishment in my life.

This year has been so much better. I haven't really struggled with friends so that's good. I feel like this year has gone right so far. But the best part is I finally completed what I have been looking forward to for a REALLY long time...

Last year I really struggled with my faith and religion and everyone was worried about my soul and if I will make it to heaven. Baptism is a really big step to make it to heaven. For my church these are the five steps of salvation Here, Believe, Repent, Confess, and last be baptized.

I never thought I would believe in God because I'm one of those people that have to see something in order to believe it. You obviously know we cant see God so I didn't really believe in him. But one day I was talking to my mom and asked her "If we cant see God then how do we know he is real?" she replied "God is like the wind we cant see him but we can feel his presence" That moment when she told me that my whole viewpoint on God changed. She was right. Just because we cant see something doesn't mean its not there.

That day everything hit me. It was kind of random. Because it was just a normal day and then it just popped in my head. God is real there's so many signs. For example the Bible, prayers coming true and so many more. Finally everything made sense and God was real. I started crying. I never thought I would get to this point where I actually might make it to heaven.

The next big step I needed to do was get baptized. I already believe, I've heard all the steps of salvation and I was more than ready to tell my family "I'm ready. I want to make it to heaven".

Once I was ready, my family and I were eating at Delias (the Mexican restaurant) and I said "I'm ready to get baptized." They were so happy we all teared up. We started texting everyone I wanted to invite to watch me after church. Everyone was so happy.

Then the day came…I decided I wanted my dad to do it and after church that sunday morning. We stayed and all my family/ friends were there. I was very emotional. It took me so long to get to this point after everything that had happened last year. All my friends and family were so proud. They all cried, including me .One of those people there gave me a bible that said "we are so proud of your decision" Now every night my family and I read the bible before bed. Right now we are currently in the book of proverbs.

This is the story of all the steps it took me to get baptized. It took a long time but I finally got right with God. I can tell you all that studying has paid off. It got me to where I wanted to be today. Getting baptized is the best and biggest decision I've ever made by far. I love waking up in the morning and flipping to a random page and reading that bible verse for the day. I love thanking God for letting me get up and see the sun. Now every morning I have something to wake up and look forward to.

The Three Little Investors

by Brian Slaven

One day three little investors who were down on their luck went to their financial adviser and asked. "Should we invest in stocks?"

The financial adviser said, "yes you should, the market is low right now and may boom in the future!"

So they all invested in three different stocks.

The first investor decided to invest in a small website called Pets. com. Which was founded in nineteen ninety four by Pasadena-based entrepreneur Greg McLemore. This investment was going well at first with the stock going up and up but the investor wanted to leave it for a week more. But then the big bad Jeff Bezos came along buying the rights to pets.com and then liquidated the company and that caused the stocks to completely crash. From the one thousand dollar investment into a total profit of negative nine hundred and fifty six dollars, This means he only got forty four in profit.So the investor ran back to the financial advisor but he couldn't afford to keep him hired so in return he lost everything. Then he ended up homeless in a random subway in the middle of New York city.

The second investor decided to go a different route investing into kozmo.com. Another small website linking to a store founded by Joseph Park in nineteen ninety seven. This investor decided to play it safe and only invested five hundred dollars. This small investment was not the best as the stock kept falling and falling but suddenly raised all the way to two hundred percent in value. He sold the stock. He then gained one thousand dollars. He put another five hundred in hoping to make even more profit, But as happened to pets.com the big evil Jeff Bezos came and ruined it all, liquidating it and ruining all the stocks. This investor still had to fire his advisor but could at least still have a home.

The third investor felt risky and decided to invest in the Washington post while it was low. He decided to invest a total of two thousand dollars. His investment was going great as the stocks kept going up and up. Then the big bad Jeff Bezos came along and decided to purchase the Washington Post, But this time he couldn't get rid of it for money from the widespread use all across the entire country. So then the stocks shot all the way up to one thousand percent and he took out his investment gaining Ten thousand dollars in stock. The Washington Post joined the ranks of amazon as some of the most successful companies in America and maybe even globally.

After about a year he found the other two investors and helped them get back up on their feet. Then after this they decided to make their company called pro-test-er a small play on words where they made calculators. But unfortunately the big bad Jeff Bezos came along and bought their company and liquidated it using their ideas for Amazon. This left all three investors rich and they lived happily ever after.

"Shining Bright"
by Brayton Campbell

Oh how bright

Yellow showing like a light

Then the orange is like the fruit

Still shining like a fancy boot

Yep, you have guessed

We saved red because it's the best

Looking out my window in my bed

It's how you thought

Shining bright, not at the top

But at the bottom of a sunset.

"Freedom, oh Freedom"

by Brayton Campbell

I was in the war

It took a turn

I had to fight

Sitting at home

You are free

Dreadful it is

But once I'm done

I will sit waiting to go

The day came for me to return home.

Glass Shards
by Bella Speller

Everyday. Emerie woke up at six in the morning to go to work. She was a dentist. It takes a certain kind of person to pull teeth out of someone! She had to drive about an hour everyday to earn her pay. This was normal for her. Emerie had a pretty simple life but one day, this all changed. As Emerie gets in her car to drive off, she notices the new fan she was meant to replace for her old one in the living room. The box was just sitting in the back so she quickly decided to put it inside the house! This only takes her two minutes, she must be fast enough so she isn't late for her early appointment. She had someone due for a check up. They hadn't been to the dentist in years! Emerie mentally prepares herself for the mouth of the client. But again, this was just a normal day for her.

On the way, about thirty minutes in, she was in a more busy area. This led her to a coffee shop that she had been wanting to try out. So she grabs a cold drink, and leaves. She usually went to the same place for coffee and had stayed loyal to it, but she switched it up today. Normal to get coffee, so still a normal day. Now she pulled into the dentist office and got out of her car. She checks in and sets up for her dental appointment client. She saw that after this appointment, she had one more client, for a little girl that had failed to not get cavities. But this again, was normal! So she gets through the first appointment.

"Alright ma'am, time for a tooth checkup! Are you ready?" Then,

"Okay, thank you for your cooperation, great checkup today!" Emerie would say.

She finishes up her first appointment like always. It was like life was a loop. Emerie didn't notice the little things, and they didn't notice her.

"Hello little miss, is there anything that's bothering you now?"

"I think I found the issue! Make sure to brush your teeth a little more and you're good to go!" Emerie finishes her second appointment. Then the rest of her day was filled with making more appointments, then a lunch break, studying treatments, and filling out paperwork. This was normal. Everything was to Emerie. She is now able to leave. So she gets her stuff from her office area and checks out. She walks out to her car and leaves. It was pretty chilly in scrubs so she made sure the car was warm. Emerie then drives from the office, past the suburbs and past the coffee shop from earlier. She is now home, where when she walks in, she notices that fan box from earlier!

"I need to get on that! I need new fans for this upcoming spring." Emerie says. Even though it was chilly now, in about three weeks, it would become so hot and humid so the fans were crucial. She gets a small ladder and removes the first fan. She removes the light bulb and carefully places it in a cloth next to her on the couch. She adds a new light bulb, then places the fan. And to her surprise it works! Now for the other fan. As she removes the fan off the ceiling, the light bulb goes with it. Uh Oh. She drops the fan on top of herself as the light bulb explodes directly near her face. Glass shards fly everywhere, including into her eyes. The pain is so unbearable. She shuts her eyes and begins to tear up. It was very blurry, but she could see well enough to call 911.

As she speaks to the operator, she tells the operator to make sure the paramedics are careful when stepping through the house.

Time is ticking. It had felt like a decade before the paramedics arrived but in reality, it was only seven minutes. They step carefully into the living room as directed. What happened next was actually a blurr for Emerie.

She opens her eyes, and realizes it was very difficult to see. But she was in the hospital. Doctors tell her that without a quick surgery, her vision will become increasingly more impaired soon which will lead to her becoming blind. Emerie had to have this surgery. If she becomes blind, how is she meant to do her job? She was a dentist! She was good at it too, and her normal life? That wouldn't be an option anymore. The surgeons carefully remove glass from Emeries eyes, but her vision would still be pretty blurry.

When Emerie wakes up from her anesthesia, her vision is impaired. She could still be a dentist, but with assistance. This made Emerie realize her *normal* life can be changed very quickly. This led her to learn that she should enjoy life. Not just let it be normal like always but to learn, grow, and improve.

Merry Christmas Elizabeth

by Ava Moore

My name is Annebell Swansen. I am a twenty-eight year old woman who works at Floshot Marketplace. I don't make good money on my part. Though my husband James Swanson, makes very good money for the two of us. Things changed for the two of us when we were both seventeen.

We had a beautiful baby girl, Elizabeth Swanson. Elizabeth is the love of my life, I would do anything for my daughter. My husband and I's world revolves around Elizebeth. Since Elizebeth was born, money has become tighter and tighter the older she gets. We try to make Elizabeth's world as good as we can for her knowing that money is tight.

We live in California, where everything is expensive. Especially bills. But luckily James' job is very profitable but we still need the extra money I make for Elizabeth.

It is now December, Elizabeth's favorite time of year! This is the one holiday where we can spoil her the most, which she loves. Christmas has always been special with our family. It has always just been us three.

December 17th, the day when everything changed. I walked into work twenty minutes early to set up my cashier as I always do everyday. I notice a woman who looks about my age setting up in my station. I brush it off and walk to the back to put my bag in my locker. Then I feel a hand on my shoulder. I turn around to see my boss. I flash a bright smile at him as I always do. Usually he would flash one back , but he didn't. He actually gave me back an unpleasant frown.

My heart started pounding. I politely said," Well good morning Mr. Ross!"

Mr. Ross responded back with " Annabelle"

He took a pause. " Can we talk?"

My heart was still racing and I began to become nervous. We sat down at the table with two chairs. I usually sit there when I'm on break.

He looked at me with tear filled eyes," Annabelle I am so so so sorry."

 "For what!?" I replied.

"I can't have you working here anymore, we found a replacement already and I have to let you go." A tear rolled down his face as my heart dropped. He knew everything I was going through. I couldn't afford not having a job. So many emotions were racing through my head I couldn't think straight.

I slammed my hands on the table as I aggressively stood up. I began yelling at Mr. Ross. "Why! Why! Give me a good reason as to why!? You know everything I'm going through and you do this to me!? You know how I need this job! How freaking could you!?" I slammed my fist against my locker as I began to sob. Mr. Ross was like an uncle to me, he's been there ever since I was a little girl.

I could feel my body fall to the ground. Mr. Ross came to comfort me but I pushed him away. I stood up, grabbed my things and began to walk out of the door. My head was spinning. All I could do was go home. All I could think about was Elizabeth.

I began to feel sick, but I waited until James and Elizabeth arrived home. Finally they arrived home but when I stood up to greet them, my world went black. I could hear Elizabeth cry faintly, my heart began to shatter. I could hear James trying to help me, he was on the phone with 911.

The next thing I remember is me waking up in a hospital. I felt drained. As I looked around I saw my precious family asleep on the hospital couch. Elizabeth was eleven now so James and her on the couch, there wasn't as much room as there used to be.

I sat there with all of my thoughts surrounding me until a doctor came in. Elizabeth and James had both just woken up. The doctor explained to me how she ran some tests when I was unconscious. Then the words ," We realized why you passed out. Which is good but, the reason why isnt." I looked at James, his face was as if it was malformed.

"Mrs. Swanson.... You have stage five cancer." I began to cry.

"There is a treatment we can do for it, but we must start as soon as possible and it is pricey." We don't have the money for something pricey. James wrapped me in his arms, along with Elizabeth.

Elizabeth...my sweet girl. I would do anything for her. I knew immediately what I had to do. As Elizabeth went to the bathroom I told James, " James my love, we cannot pay for the treatment." "We will find a way, Annabell." James said softly. I had a faint smile." James, I can't do the treatment. I'm saving the money for Elizabeth and her future." " But you'll die!" James says.   " So be it. It's not like I want to leave James. But it's for her, darling." My husband began to cry. I cradled him in my arms as they were nearly limp. My time with them would be gone before you know it.

December 23rd, almost a week from when I was diagnosed. I knew I was dying. It was painful. Elizabeth and James had to leave the hospital, but I wanted to say my last goodbye. I picked Elizabeth up with every bit of strength I had left. She cried and I hugged her for at least thirty minutes. I told her, " You are so beautiful Elizabeth. I would do anything for you my love. Just know that. You are perfect in your own ways." I handed her a necklace to always remember me. It was a necklace of wings with an "E" In the middle of it. I plopped her on the ground as she shuffled back. James came forward and squeezed me. He kissed me on the forehead and rubbed my cheek. " Forever my angel" He said as he kissed me again.

My heart shattered as I saw the two walk out of the room. I knew this was my last day to see my family . I turned to the nurse, gave a soft smile and said " I'm done fighting." She looked at me puzzled , " Would you like to go off all medicine?" the nurse asked. " Yes Ma'am" I replied. I closed my eyes and let my brain relax. I opened my eyes. I see the white essence surrounding me.

Merry Christmas Elizabeth.

Why Did It Have To Be Spiders?

by Abigail Green

It all started on a normal day, you wouldn't expect to die on a normal day...

It was rainy outside, but that was common where I lived. The living room was dark; only the dim light of the TV lit up the room. Figures danced across the TV screen, and bright lights shone through the darkness. I was cozied up under blankets watching the horror movie currently playing on the screen, and that's when I spotted it...

A big, hairy, long-legged spider crawls up the wall. Immediately my heart rate speeds up, my nerves go haywire. One thing about me is that I'm deathly afraid of spiders. Luckily we have an in-house vacuum, so it makes it easy to vacuum up the spider. I slowly get up and grab the vacuum and suck up the huge arachnid. I wiped imaginary sweat off my brow, relieved that the spider was dead now.

Just when I turned around I spotted two more spiders, I let out a small squeal, I was petrified. Why did it have to be spiders? I was basically Ron Weasley, I could do anything, but I'm bolting when it comes to spiders. Now I had to get rid of two more spiders, just great.

I make my way over to one of the spiders that were tormenting me. I suck it up in the house vac. "One more to go," I say only to be met with the silence of the room. When I look over at the spider I notice that there are four more gross, harry, huge spiders crawling all over the wall.

Immediately I freaked out about why more and more spiders were spawning, I didn't know what to do so I sucked up one of the spiders. Now there are two more spiders so I suck both up in one swoop. Suddenly four more spiders appeared out of thin air. I didn't know what to do, spiders were swarming me left and right. I kept killing them but more and more kept showing up, eventually, they swarmed the walls none of the paint was showing through the spiders.

This was torture, the sound of their legs on the walls the dark down blurs of arachnids eventually, the spiders ran out of room on the walls, and the spiders started crawling on the furniture making their way down to the floor I kept fending them off, but more appeared. The spiders slowly crept their way to my feet, crawling on my socks. I jumped to try and get them off, but it was no use. I squish some of them underneath my feet, but more keep showing up. There was a look of pure panic written on my face as spiders made their way up my legs. An uneasy feeling settled in my stomach, I knew there was no escape...

I let out a small squeak finally accepting my fate, there was no running away, spiders were covering the door. At this point, spiders were crawling up my torso, and to my neck. "Is this really how I'm going to die? Probably." That was the last thing I said before I was encased by the spiders. The whole room was covered in spiders, with nothing left to be seen I tried to shake the spiders off of me. A few of the spiders fall off but more and more appear. At this point, I couldn't breathe the spiders were crawling over my face, and I was scared to open my mouth.

That's when it happened, I blacked out, with no sight, no sound, only the feeling of tink legs crawling all over my body.

That is the tragic tale of how I died from a spider infestation...

The Three Little Crocodiles

by Henry Williams

Well, I woke up this morning to find my brothers awake and in the water already. I asked what they were doing and they said they were going to build forts to hide in. Well of course I was going to be a part of that challenge in some way. But they don't like me because I always win, so I'll let them decide the way of some sort I'll play

Well my youngest brother Danny isn't the brightest and decides to build his house out of plain pillows. Well, turns out I was the judge, and I knew one big push will make it all crumble. So I tell him he may want to fix it before I try to knock it down. Well, Danny's super stubborn and decides he doesn't want to listen to my advice. So I walk within three feet of his fort and with one big blow dead center of the wall it all crumbles down with him inside it. He says I cheated but he's just a sore loser and doesn't like to fail when we play these types of games. So with sadness, anger, and shame he walks to his brother's fort to hide from defeat.

Well, my next brother, who's the middle child, Jon decides to follow a different path than Danny. He decides that he will build his out of tree planks. He waits for the right moment then all of a sudden BOOM a huge ditch covered all around his base. Well now I had to find a different way to knock it down because I'm nowhere near close enough to reach his base. For a second I thought he was going to win then I thought of a plan. Danny showed me some spare planks. So with help from Danny and a hammer and nails we created a bridge to get across. So I get to the other side and Jon is in disbelief at this point. Well, with my first punch it doesn't budge. Then with a kick I create a little hole. With my last kick I finally break the wall down revealing Jon and his surprised face. Well again they think I cheated because of me taking more than one kick or punch to break his wall. Danny even thinks I cheated, because of me using Jon's extra planks even when he was the one who pointed them out and helped me build it.

Well, they ended up running to my oldest brother Nathen. He is the smartest person out of them because he builds it out of plain concrete. He doesn't have any traps or plans, just a plain concrete box around him. Well, I know my kick won't get through or my punch so, I crawl into the den and grab a hammer from my dad's work bench. He knew what I was up to because he started laughing at my idea. Well it turns out this plain concrete box was three feet thick. So I just knew nothing was getting in or out of the box.

So it turns out he had a trap door leading outside the box behind it and no one told me. So I guess sometimes plain and simple may lead to a better outcome than expected.

royed
Tired
Angry
Depre
Ruined
Afraid
pty
Foresa
Scared
Hopeless
less
Useless
Fearful

Million Dollar Mystery

by Anslee Parker

When I went to the case to turn the lights out for the end of my shift and noticed the glass case was open, I knew something was wrong. This was the case that held the queen's most expensive valuable and prized possessions. I started rummaging through all the items in the case to make sure nothing was missing. Her ruby and diamond necklace, earrings and bracelets were all there. Next, I looked for all her clothing items and saw her dress and shoes were there as well. There on the shelf was her pocket book, matching wallet and travel bag she carried to all her events. Now that I have checked everything and see nothing is missing I reported the open case to my manager and he came and double checked to make sure everything was there and to lock it back. When he arrived he checked the case and immediately realized the crown was gone. I asked myself how I did not see the missing crown ? How did someone get in here without me noticing when I stood guard to this case all day long? This crown made of real gold, 278 diamonds, and 112 rubies was worth a fortune. I just knew I was doomed and going to lose my job. I asked my manager, am I fired and his reply was, "Not yet you have 4 days to find the culprit of this mystery".

After this discussion I knew my job was in my hands and I had my work cut out for me. Detectives were called to start the investigation. They closed off the area with caution tape and allowed no one in there. Three detectives started watching the security cameras and the other three were trying to find evidence of fingerprints on the glass case. This made the job a little easier, but I still had no idea where the crown was or whose hands it was in. I tried to remember all the people that came in and out of the queen of France's Hall of Fame room, but there were so many people it was all a blur. I then remembered a sketchy guy with all black on and a huge backpack that asked how much everything was worth in the case. I thought it was weird, but I was being nice because that is my job.

The next day came and I was at home thinking about the case. Suddenly I get a call from the detectives and they have found the culprits' fingerprints on the glass case. They ran them through to check for DNA. Tuns out this guy was a criminal and had a record for stealing things, for the most part expensive items. They found a match in the system that told where he lives. Police went to the address and knocked on his apartment door. Sure enough there was the guy, the one I remembered with the black backpack. They searched his apartment and found the crown. It was not a good day for him. He was arrested and put in jail for robbery over a million dollars. I must say we gained the crown back to its case and he was put in a case with metal bars.

The Right Time For A Police Officer To Use Force

by Ayden Jules

When is it right to use force against something reasonable(legal)?Does it affect the environment or destroy it? Let's find out...

So, why is it important to know the right time to use force, as you are a legal force? Well, yes it's commonly necessary to use force against something that can potentially be a threat, to society.

Police use force when necessary to uphold the rule of law and protect citizens. They have a duty to arrest and detain fleeing suspects and defend themselves from physical aggression. However, they should only use force when an unwilling perpetrator resists their control. Officers have the right to defend themselves against injury or death. The force used should be objectively reasonable and proportional to the threat posed by the suspect. Citizens prefer a fair government based on the rule of law, supported by public support and impartial courts.

There are many reasons why police use force even if they don't get enough details. Here are some instinctive ways that policies act, persistently to quick resolutions.

The rule of law demands fairness and equity from the government, and the killings of Black citizens have lost trust. Rebuilding trust requires education about police reactions and training, as well as understanding the United Nations' belief that the rule of law must allow for police use. Contrary to popular belief, many police departments do not train or approve choking as a compliance technique.

Sometimes police need to be well-trained to handle/control the situation,while being less-lethal(elimination).Police officers are trained to use less lethal weapons like batons, pepper spray, and stun guns when verbal commands fail. These weapons can cause severe medical complications, especially for those with respiratory conditions or heart patients. The Marshall Project suggests that if less-lethal tools were used, people like Michael Brown, Walter Scott, and Tamir Rice may not have died. Officers must be trained to render medical aid promptly to prevent serious injury.

The Weird Cat

by Elijah Morrow

One day I was doing my homework then I got bored very quickly, so I went outside to get fresh air. Suddenly it started pouring down rain, it was raining cats and dogs outside. I went back inside to finish my homework, when I got done. I picked up my cat and started playing with him. His name is Ted and Ted was a cat that we found on the road. He had brown eyes, patterned skin and a white spotted ear.

I woke up the next morning and got ready for school. I was very excited because it was Friday and that meant it was the last day of school till the weekend. We pulled into the school I hopped out of the car rapidly. I ran into the school I wanted to be the first one to class. When I got in there my teacher said "hey hey hey! Why are you running?" I said "I wanted to be the first one to class so I ran from my car to where I am now." So I sat down and got ready for class, the bell rang. Good morning class today we are learning about your family's nationality, my teacher said. I thought to myself what nationality is, so I raised my hand and asked.

He said "It is your ancestors' original race. So I thought of it and I don't know mine."

When I got in the car I asked my mom what my nationality was and she said I don't know. My mom said when you get home look at the pictures then you will find out. We pulled into the driveway and I ran inside to find the pitchers, I ran to the basement and started to sort through the buckets. Finally! I found it and went downstairs and started flipping pages. One thing I noticed is there is the same cat over and over. When I looked closer it looked like my cat, then it hit me.

I ran to show my mom she said "Oh my gosh, it is, so that means that this cat is like 1000 years old." Me and my mom were very freaked out about this so we called the pound on the cat, they took it away and we felt so good that we felt like we had to go out of town. We arrived in Paris when we got there my mom said let's take a pitcher so I asked a nearby person to take it. When I looked at it closely it was the cat that we called the pound on. My mom and I both freaked out and hid for our life. The End

The Clown Motel

by Edward Milligan

May 23,1991. Ian, Caleb and Christian are diving and they're heading to Las Vegas for a vacation. But they all are getting tired.

Caleb says " It's getting late guys I think we should stop at a motel or somewhere for the night and then in the morning we'll continue on the road."

Ian who is driving says " Ok when I see somewhere we can stop we stay there for the night."

Not that far later they see a motel to stop at. They park and head into the lobby and as they step in they see. All of these clown items and statue's of clown everywhere, so they ask the room clerk why there is so much clown stuff around

The clerk laughed and said "OIh i'm just a really big fan of clowns."
So they say ok and take their key to the room and leave.

After they check into their room, they go and grab their stuff and bring it to the room, they go to sleep. A few hours later Ian wakes up to a sound and he sees that Christian is gone and Ian goes over to Caleb and says "where did Christian go" then Caleb says mumbling " He went to the front counter." Right after that Ian hears the door open and there's a black figure standing at the door. So Ian turns the light on and it's Christian and Ian says to Christian"where did you go." and Christian after closing the doors says" I just went to the front desk and asked if we could get another nights stay and he said yes." so Ian says okay and they go back to bed but what they didn't realize was that there was someone else watching them near their car.

The next night. After taking a long time to rest they came back at the end of the day and as their about to get back to the room Christian says"while I was going to the front desk last night I saw a graveyard and I was wondering if y'all wanted to check it out and both Ian and Caleb both say "sure." so they check it out and they don"t see anything but as they're walking back someone in a black and white silk suit is following them back to their room but they don't see anything. After a while as they are all sitting around Christian see's out of the corner of his eye see's someone run by and he says " who was that just ran by." so Christian opens and checks out the door and in that moment A tall clown in a black and white suit grabs him and take. Ian and Caleb run after him and the clown screams for him to stop and as they see the clown with Christian turn the corner, they turn the corner and they see. Nothing there is nothing and nobody there. So they end up going back to the room and locking the door and closing the blinds. After a while Caleb says" I forgot something in the car I need to go get it." so they both go but when they get back to the room they see the door open and another clown standing in the room. The clown was wearing a multi-colored suit and was tall and big. So they ran but the clown was able to catch Caleb , dragging him away into the room and closing the door. Ian, still running to his car in horror, hears the screams of Caleb and Christian. Ian starts the car and drives out of the parking lot onto the road he Looks back at the motel to his horror. Both the clowns with Caleb and Christian not moving and

The clowns waving, he drives away reading the motel sign.
It reads THE CLOWN MOTEL.

Olivia
by A. N.

Today was like any other day: I woke up, got ready for the day, went to school, got food, and drove home. Pretty simple, right? Yeah, I know. Anyway, on my way to school, I noticed that the flowers looked wilted. Like it needs water. It was in the shade, too. I felt kinda bad for it.

I continued in to school. When I arrived, I put my stuff in my locker and grabbed my stuff for my first period. Then walked to my first class. I sat down in my regular seat that day. As I sat down, I noticed my seat was warm. Uhm, who in the world was sitting in my seat??

I decided not to worry about it and listen to my Biology teacher's lecture on and on and on about how to use a microscope. He told us that they are used to seeing tiny plants and animals structures all that weird stuff. Then we got to the cool part of the lecture. We were gonna learn how to dissect a pig. I got so excited.

I finally left Biology class, and all the other classes went by in a blur. Soon, it was time to go home. After school, I have the same routine. Take a walk through the halls, then walk outside to the huge willow tree and read.

After roaming the halls for a bit, I grabbed a book from the library and headed outside. I have been obsessed with this one writer; her name is *"Holly Jackson."* She writes murder mystery books. After I grabbed a new book that she had written, I started to walk outside. When I reached the tree, I noticed that it looked a little different. I tried not to think about it. So I sat down under the tree and opened my book.

As I was reading my book, a teacher that I had never met before came over and introduced herself. She shook my hand after telling me that her name was Mrs. Johnson, which I thought was an odd name for a teacher. Obviously, I didn't tell her that. As soon as we shook hands, something was off. I got this weird feeling, and then all of a sudden I could hear her thoughts?!?! She was saying weird things like this girl hasn't even told me her name yet, how rude, and why is she still shaking my hand it has been like a minute. When she said this in her mind, I quickly let go of her hand and backed away. I told her my name was Olivia. She looked at me and started talking about random things. She left about thirty minutes later. I sat back down and started reading again.

I finished reading, packed my stuff up, and left. I was on my way home, still thinking about how I could read her mind. Maybe that's why the tree looked different today. When I got home, I told my mom all about it, and she just shrugged it off. She told me to get ready for bed. I walked to my room and got ready for bed, then went to sleep.

I Hate Bigfoot
by Corbin Ooten

My Uncle finally arrived home after five years of being missing. My name is Kyle and I'm fifteen years old. I never really knew much about my Uncle, all I knew was that he helped raise me ever since my Dad abandoned me at only two years old. He worked late shifts and wouldn't come home till far past my bedtime; sometimes he'd wake me up by barging through the front door. I remember distinctly the night my mother died, he stumbled into the house covered in blood and cuts, it looked like he'd been beaten. That was the first night I ever saw my uncle cry.

My Uncle was a giant man. I remember he had a large black beard and had to duck before walking through regular doorframes. He reminded me of a large brown bear or a Viking I saw on TV once. He was always a kind man, as my grandma says, but everyone else who knew him often said he was as strong as an ox and he had his reasons to leave. I never knew why or when he left, I just woke up one morning and he had vanished, I often resented him as life went on for leaving me when I needed him most. I felt as if anyone I loved either left me or died.

Then all of a sudden, I woke up to a knock on the front door. After five long years, my Uncle decides to show up. We stood there looking at each other for what seemed like forever, I couldn't believe my eyes. His beard was grey and his long brown hair was now grey, his face was wrinkled like he'd aged fifteen years in the past five. I let him in the house, and he soon apologized for leaving me when I was ten, but he also said that I'd understand why he left when I was older. I don't think I will. Before I could say anything, he stopped me and asked where my grandparents were.

They were out at my cousin Edward's house. He fled from the house, not saying another word to me. I was so shocked he could do this to me, after five years, and thinking he was dead all this time, he left again. I was devastated, but he left his bag at the house and maybe I could find some answers there.

I regret looking in his bag. The things I found in the bag disturbed me and left me with more questions than answers. There was a map of the Himalayan mountains, several fur coats that smelled rotten, and a newspaper article about the search for bigfoot in Tupelo, Mississippi, the town where I grew up. I'm so confused, I always thought my uncle looked more grizzly than man, but I'd never guess my uncle was Bigfoot. I need to tell my grandparents before it's too late, or did they already know? This whole time they've been keeping this from me.

The Three Musketeers

by Bentley Painter

It was a normal day with LeGoat, LeSunshine, and LeBron. They were out in the woods thinking of something to do. They wandered all around the woods. It was beautiful weather outside, sunny with clear skies and not a cloud to be seen. They were just as happy as could be.

LeGoat went off to go sit in the pasture. He decided to build a house out of straw. He had tons of it on his pasture. There he went into the barn to collect his harvesting tool. Slowly he chopped down many pieces. It took a long time just to get his harvest. Now it was time to build.

He slowly placed every piece of straw onto each other. The structure was not very sturdy, so he had to be very careful. LeGoat was making an igloo-like structure that would not hold up. After a while he had three fourths of it completed. He was sweating like crazy due to the hot weather conditions he had to build in.

Finally LeGoat's house was complete and fully made of straw. It was shaped just like an igloo. When night had arrived he was very nervous due to the fact his house was not strong enough to stand a big wind. Then he heard the big bad wolf.

Steph Curry said, " I'll huff and I'll puff and I'll blow your house down."

LeGoat was terrified as his house started to fall down on him.

The next day arrived and LeSunshine decided to build a house made of wood. He went to the shed to grab an axe. He chopped wood for hours as the day went on. He had a giant wood pile stacked up ready to build his house. He started placing stick by stick to eventually build his home.

He had many hours put into this house as he worked all day. Then he heard the same thing LeGoat did.

Steph Curry said, " I'll huff and I'll puff and I'll blow your house down."

There went LeSunshine's house as it fell on top of him. He felt like he was crushed by a hammer watching his hard work being destroyed.

Here went LeBron is building his house. He was approaching it in a different way. It was very smart of him to build his house out of bricks as they could hold almost anything. He started collecting bricks and loading them into his wagon. He grabbed some cement and went to work. His house was coming along great. It was a very strong structure and actually looked like a house. It was very strongly built. It could almost hold anything that came at it. He was very confident in his new house.

There Steph was sitting in the woodline waiting for night to come. Eventually the sun went down and he was on his way. Something felt different to him as this house didn't look weak. He said, "I'll huff and I'll puff and I'll blow your house down."

LeBron did not fear as his house was holding up strong. Steph finally gave up and ran off. LeBron cheered in success as he had out done Steph.

After all had happened, LeBron was the smartest of the three. He succeeded in the greatest challenge of all. The other two LeSunshine and LeGoat had failed and were very disappointed. But at the end of the day they all had succeeded in beating Steph.

The Robot Takeover

by Tucker Dalton

It wasn't a special day or anything, just Saturday. I woke up and went downstairs to eat breakfast. I was ready to get started on the normal Saturday things, clean my room, mow the lawn, feed the dogs, and those sorts of things. My parents had already left for work, and they both worked at the robotics testing facility downtown. My dad is part of the engineering team there. He came up with all of the codes and designs for the robots. The company wants the robots to help with the military, and just be around the house.

My dad has an office downstairs where he does some of his work. He says I'm not allowed to go down there, because there is some classified files and software that I'm not allowed to see. I am only 11 years old but I think I know what he means.

I had just gotten done eating my cereal when I heard the siren. It was a lot louder than you would think, and shortly after I got a call from my dad and he said that there was a malfunction at the lab when they were testing a new AI robot, and now it's self aware and is ordering the other robots to take control of the city and destroy anything in their way. He told me that him and my mom probably wouldn't make it out of there but that there was a flash drive in a vault in the basement of the facility that holds all of the data and codes for the robots. He said that if I could get to it and back to his office in our basement, then I would be able to destroy all of the robots. I tried to ask him how to shut them down from our basement but suddenly there was a loud explosion in the background of the call and all I could hear was static.

I was beginning to cry when I heard a knocking at the door. I looked out the front window to see a large robot standing with a machine gun resting on his shoulder. I got scared and went down to my Dad's office to see if there was anything down there to help me. When I got downstairs, there was tech. like I'd never seen before. There were so many buttons and holograms that I would have no idea how to operate this if I did get the flash drive. I saw this closet in the back corner that was glowing, so I went over to it, opened the door, and a bunch of weird looking things fell out. I wasn't sure what they were at first, but the I saw a trigger and a scope and I said, " oh yeah ".

There was a bunch of different guns, but of course I took the biggest one. The robot that was on the porch got tired of knocking, so it decided to kick the door down. But when it did, I was ready. When the door flung open I was holding the biggest gun and pulled the trigger, and I kinda wish I had used the smaller one because when I shot it launched me about 10 feet backwards, but it sure took care of that robot because he was nowhere to be found.

I started towards the facility and on the way took care of some more robots and when I got inside I was able to sneak down to the basement. The basement, was a whole new level. There were robots everywhere! I switched to my machine gun, only because it felt right. I probably destroyed around 300 robots on my way down but when I got to the bottom I found the flash drive. I grabbled it and used a grappling hook that was in my dads office to get out.

I stole the companies helicopter and had it auto-fly me back to my house and when I got inside, I heard this very loud siren, kind of like the one I'd heard earlier. Once it started blaring I could see a whole bunch of robots flying to my house. I ran downstairs and blocked off the door with as much stuff I could find and began trying to figure out this tech. Out. It was so advance and my dad never told me how to operate it, so I just plugged in the flash drive and started pushing buttons.

After a minute or two of pushing buttons a bit screen popped up that said, " POWER DOWN ALL DEVICES?". I started pushing more buttons when the robots started pounding on the basement door. I looked back to see one of their arms punch right through the door and start pushing the objects that were being used to block the door right at me. At that point I was waving my arms across the keyboard pushing every button possible. Just as they had gotten through the barricade they were about to shoot me and they all fell to the ground and there was a big green check mark on the computer that said, " All devices powered down ". I had done it.

The Guy Who Never Left

by Griffin Harmer

This boy lived in a big city that had nothing but traffic. He lived on the top floor of this skyscraper, which at the time was the biggest out of all of them. So this guy could not go on the street and could only work in the building. The only problem this guy had was that he had no food to get since this building was just an office.

The boss said that he could stay in the building if he did a lot of work and did longer shifts than all of the others. So every day this guy would just work and work and never leave that building. The only time that he left the building was when he had to go and get food so that he does not starve and die. Though today was the day he would have to go out and buy food because he had run out of all of it. He did not have a car or bike to ride on to get to the store. He also has never seen the outside world in ten years, so he has no clue what is going on out there. The only information that he got was from his other employees.

His only way to get an uber was from his computer which is on the top of the building. So he takes a long walk up the stairs, since the elevator was broken. He gets tired and falls asleep on the stairs. He stays asleep for a while, and when he finally wakes up he looks up and finds out that he has not moved up at all. The guy sits there on the stairs when then the boss comes out the door and sees him. The boss asks "Why are you all the way down here?"

The boy says "I have run out of food and am going to buy more at the closest store." He orders his uber and it says it will be there in an hour. He says that is how long it takes to get down the stairs. So when he got to the front of the building the uber was right there ready for him so he took his first step outside the building. He finds it a little weird that it looks the same it always was. He goes to his uber he ordered and the uber takes him to the store which was a mile from the building which made him surprised, and said sorry to the guy that did that just for him to drive two minutes.

The man told him that it was fine and that he could just use an electric bike or scooter back to the building. The boy looks at the man and says what is that. Before the man can speak the guy said that he will just walk and said thank you and left his uber. The boy gets the food he needs and starts to walk back to the building. The boy asked himself why did it look the same for ten years?

The Wine Bottle

by Aaliyah Shaw

Gwenyth sat on the window seat, looking out over the rolling hills of her backyard. She let out a long overdue sigh as her music flowed through her headphones as she looked over the bustling hills of the ranch. Before she knew it she had drifted off, waking to the sound of her parents yelling and a door slamming. Instead of doing anything to check on her mother, she got up from the window ledge, and slid into bed.

Gwenyth woke up a few hours later, her hair frizzy and tangled. Gwenyth looked out the window, seeing an illuminated lantern in the cornfield by a large rock. Curiosity seemed to get the best of her as she stumbled like a newborn gazelle. It was like a large hole, her mother standing by it's side with a shovel. "What?" She whispered, looking at her small siamese cat at her side. She had a look of fear as she watched her mother push the large rock over the grave sized hole. She closed her eyes as she shut the light blue curtains closed, praying that this was some murderous dream of hers.

Gwenyth laid back down and back down into the satin sheets that were still warm from her body laying in them. Gwenyth drifted off to sleep in her bed, the sight still ghosting her thoughts. She woke up the next morning to the smell of pancakes and bacon, a smile ghosted her face as she simply smelt her mothers wonderful cooking. "Gwenyth, honey! Breakfast is ready!" Her mother yelled.

Gwenyth sighs, deciding to just lay down her stress and fear before standing and opening her bedroom door with a creak. "Coming, momma!" She yelled, rolling her eyes slightly as she walked down the steps from the attic. Her mother had converted it to her bedroom when she was little. She saw the little table full of food and a pitcher of orange juice on black and white table cloth with the little wooden chairs on each side, reminding her of the times when she was little when her father held her on his hip as they danced to music on rough days on the checkered linoleum floors with the kitchen light on with the candles lit in the window seal. A sigh fell from her lips, "Hey, momma, where'd daddy go this time?" She muttered.

Gwenyth's mother's face went red as she stuttered on simple words. "O-oh! Your father went to stay with his mother...permanently..." Her mother smiled, reaching for the cross on her neck to fiddle with.

"Hm, well alright, tell him I love him." She muttered as she grabbed a plate from the table with a piece of toast in her mouth as she walked away. Her suspicion growing as she walked up the stairs to her bedroom 'What is going on' is all that went through her head.

Gwenyth slid into bed with a book and turned on the radio on her nightstand with a smile. She listened to the song that her father favored in the car, "I'll miss you, daddy.." She muttered, a tear falling down her cheek as she fell asleep.

Gwenyth woke up hours later, not realizing she fell asleep as her food and glass of juice sat on her nightstand, a sigh left her lips as she sat up to eat her food as it was midday and she was starving. She got the plate off the nightstand and proceeded to scoop all the food from the plate into her mouth. As she did so, she couldn't help but think of that dream she had the night before. She looked out the window before looking to her dresser where a picture of her dad sat with a glint from the excruciating bright light of the sun on it. "Time to see what you're hiding, Malory Harris." She hissed as she got dressed and slid open the door quietly, knowing her mother was sleeping.

Gwenyth opened the front door to see the plywood wrap around porch, her old dogs snoring on the porch with their water bowls sun dyed. She stepped off the squeaky steps and headed off to where the huge boulder sat, behind it was a hole that was about the size of a grave.

"Oh lord...I need a shovel..." Gwenyth muttered, looking till she spotted one and grabbed it, looking at the hole before she got to work. Once she got to the bottom of the hole, there was her father with a wine bottle embedded in his head. A look of plain terror crossed over her face, she stumbled backwards into her mother.

"What're you doing out here, Gwenyth?" Her mother asked with a psychotic smile on her face, "I see you found your father."

"Momma, what'd you do..." She mumbled, looking at her father, tears welled in her eyes as she reached for her phone. Her mother reached up, a kitchen knife in hand at her own neck.

"Don't you call the cops, if you do, I'll cut myself!" Her mother yelled as a small droplet of blood dripped down her neck, a smile darkening.

"You're crazy!" She yelled.

"Darling, your father was just a no good drunk!" Her mother hissed. Hearing those words made her heart shatter, knowing it was true but she refused to believe it.

"No, he wasn't!" She yelled, tears streaming down her cheeks.

"Yes, he was. Where do you think that broken picture frame came from and all those beer bottles? 'Cause if you know, I'd feel bad for killing off daddy dearest here." Her mother smirked as she continued to playfully pull the knife over her neck in meer imitation.

"NO!" She choked out, falling to her knees in fear and defeat as she cried.

"Yes, honey. He wasn't good to us!" Her mother yelled.

"What about all those nights when we'd dance in the kitchen after I had a rough day or vice versa? Were those all fake as well, because I truly think they were real!" She hissed at her mother, eyes glazing over from tears that she refused to let free.

Her mother dropped the knife for a moment, so Mallory grabbed it. Blood poured from holding the blade as she called the police. "Help! My mother killed my father!" She yelled into the phone.

"We will have officers your way in fifteen minutes ma'am!" The operator said into the phone. Around fifteen minutes later, she heard sirens and tires screeching to a stop around her. It felt as though time was stretching on and on like an endless ocean.

"Drop the weapon!" The police yelled, aiming guns at them. She sighed in relief before turning to her mother.

"I won." She muttered, a smirk coming to her lips as her mother was put into the back of the cruiser.

Sad
Dipressed
Emotion
Mad
Stress
Act
Hurt
Secret
Grief
Fear
Lie
Apprehensive
Anxiety
Hidden
Alone
Pain
Trapped
Angry

Angry Birds: The Plot to Kill King Pig

by Kolt Cobb

"So what, they stole some eggs? They do that all the time and we always get them back."

"Chuck, this time is different. These aren't any old eggs, these are the Mighty Eagles' own offspring."

"Red, I believe we should consult Mighty Eagle first, to see what he thinks should become of this matter."

"Wise words, Terrance. Hal, Chuck, Bomb, Terrance, Blues, you all come with me. Stella, stay here with the rest of the flock to receive our incoming transmissions."

"Yes sir." Red's hallowing leadership was unmatched on Piggy Island by any creature. The Angry Birds were sure to snag yet another victory for Bird Island.

"Mighty Eagle, sir, ARER (Advanced Recon Egg Retrieval) Trooper 'Red,' along with A-B unit 01 Reporting for duty."

"Men, I am sure all of you are aware of what has happened to my beloved children. Yes?"

"Yes sir, we are."

"Very well then." Mighty Eagle flops a folder down onto the desk in front of him labeled 'OPERATION PORKCHOPS.' Red opens the folder, skims over various pigs' writing, diagrams, and mugshots, and passes it around his squad.

"So, Red, I want my children back. But I don't just want them back. You see, King Pig has been stealing eggs from our island for years now. This shall be his last time. I want him DEAD! TODAY! This is no ordinary mission, Angry Birds. Go to the armory and fetch the finest equipment."

"Sir, will you be joining us at all for this mission?"

"I might. Everyone bring a sardine can in case any of you need my help urgently. It will tell me the exact location to impact, but only use it in dire emergencies, per usual."

"Yes, sir. Hal, take the unit to the armory and get suited up in tactical gear. Make sure everything is perfect."

"Right away sir."

"CHUCK, PREPARE THE SLINGSHOT!"

"YES SIR!"

Streeeeeeeetch "SLINGSHOT READY SIR!"

"Launch at Latitude: -31.92024, Longitude: -49.06332.

See you on the other side, boys. FIRE!" The slingshot fired Red to Piggy Island to observe the surroundings. The rest followed behind him and soon were all there.

"Bomb, as our explosives specialist, you will blow a small hole in the side of the castle, then Bubbles will squeeze into it and widen it QUIETLY. Then Blues, being the smallest, will go in first to take out any nearby pigs and make sure the coast is clear."

"Yes sir." They all say in unison.

"Matilda, come in, this is Red. We have successfully landed and infiltrated the Piggy Island Palace. Making our way to the vault now. Over"

"Wonderful news Red. We'll be here to receive and respond. Over"

"Chuck, use your speed to find the vault and secure a perimeter around the eggs. Blues and Bubbles will come find you and get you into the vault."

"Yes sir."

"Hal and Bomb come with me. King Pig dies **today**."

As Red, Hal, and Bomb made their way up the stairs, they finally arrived in King Pig's throne room.

"So, you've come for your eggs, have you? Well, you're going to have to get through my vault first!"

"Red? This is Chuck, we have secured the eggs, over."

"Looks like we already have, *your highness!*

"This can't be!" King Pig said with distress.

"Red, we are prepping the slingshot for our departure, over"

"Happy trails Chuck! Over. What now, King Pig?"

"I- I-"

Hal had snuck behind King Pig and had a gun to his head, ready to splatter green blood all over the floor in front of him.

"Hal, ready your firearm while I tell Mighty Eagle of our doing. Mighty Eagle, sir, this is Red. We have King Pig in a vulnerable position. Do you have permission to shoot?"

"Get out of there. Launch the sardines on your way out."

"Sir, I understand this is personal for you, but this could be our best shot at ending his reign."

"THAT WAS AN ORDER, RED. GET OUT AND LAUNCH THE SARDINES. OVER."

"Yes sir... Over. Hal, leave him."

"Fine then. Matilda, come in. We're exiting the island now. Over."

"Wonderful! The landing pad is prepped for your arrival, over."

"Mighty Eagle, we've launched the sardines."

"I'm on my way."

"Sire, they've launched the sardines! What are we going to do?"

"There is nothing we can do."

And so the reign of King Pig ended, and a new generation of Mighty Eagles was born, forever instilling the raw power of the Angry Birds into the feeble minds of Piggy Island *forever*. And the Birds indulged in some very tasty barbecue.

Scary Things That Move In Mirrors

by Kendall Allen

A crash of lightning thundered down on an old crooked oak tree in the creepy town of Birchwood where Emily Hoppkins quickly tip-toed into the broken down flea market door. When Emily got through she heard the door slowly closing back after her. She heard the thundering rain splattering down on the roof, she thought it was going to fall through on her. She looked around at the old building that had been there for many years. Stuff was packed up to the ceiling there was no way that she could possibly see everything the store had in it. She took a few steps and noticed that the wooden floor boards bent with every little bit of weight that was laid on them.

She was walking past the costume area which had every costume you could think of in it, and noticed a beautiful antique mirror. She looked at her reflection, her hair was still in a french braid but it was soaking wet, her pink and white striped dress was wet but it wasn't dirty. She straightened out her dress where it had been wrinkled from the rain and tucked the loose strings of hair back into place on her head and continued looking around.

When she didn't find a costume that she thought was good for her, she turned around and started walking back towards the door. On her way she passed the mirror again and looked at it one more time before deciding to buy it. She pulled it off the shelf that it had been resting on and tucked it under her arm. After she paid for it, she ran back out in the rain and jumped into her little red car and drove home. It was pouring rain outside and it was dark, Emily stepped out of the car and jogged to the front door. She had to set the mirror down so that she could find her keys. She started jumbling them around looking for the one that fit her front door.

When she found the key that unlocked her door she felt a shiver run down her spine. She set the mirror down by the fireplace to let it dry off and went to go make herself some dinner. Her house was little but somewhat cozy. It had a nice warm fireplace and two bedrooms even though she was the only one who lived there, and one bathroom. When the mirror was dry she found a nail and a hammer and hung the mirror up on her living room wall.

She walked past the mirror a few other times that night and it kept getting more interesting each time she did. Sometimes she would walk past it and she would have her hand scratching at her head even though she wasn't doing it as she walked, but she just thought that she saw it wrong because as soon as she would face towards the mirror it would go back to normal. It did this a few other times and she was beginning to get creeped out.

The final time she walked past it she turned around and saw the most horrifying thing she had ever seen in her entire life. The reflection was smiling at her! It had a huge Grin with enormous yellow teeth, the face had turned white and instead of Emily's brown eyes, the reflection had green eyes that looked like they were going to pop right out of the thing's head. Emily screamed and ran into the closest room and hid under the bed. She waited for it to come after her but it never did. She slowly crawled out from under the bed and cracked the door open so she could see the mirror. The thing was still in the mirror and it saw her and yelled something through glass but Emily couldn't understand.

Emily creeped closer to the mirror and noticed that the thing was caged up in the mirror and obviously was calling her to help it out, or so she thought. Emily didn't know if she should trust it or not. She didn't know why it was caged up in there but she knew that if it was her in the mirror she would want out too. She grabbed a piece of wood from the kitchen that was off of a chair and went back to the mirror where the thing sat staring hopefully at her. She reared back and swung with all her might and busted the mirror's glass. She stood for a split second looking at the thing that was in the mirror. It was terrifying and it had that enormous grin on its ugly face. It said to her then with a low, scratchy voice, " I told you not to trust me, but I guess you didn't hear me, hahaha" Emily, shocked didn't know what was happening until the thing leaped out of the mirror and chased after Emily who was running for her life.

Emily ran down the dark basement stairs. She thought that she lost the thing. She hid behind boxes that held some bats and softballs. She was just about to get one of the bats when she heard the sound of the thing's feet hitting the steps leading down to the basement. The thing said in that same voice, " Come on out and play with me, I won't hurt you." Emily was too smart for that, she continued to stay in the place that she was and with no warning the thing shoved the boxes that she was hiding behind and laughed again, " Hahaha, now it's time to get revenge on the humans for trapping me in that mirror. I have been in there for over a hundred years and now it is your turn to get stuffed in a mirror.

Just as the thing was reaching for Emily she saw a bat laying on the ground beside her and in a split second she grabbed it and swung it at the thing's legs causing it to fall backward with pain. Emily hit its head too, knocking it unconscious.

Emily managed to drag the thing back up the stairs and threw it back in the mirror. The thing woke up and saw that it was getting sucked back into the mirror for good. It screamed, "No! I will be back!" Then it disappeared for good. Emily knew that she was safe and the mirror was a normal mirror now. Emily lived in peace for a few days after that, but Emily was walking over to her chair in the living room one day and turned around at the mirror and heard a sound that disturbed her, " I told you I'd be back. Hahahaha"

No Caller ID
by Bailee Arnold

It was June 26, 2016. As I was packing up the car to pickup my best friend, Sage, for our yearly beach vacation, I got the phone call. What started out as an amazing day suddenly took a turn for the very worst.

It was a stormy day, I vividly remember the terrible weather. I was getting ready and I couldn't find the dress she wanted me to wear on this very special and specific day. I wasn't looking forward to this day at all. The dress was black and had pink and violet flowers on the very bottom of it. It was long and had sparkly glitter on the flower petals, truly, it was beautiful. After what seemed like forever, I finally found it. It was in a box that we were never supposed to open, never in a million years.

My mind keeps racing, I don't know how this had happened. People keep telling me that it was all a part of God's plan, but she was my very best friend. Why had this happened to her? She didn't deserve this.

I had to write a speech, her mom requested it specifically from me. It was the hardest thing that I ever had to do. One of the hardest things in the world for someone is to write is a goodbye letter to their very best friend. I just kept telling myself 'at least I got to be by her and talk to her one more time'.

It was the day of the funeral and I could not believe my eyes. I walked in and couldn't take that pressure. I couldn't breathe. I was trying to swallow my sadness. I couldn't see. The whole world was spinning through my teary eyes. She always had a beautiful smile on her face. We hung out all the time, almost every single day, and it came to an abrupt stop. Please, don't take her away from me like this, PLEASE DONT!!

Her mom helped me inside. She is like a second mom to me. In the summer time we would always go to the beach together and just do alot of stuff when we were little. I couldn't believe it, seeing her like that tore me into pieces.It can't be. It can't be.

It was my turn for my speech. I couldn't do it. I just couldn't. I built up the courage to go up there. I couldn't spit out one word without sobbing. I was trying to swallow my sadness and blink the stuff that was in my eyes away.

After the service was over I went to her house to get the thing's she left for me. What I   would give to see her one more time; anything in the whole world. I stayed at her house for a little while, just being in her room made me feel like she was still here with me; like she never left.

These next seconds, minutes, hours, days, weeks, months and years are going to be hard without her being by my side. She was always there for me. I wish I could have done more. But it's too late now. Every morning and night I write her a note and put it in her bed (she told me before she passed she wanted me to do that, if it were to ever happen).

Now it is August of 2025, just a regular Monday, I still think about her everyday. Not one minute goes by without me thinking of her. No one knows how it happend. It's still a mystery that is too late to solve. People have been trying to solve it for years now but it's just too late they said. I mean, hey, at least she didn't have to go through Covid. That girl wouldn't survive one day in Covid quarantine.

One day, when I was at the store trying to get some cherries for my new pie recipe, I got a call from a no caller id. I didn't answer. Another call again with the same no caller id, and again I didn't answer. This went on for about 5 minutes, then I finally answered it.

On the other end of the phone I heard her weak, soft-tone voice say my name through tears and a studder in her voice.

Mistake

by Oliver Woodard

Two days ago:

As I walked into the Vet-Homo Fuze Institution, I would soon find out this would be the biggest mistake of my life! "Hey," I exclaimed to the security at the entrance of the institution. It was kind of bright but very clean-looking. Almost too clean.

I walked into the room titled "Fuzion Dorm ". It said this above all the doors down the hallway, but I had to walk into the one with "26" on the side. As instructed in the email. Then three doctors covered in blue clothes, with the blue face mask. They instructed me to the shower connected to the room that we were standing in. They said to use the soap and shampoo available sitting on the side of the shower. After I was finished I was told to put on a blue gown with only a string keeping it all from falling off. Once I did that, I was supposed to come and let one of the nurses who had been walking around know that I was ready for the survey. Before the Fuzion.

I did the following and was shown into a room with a lot of medical materials and a mask to cover my mouth and nose. The mask was attached to what stood out like a sour thumb. A metal coffin-like tube that had a glass door reaching from the top to bottom. They told me to lie down in it and that it would fill up with a liquid and I would be hooked up to IVs.

As they placed the mask on me it quickly became hard to breathe. It was very uncomfortable, but I knew that what I was breathing was anesthesia. I became very tired and everything started to slowly fade. Right before I was fully in the sleepy trance I felt multiple needles go into my arms, and the liquid that filled the chamber had a burning sensation.

As I woke up it was now nighttime. I had arrived early in the morning. I felt extremely sore, and almost like I was changing. Then I thought about the survey I took. It had some weird questions. It asked what my favorite animal was. I answered a kangaroo. I thought to myself that I had to be paranoid. But the name was also Vet-Homo Fuze Institution. Vet means animal, homo means human, and Fuzion means to join together. I suddenly fainted.

Only two of my senses were working, hearing, and smell. Then I shot awake in the woods. Except something was off. I ran around the large rock in the center of an opening in the woods. Not long after I fell to the ground. Where I began to look at myself... I had become a kangaroo! This was not good. I didn't expect that I would be a monster. I can't do anything anymore in my life. Nothing I learned or thought matters now. I am a kangaroo.

The days became long and the nights hollow. I began to think the worst. Will I be trapped like this forever? I kept waiting for the nurses to come rescue me but that was only a fantasy. With each day that passed I began to feel less like a person. I couldn't remember things past a certain date before the surgery. It was hard to think in English. I tried to yell for help but what came out was a loud squeal. This is the end.

Three Little Pigs Remix

by Mario "Rio" Padgett

One day the three pigs wanted to get out of the house, so they decided to go to the market. One is named Juju, another is Lulu and the other is named Coco. And They decided they were going to go to the market to get groceries for all three of their houses.They needed a lot of groceries. When they got to the market they got out of the car they noticed something, and kinda felt like they were being watched. It kinda felt off to them because they always went there and usually felt safe. So as they got in the store a worker greets them, but it is not a regular worker. The worker looked like he hadn't shaved in years and his voice was deep and scary.

They tried not to think much of it. As they shopped around finding things they needed, they started to notice the worker they saw at the front was following them around. They started to have the chills not knowing what was going on and was confused why that worker was following them around the whole store. So they decided to go find the manger and ask what was wrong with this worker they had, and the manger was very confused on which worker the pigs were talking about. So everyone was all confused and kinda creeped out at the same time.

They knew that they needed to get out of there fast so they checked out quickly and got in their car. As they look back, standing there in front of the back up camera is where they see a six-foot standing beast covered in fur. It was the wolf. They speed forward opposite ways from the wolf. And then behind them they see an all black car. In the black car was the big bad wolf. They didn't know what to do so they tried going down different streets to try to lose him.

They then turned down a street noticing he was not behind them anymore.

So they knew it was the time to rush home before the wolf found them. So they finally reached home and they were so relieved until they heard a loud rev sound like the wolf's car, so they quickly ran into their houses. One of the pigs' houses was made of wood, the other one was made out of hard plastic, and the third one was made out of brick.

The wolf noticed they ran inside so he goes to the first pigs house built with wood and tries breaking down the door, but that didn't work. So he then ran back to his car and got his trunk and came back with matches and a flame thrower so he lit a match up and started shooting his flame thrower and shot it at the wood house. The pig thought it wasn't going to do anything until the houses started to be taken over by flames. So he ran out the back door to the second pigs house knocking on his back door hard.

He let him in and they thought they were completely safe there in the plastic house that they were in. The wolf tried to throw flames at it and it didn't work. So then the wolf thought since it was plastic it could crack with a baseball bat, so he went and got his bat out of his car and started beating the house and started cracking the plastic. So the two pigs then run to the third pig's house which is made with straight bricks. He tried the same methods he did on the first two and neither did not work at all. So they decide to call the cops while he was distracted trying to get into their house. The cops decide to show up silent instead of with sirens so they could sneak up on him. So they snuck up on him and arrested him. And the three pigs lived happily ever after.

The Road Trip
by Makayla Huckabee

One summer morning, Heather got out of bed and went downstairs for breakfast. When she was done eating breakfast, she called some of her friends, Sheela and Piper, to ask them if they wanted to come over for the day and have some fun together. Then she got off the phone and started to clean up a little bit.

Right when Heather finished cleaning and went to sit down her friends were at the door. Instead of sitting down she went and answered the door. When her friends came in and sat down they had asked her why out of nowhere she wanted them to come over.

Heather said," Well the reason I wanted y'all to come over was because had this amazing idea since it was summer break."

Piper said," Well what is it, you know I have a short attention span."

Heather says," Ok, ok here it is, what if we went on a road trip to Minnesota?" They said in unison.

" OMG, that is an amazing idea, what made you think of it?"

Heather answers," Well you know how we all have been saving our money up for something enjoyable. Well I thought that this would be that really fun thing we could do."

The girls were so happy that all they could do was smile and scream. Later on, they finally stopped screaming and sat back down on the couch. They watched a movie and then decided to start packing for the trip.

Then Sheela asked," What do we need to bring for the trip?"

Heather answered," I'm not sure but take everything you would to go out of town for at least three weeks."

Sheela said," Ok, sounds about right for me."

So all of the girls continued to pack. Heather decided that she was going to bring her own blanket and pillow because she didn't like the idea of using someone else's pillows and blankets. After everyone had got done packing they decided to have some lunch.

"So Heather, what do you have around here for lunch?" Piper asked, going through the kitchen.

"Almost anything you could think of." Answered Heather walking over to Piper.

They all started to look and find ideas for lunch but no matter what they came up with no one wanted the same thing so they decided to do personal pizzas. After they decided on that they got to work and they had fun making the pizza but it also made a very big mess to clean up afterward. So while the pizzas were cooking they decided to go ahead and clean up so they didn't have to do it later.

"Our pizzas are done," Sheela says as she walks to get them out.

"Thank god I'm so hungry it's unbelievable," Piper said, getting ready to eat.

Heather got up and started getting the table ready while Piper and Sheela got the pizza out of the oven and cut it into slices. They all decided they wanted to cut the pizzas into sixths because they were going to have two slices of each pizza.

Later Heather tells the girls to go home and finish getting ready and get some rest over the night because first thing in the morning they are leaving for the road trip to Minnesota. So they do the girls rush out of the house out of excitement to go on the road trip in the morning.

After a good night of rest, the girls wake up and get ready for the day at their own houses, and then all meet up at Heather's house for the trip. When they get to Heather's house and start putting all of the bags in the car so they can leave as soon as possible. When they got everything in the car they double-checked and made sure they had everything they chose a playlist to listen to on the way and left for Minnesota.

On their way to Minnesota, they stopped several times for food or bathroom stops. When But when night came they stopped to stay overnight at an air bed and breakfast. They all checked into one room because it was cheaper and they wanted to stay together.

When they all laid down to go to sleep Piper realized she had to use the bathroom so she went downstairs and passed the basement door she realized it had a sign on it not to enter so she just ignored it and went on to the bathroom. On her way back she stopped at the basement because she was wondering why it had the sign saying not to enter but she decided not to go in because she thought it had a sign for a reason.

So Piper goes back to their room and goes to sleep for the night. When they wake up in the morning they all go downstairs and get some breakfast together. But when they get downstairs Piper tells them about the trip to the bathroom last night and how the door had the sign. After she told them the story they wanted to go see the door for themselves but when they got to the door it was open with the sign down and the lock on it was broken.

So they were so confused thatconfusedceruse that they all went down into the BASEMENT!!! The first ones to go into the basement werewas Piper then, Sheela, and Heather. When they got into the basement there was a switch. Heather flipped the switch and a light came on. After the light was on it wasn't as scary as they thought it would be. But what they didn't know was that there had been reports of people going into that basement and never coming back.

They all stood still for a minute and heard something they had never heard before. It sounded like screeching. The sound of horror. The most terrifying thing ever. They were all fixing to run up the stairs and get out of there but then the door slammed shut. When they turned around they came to see a werewolf. They all screamed out of fear. The werewolf enchanted them and turned them into werewolves and they became a part of the pack and were never to be seen again.

Devil's Angel

by Landon Sims

The grass trampled and snapping, hearing the swiping of it, I ran and ran till I felt my lungs collapse. A rock betrayed me and I fell face first, I then saw one black feather fall to my face and then a slash of blood.

In golden letters "Museum of Fredrickson Raven" I sighed thinking "I'm too old for this…" I walk up flashing the gold badge being allowed to cross the line. I walked in smelling the stitch of dread, I pitched my nose never smelling something this bad "Jesus christ!" I say. Detective Brooke walks up to me "Detective Hax! It's been a while. How was the vacation" I chuckle rolling my eyes "I was sick one day and everyone thinks I'm dead!" I laugh it off going into the room where all eyes are on.

I walk in and see the room of the 1300 plague, plague doctor suits, plague equipment and an empty stand.

I asked a detective "So what happened here?"

he responds obviously tired "Someone stole the devil's cloth"

I look at him as if he was joking, then see he's being serious "What in the devil is the devil's cloth?"

He responds slightly surprised "Right your new in town, the cloth is some folk tell of the crow, a story where some crow man been killing people, but yet to be found some say he had the plague and was hung for witchcraft" I look at him and laugh, and respond sarcastically "Sure sure whatever!"

I grab the first lead, it being a small town stuff like this never happens we don't have a lot. I start heading there to an old farm house in a field there, seeing an older man maybe in his 40s in red plaid.

He yells out "Who goes there!?" I begin to step out of my car, flashing my badge saying "Detective Hax, but I advise you to call me Victor" I say walking up to him, I then say sternly the fog closing in, strangely feeling worried and closed "You have been suspected as a man who stole the Devil Cloth, reasoning is your the first person we was instructed to suspect"

He raises an eyebrow surprised and puzzled and says "Excuse me! Me? I haven't been in this town for a month and you're suspecting me of a crime! This is barbaric!" I sigh.

Before I say something my radio dings and someone says "I'm watching you victor" I raise an eyebrow,

 pressing the button then saying strangled in my own voice "Who's this?" the man speaking through the radio says "I'm the devil's angel, and your gonna be hell and back if you keep going down the route your heading, don't go to the old jurnleen house if I was you"

I don't think for a second, I hop in my car and start driving, but see the plaid man and swear I saw him crack a smile. But I had no time for that so I drove there knowing the stories of a man breaking into that family's house and all burning alive inside so why was there, that was in the 90s what could this have anything to do with the devil's cloth I kept thinking. I stop my car making a sharp turn and hop out, seeing the house still down I keep my hand near my holster as I walk up there looking for any clues for what's happening and then I step on something.

I look down to see a radio with a black feather on it, I pull out some gloves but hear someone say in crackling broken voice "Great job" I pull out my gun but it all goes to black feeling a thud in the back of my head. I wake up in a basement of some sort confined in this room, I turn to the exit of this door seeing someone peek from a hole in the door. I run and bang on the door and then the door falls down and I look at my hands thinking "did I do that?"

A man to the side, burned black wearing a old burnt coat and torn pants says "Don't flatter yourself chump by the way, I would run" he says reaching for something, I reach for my holster noticing my belt is gone, I then run down the narrow hallway feeling like it's closing in on me then notice it is closing in. I panic and see the door at the end of the hallway and jump for it barely making it then see something I wish I had never seen, "MORE DOORS!" I yelled, seeing a big hallway of doors, some saying exit but being locked, all being just metal doors but after an hour I made it down to the end of the hallway with a door opened.

I hear a crackle seeing that burned man waving bye. I go out and see the stars sighing in relief but a feather falls down, I then see standing in front of me a man in a plague doctor suit with black raven wings it says "Welcome to Raven-home the homes of ravens and freaks" he lunges at me but I dodge and booked it out making it into the trees, laughing in the distance. The grass trampled and snapping, hearing the swiping of it, I ran and ran till I felt my lungs collapse.

A rock betrayed me and I fell face first, I then see I'm at the burned home, I stand up and see one black feather fall to my face and I turn around seeing it, I try to lunge at it tackling him but I felt a sharp pain in my stomach looking down seeing it's arm pierced through my stomach right through, I start gagging choking on my own blood, it says "Don't worry your fit right in, plus you won't be going to hell, your be staying with us" it starts cracking up.

I felt as if I was a new man, stitched up with random mens' skin stitched on me, I felt happy. The crow, my new savior as the root of all evil has found me and made me and saved me from humanity. The Devil's Angel has become the evil of raven-home.

Friends

by Troy Fisher

Friends make life very enjoyable but how do you know if you are a good one? In this article, I will be talking about how to be a good friend. Friends do things like checking in on their friends if they have not heard from them in a while. Also, they are good listeners and communicate with them honestly and openly. These are a few different ways that I will be talking about on how to be a good friend.

One way to be a better friend is by checking in on your friends if you have not heard from them in a while. Doing this shows that you care about them. In the text, "The ultimate guide on how to be a better friend," it says "checking in on a friend you haven't heard from can strengthen your bond, offer support, and potentially help them if they're struggling, all while reminding them you care and are thinking of them." This shows that checking in on them can make you a better friend because it reveals that you care about them.

Another way that you can be a good friend to others is by being a good listener when they talk to you, especially when they are upset or frustrated about something. In the same text from the last evidence, "The ultimate guide on how to be a better friend," it says, "When you actively listen to your friend, they feel heard and valued, which strengthens the foundation of trust in your friendship." This shows that when you are listening to one of your friends talking to you it makes them feel valued and cared about when they are talking to you. It also shows them respect when you are listening to them. In the same text, it says, "Paying attention and listening to your friend when they speak is a sign of respect and a skill that will lead to deeper and better relationships." This shows that listening can make you a better friend and strengthen your friendship.

The last way you can be a good friend is by communicating with them honestly and openly, which can be tough because you do not want them to hate you. However communicating with them honestly will not only strengthen your relationship with them but will build your trust with one another. In the text "The ultimate guide on how to be a better friend," it says, "Open and honest communication with friends fosters deeper connections, builds trust, and allows for better understanding and conflict resolution, ultimately strengthening the bonds of friendship." This shows that being open and honest will strengthen your friendship and will make you a better friend overall.

Having friends is important because they make life more enjoyable. Those writing explores ways that you can be a better friend to others and strengthen your friendship. A good friend checks in on your friends to let them know you care about them. Being a good listener when they speak to show that you care about what they have to say and show you can be respectful. Also, communicating with them honestly and openly shows that you are trustworthy. Those are some of the many different ways you can be a good friend.

She Found It In The Back A Desk Drawer

by Harper Imami

S he found it in the back of a desk drawer.

"Anne? Where are you?" a woman shrieked,

Anne shoved the paper in her pocket and shut the drawer.

"Anne! What are you doing here? Dad's not here right now, you're not supposed to be in here anyway!" she said,

"Uhm, sorry. I was just...looking for a phone charger. My phone's almost dead." Anne lied,

Her mom glanced at her phone and saw it was at 89%.

"Why are you lying Anne? Your phone is at 89%, what are you doing in here?" She said with a death stare,

"Okay okay! I'm looking for...uhm...paper. For my art drawing?" Anne said confused on what she said,

"Still. You know you're not supposed to come in here, this is dad's work stuff. He would be really angry if he found out that you came in here without permission. Where'd you even get the key…Whatever, just go to your room!" she yelled.

If you're wondering what is happening, I will explain it. It all started when Anne was late for her doctor's appointment that morning.

***

"Anne! WAKE UP! WE'RE LATE FOR YOUR DOCTOR'S APPOINTMENT!" Anne's mom screamed. Her mom hated being late so she knew that she had to hurry. Anne slipped on a pair of blue ripped jeans and a pink spaghetti-strap shirt with a star in the middle.

"You look just like me! I used to wear those shirts all the time!" she smiled,

The weird thing is that Anne looked nothing like her mom or her dad, and that made her wonder.

"Okay, come on! Let's go! Put on some makeup because you look like The Walking Dead. And brush your hair, it's greasy!" she said.

Anne's mom always treated her differently than her sister. Sure, she was nice sometimes but she always gave her sister the benefit of the doubt. For example, Anne had been wanting a Range Rover for her birthday, and guess who got it? Her sister, Marie. Even though Marie is 4 years younger than Anne! It didn't make sense and Anne always started overthinking if she was their daughter. She slathered makeup on her face and brushed her hair and ran out the door.

"Isn't Marie's car so pretty? Why haven't you asked for a car yet?" she asked,

"I don't know, maybe because you already got my dream car for MARIE?!" I replied,

"No need to be so salty, she's my daughter so I got a nice car for her!" she screamed,

"But, I'm your daughter too! Right?" Anne asked. Her mom stayed silent, and so did Anne. The silence filled the car as they drove to

Anne's doctor's appointment and Anne decided to find out what was going on. She slid her phone out of her back pocket in the waiting room and pressed the on button. She typed in her passcode and clicked on Safari. She typed in seven simple words that formed into a question. How. Do. I. Know. If. I'm. Adopted. The results all said different things, but she decided on something that was not one of the results.

"Mom? Can you drop me off at home and get me a Starbucks drink? Please?" Anne begged,

"Why can't you come with me?" she replied,

"Uhm....well. I'm...SICK! Yes, I'm sick and need to get home immediately. I want Starbucks because I haven't had food all day, and I want a cake pop. Please?" Anne kept begging and begging until her mom finally gave in.

"FINE, fine, just stop begging your voice is like nails on a chalkboard," she said.

Anne saw a shiny gold bobby pin, grabbed it, and shoved it into her hair. Then she hopped out of the car and ran inside. She ran upstairs and started walking down the dark hallway leading to the big brown wooden doors that would eventually lead her to her past that had been tucked away by her parents. Her feet stop moving and her eyes slowly look up to the huge golden handles. Each door had special markings that were engraved in the wood. Anne saw the lock and wiggled it in between the crack with the bobby pin that she pulled out of her hair. The door opened slowly and a big flash of light came through the window. She walked through the doorway and softly walked on the creaking floorboards.

"Where could the papers be? Think Anne THINK! If I were adoption papers, where would I be?" she whispered.

Anne opened and closed almost every drawer except one with a silver lock. She grabbed her bobby pin and wiggled it, but it wouldn't budge. She put her hand under the drawer and felt a key. She slid it out and twisted it through the keyhole. She found it in the back of a desk drawer - a birth certificate. Anne Marie Kent, the daughter of Mackenzie Faye Woodland and Jackson Emmett Woodland.

"Wait a minute. That's my name. But those aren't my parents." Anne said in disbelief.

Anne kept rummaging through the papers and found adoption papers. Anne Marie Kent. Adopted by: Margaret Elizabeth Kent and Duke Reese Kent.

"I cannot believe this. This all makes sense now. I am adopted and no one told me! When were they going to tell me? Were they even going to tell me?" Anne gasped,

"Anne? Where are you?" a woman shrieked,

Anne shoved the paper in her pocket and shut the drawer.
***
"Anne! What are you doing here? Dad's not here right now, you're not supposed to be in here anyway!" she said,

"Uhm, sorry. I was just...looking for a phone charger. My phone's almost dead." Anne lied,

Her mom glanced at her phone and saw it was at 89%.

"Why are you lying Anne? You're phone is at 89%, what are you doing in here?" She said with a death stare,

"Okay okay! I'm looking for...uhm...paper. For my art drawing?" Anne said confused on what she said,

"Still. You know you're not supposed to come in here, this is dad's work stuff. He would be really angry if he found out that you came in here without permission. Where'd you even get the key...Whatever, just go to your room!" she yelled.

Anne quickly walked back into her room and sat on her bed. She noticed her outlet sparkling under her nightstand as she tried to catch her breath. She curiously put her head under her nightstand and touched the outlet. *BANG. Everything went black.

The Beautiful Sunset

by Rose Stewart

The luminous sun is going down, a fiery and feisty red.
Apricot colour flows where the sun now fled.
purples, pinks mix into the last sight of sky blue.
The sights of a night slowly come with a dark hue.

Beautiful auburn and gold shadows start to sway,
As they quickly paint the sky
Letting everyone know it's close to the end of the day.
A swift masterpiece
So bold, so pretty, so bright,
Shows the sun shining its last light.

Bad Mood

by Elijah Smith

One day it was sunny and clear. JaQuavion was so excited to be able to play outside with everybody in the neighborhood. He was playing until he tripped over a rock and broke his leg. That same day, it started to thunderstorm. He had to get rushed to the hospital. Since it was so intense, he had to spend the night there.

The whole week he was in the hospital, there were thunderstorms the whole time. When he went into the room to get surgery, he was happy. So, the weather was sunny. When he came back out. He was glad that he could walk again. Since he knew he was coming home and he could walk, there were no more thunderstorms after he came home.

All his friends were telling JaQuavion, "Your attitude controls the weather! Take the other day as an example, when you fell, there were thunderstorms. When you came back, it was sunny." JaQuavion didn't believe them at all. So he went to tell his parents what they said. His parents knew the truth but never told him. He thought his friends were just tricking him like they always do.

JaQuavion had to go to Physical Therapy, so he can walk without assistance. When he went, he asked the doctor if the mood and weather was real. The doctor replied, "Well." Then JaQuavion fell asleep. The parents told the doctor, " Don't say anything to him about it.

He will try to always act happy when he is really angry." The doctor nodded.

His friends kept trying to tell him about it. His parents heard it this time and told the friend's parents. Their parents told them the same thing. Then after that day, the friends didn't say anything about it.

The next day, JaQuavion lost his championship and was mad about it. He was mad for over a month. So guess what? There were thunderstorms for over a month. He started to notice that there were thunderstorms when he was mad. Then sunny and clear when he was happy. So he asked his parents about it and they told the truth.

JaQuavion knew he was right. He told his friends they were right. He tried to act as happy as he could be. Nobody wanted JaQuavion to feel this way. When he was mad, nobody knew because he always acted one way. They all hated how he was acting. Nobody knew the real JaQuavion. He never came out of his room to talk to anybody.

When he started to come out of his room, he seemed fine to everybody. He talked to everybody like it was normal. The truth affected him like if he had a family member die in his family. Nobody wanted to talk to the fake JaQuavion. He was like a kid on Christmas morning, getting coal and being happy about it.

When JaQuavion started to talk to the doctor to see if they could fix his bad mood disorder. The doctor said, "Yes. They can do it but he needs to go into a long surgery." JaQuavion was happy with that.

JaQuavion got done with his surgery. He was in a bad mood when he got home. It was sunny. His mood disorder was gone. He never had to deal with his disorder ever again.

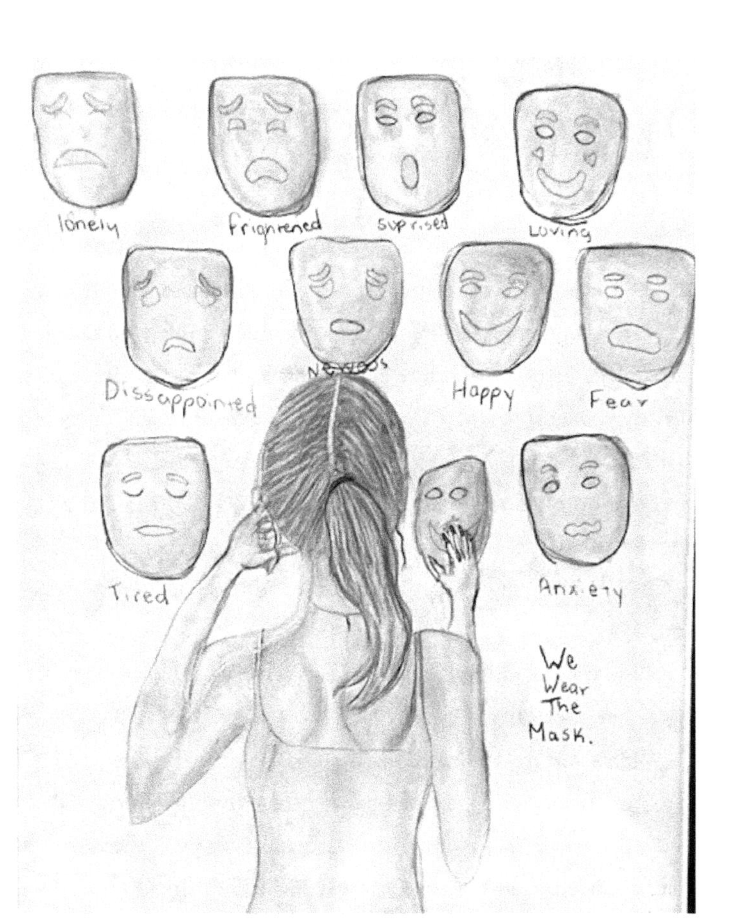

lonely
frightened
suprised
Loving
Dissappointed
Nervous
Happy
Fear
Tired
Anxiety
We
Wear
The
Mask.

Heir To Fortune

by Alyssa Reavley

The loud noise of the train station rings in my ears, making me feel slightly disoriented. I enter the noisy crowd and take my place in the identification line. The identification line is where they identify you, ensure your ticket is accurate, and ensure you are going to the right place. I think it's a long and boring moment. Soon enough, fifteen minutes passed, and the loud clock hit 1:00 PM. The clock rings in my ears, making me lose my focus for a few seconds.

I finally made my spot at the counter, and I sighed with exhaustion.

"I'm waiting for Train 35," I say politely because I know a job like this can be a total bore.

"Here you are, Hellen Lewis, right?" The trainman says politely.

"Yes, thank you," I say as he hands me my freshly stamped ticket. The red ink catches my eye, then the trainman's eye. The stamp is different; it's the same as others at first glance, but then I look closer and see a smaller logo in the middle. It's a little package logo in the middle, it's confusing me. I look at the person behind my stamp, and it's the same at first glance, but then no package logo in the middle.

The trainman gave me a peculiar look with a worried eyebrow scrunch. "Good day," I say to him strangely. I need to get to the bottom of this stamp. I see the trainman smoothly put the peculiar stamp back underneath the counter. I walk forward and try to erase the stamp from my mind, but I can't.

I walk through the train's door and make my way through the narrow hall. I pick a seat right in front of a window and set my brown leather clutch purse down on the train floor. I see in big black font above the train door "TRAIN 35". I look out the window, and all I can see is the harsh winter sky.

The snow falling against the cold bitterness outside makes me shiver. Then, with a cheery smile, a tall, slim brunette strolled down the narrow hall. Humming Christmas carols, she offers me a steaming cup of hot chocolate.

"Care for a cup? You look quite cold; after all, it looks so bitter out. Please, have some. It's the least I can do." She says with a warm smile.

Her warm smile slightly comforts me in the bitterness of the day. I accept the cup with a warm smile and thank you. "Thanks," I say warmly.

The train is simply beautiful. I've never been on one this nice. It has warm wood walls, red velvet seats, delicate wall candles, freshly washed windows, warmth and comfort, and a beautiful green and brown checkered floor. The attendant pulled out a side table that I didn't even know was there and gently set my cup of hot chocolate on the petite white plate. I smiled at her, and she walked away.

Her heels are not making any noise, surprisingly, and her energy still lingers behind her. I've always been a nervous traveler, and I always will be. Except this once, something about the train is just different. Warmer, cozier, just something amazing, and I can't figure out what. I blow on my cup of hot chocolate and then take a small sip. *"Mhmm."* I think to myself. The hot chocolate is so warm I can feel it trickle down my throat and feel the chills in my body slowly disappear.

The hot chocolate is perfectly sweet, at the right temperature, and with the proper amount of whipped cream and marshmallows. I love it, it reminds me of home. Venice has cold winters but warm and cozy homes. I was adopted as a child, and I am 18 years old. My adoptive parents never told me about my parents, and maybe that's for my own good. Small things like this truly mean a lot. I am headed from home to Buckinghamshire, England. I am headed that way because I am going to the University of Oxford. I was accepted due to my musical abilities, but it will be a long journey.

Maybe I won't be as uncomfortable on this train, it's cozy and warm. Not sketchy and dewy. The seat is very cushioned and comfortable. I am enjoying the ride. Soon enough, people start to come onto the train. But from what I notice, all these people are dressed very luxuriously, and I'm dressed semi-formally. I feel so underdressed. A man sits next to me, about age fifty. He is wearing a brown leather hat, a black and beige checkered coat, and black slacks. His shoes are as shiny as the gold on the windows.

The train is comfortably full, and I settle in for the ride. The seventeen-hour and nineteen-minute ride. I think I will enjoy it, *I hope.*

Already two hours in, I see the mysterious man pull out his pocket watch. I peek over and see the time: "7:55 PM". My eyes widen at how quickly time has passed. But soon enough, I feel myself slouching slightly in my seat and my eyelids weighing down. I am exhausted. This past week, I haven't gotten any rest worrying about my letter back from the University of Oxford. I decided to close my eyes, and soon enough, I caught myself dozing off, my tense shoulders finally relaxing.

A loud whistle fills my ears, the sweet attendance lady walks up to me. I wake up to her hovering over me, picking up my empty hot chocolate cup. I seem slightly startled, and I grab my bag and thank her for her services. I looked over to my right, and the mysterious man was gone, but wait, he left something.

A small brown paper bag with a white string wrapped around it, tied in an almost perfect bow.

"For Hellen Lewis"

My eyebrows scrunch in confusion, and I pick up the bag. I unbutton my brown leather clutch and slip the small package into it. The package is the size of my wrist to my fingertips. I button back up my brown leather clutch and move forward. Weaving my way through the crowd, I spot the mysterious man. I speed walk forward, my heels echoing throughout the train station.

"Sir! Sir!" I yell out to him.

"You forgot something, sir!" I practically screamed out to him.

I finally catch up to him and tap him on his shoulder once. He turns around and looks at me. But not with any look; he looked clean through me, almost as if I didn't exist. We made eye contact for a split second, but why did he walk off? Thoughts and questions race through my mind, and I can hear my heartbeat in my ears. I take a few deep breaths. I finally determined what to do: just keep going.

I remember to myself why I am truly here, and it's not for some strange man on the train and some petite little package he left behind to confuse me. I think again, I am here for success, I am here for progress, I am here to be the best of the best, and now is not the time to get thrown off.

I leave the train station doors and find a spot in the crowd to cross the street. The traffic director signals that we can cross the street, and we all crash around each other to fit in the tiny white lines. A few seconds later, I'm on the other side of the street. My apartment should be only about ¼ a mile away.

As I walk, I breathe in the beauty of England. Tall clocks, beautiful flowers, the smell of freshly baked bread and pastries, and so much more. Granted, it's about 7:00 PM, but I still wanna make it to my apartment.

I finally make it there, and a relieved sigh escapes my body. I gently brush the hair out of my face and walk in. I make my way to the lobby and walk up the stairs. Halfway through, my legs begin to hurt, and my eyelids feel heavy. *"A few more steps."* I think to myself. Tiredly, I opened up my apartment door. No creaks, thankfully. The floor is just as nice as it was described to me: polished, shiny, and pretty. The room smells of vanilla and cinnamon, making me feel at home a little.

I take a few steps into my apartment and set my bags down as I take a deep breath, and then the thud of my bags onto the floor echoes the room. I shut the door behind me and took a seat on the couch that was set up. It has a fine, warm white color with a velvet touch. It reminds me of the inside of my brown purse, which also reminds me of the mysterious brown package. I reach for my purse and unwrap the small, mysterious bag.

Anxiously untying the strings, my fingers moved quickly along the brown package. I finally untied the strings, and I tore open the brown package. There was a box inside, covered in black velvet with my initials inscribed. My fingertips gently rubbed across the black velvet, and I smoothly removed the lid of the box, air releasing from the box. I see a dazzling sapphire necklace, sparkling as blue as the ocean. It has a diamond chain and diamonds around the edge of the almond-shaped sapphire.

My eyes widened at the beautiful sight, and I slowly removed the necklace from the box. The diamonds twinkle as I rotate the necklace, reflecting the light in the room. As I rotate the necklace, something catches my eye, an engravement in the sapphire. I look closely and even squint my eyes a little, but the engraving says *"Heir To Fortune."* This leaves me completely clueless, but then it reminds me of the famous book written by an English Author, George Matthew. That book is not any book, it's the infamous book I have to read for my college study on writing.

I think this is all so weird, almost like *a setup*. Peculiar, how the book I am reading is engraved on a necklace that I received from a mysterious man on a train, with my name on the package, and with no other clues. I don't know what to do, *I don't*. I have all these random events all out of the randomness, and I must say this must be quite seldom for something like this to happen to anyone.

I get ready for bed, and I walk into my new bedroom. The bed is made, thanks to the maids. The room is spotless, and the lighting is very gentle on my eyes. I have enjoyed it here so far.

I finish getting ready for bed, and as I finish, I return to the living room to grab something. The necklace. I pick up the necklace and carry it to my bedroom. I feel the cold, fresh chain drop onto my fingertips as I walk to my bedroom. I open my bedroom door, and I walk over to the bed.

On the right and left side of the bed, both have lamps. I just set the sapphire necklace on top of my nightstand, leaving it alone. I walk over to close my windows and shut my door. I make my way back over to my bed, and I start to roll down my blankets. Right as I make my way under the covers, I give one last glance at the necklace. I then roll around and close my eyes, but I have thoughts racing through my mind. I can't go to sleep. I ponder and wonder why the necklace came to me and how strange all these signs are. I just try to go to sleep and empty my mind.

After all my panicking thoughts, I finally got some sleep. Soon enough, I woke up to the bright sunrise of Buckinghamshire, England.

It felt like an extremely restless night to me, but I still forced my body to get out of my bed. I look over to my right, and the strange necklace is still there. A shudder went through my body, and I could hear my tired heartbeat in my ears. I turn away to see if that helps, and all of a sudden, I get a hot flash, causing me to stagger across my room.

I retrieve my balance by holding onto the brown and gold dresser, and after a few seconds, I finally feel okay. I think to myself, *"What an awful way to start my morning."* I take a deep breath and take a few steps over to my window. Finally, over there, I open the curtains and open the windows for some fresh air. The air is very fresh, crisp, and pleasant. I can already smell the bread and flowers. A smile slowly appears on my face, and I feel okay again.

I grab my clothes from my closet, putting on a sage green silk dress with a brown sweater that matches. I pick out my white heels with the silk bow on the toe, and I grab my sage green and white pearl purse. I grab the strange necklace off my right nightstand and attach it to my neck.

I make my way out the door to the coffee shop, and I can smell the espresso from here. I enjoy the smell of freshly brewed coffee and steamed milk. It reminds me a lot of home. Home. Venice, the crisp summer air, the cold summer water, the winter treats, the spring flowers, and the fall leaves getting swept off the streets.

I make my way across the street and stop near the espresso shop. I walk in, and I hear a loud "Ding!" from the doorbell. I take my spot in line and look at the black-and-white chalk menu. I decide to order a sweet espresso with five thumbprint cookies with vanilla icing. I finally get up to the counter and greet the barista with a warm smile, "Hello! Can I get a vanilla espresso with five thumbprint vanilla cookies to go, please?". The barista quickly writes it down on paper in messy cursive that even doctors can't read. He goes into the back, passing through a white door and yelling in French my order. I am assuming that this is a French-owned coffee shop, considering I can barely read half the menu.

I receive my order and give a few smiles to visitors as I walk out the doors; now, I need to get to school. Today is my first day at the University of Oxford, and it's a lecture day. I have a lecture in history, and I can't wait. History is my favorite subject of all time; it makes me think and gives me a challenge. I finally make my way through the bustling streets of England, and I am finally at the University of Oxford.

I make my way through the doors and see the massive, sparkling, marble floor. I look all around, and I find little signs across the lobby that point toward different directions. Some say *"Bathrooms"* or *"Lecture Hall"*. Which is the one I need to go to, so I make my way in that direction.

My heels clicked down the hall, not too loudly, nor silently either. I finally arrived at the lecture hall after a solid five minutes of walking. I place my purse and items on a desk and settle in my seat. I've never imagined myself to ever be here, in the University of Oxford lecture hall. I've had this dream ever since I was little, and I just can't understand how I made it here. I can only imagine how excited my step-parents must be. Or how worried, I won't know immediately.

About thirty minutes later, the lecture finally started. The professor places his things on his desk and picks up the chalk on the board. He quickly writes his name in cursive, spelling out *"Dr. Smith"*. It is very messy, but at least I can still read it. He finally started his lesson, and I was instantly intrigued by my ears. My hand, without thinking, is quickly noting things. My hand moved so fast that I could hear my ballpoint pen quickly racing across my paper, left to right. Over and over.

The lecture is finally over. I take one look at my notes, and I am instantly in awe of them. Sectioned off, neat, and helpful for tests and assignments. Dr. Smith did say one thing: that I needed to receive that book today. I asked him after the lecture if it was in the library, and he said yes, so I decided to make my way to the library. The book I need is *"Heir to Fortune."* By English author George Matthew.

I am finally at the library, and I am short of breath. Nobody told me this school was going to be this big. I look for the aisle that I need to go to for my book, and I quickly arrive. *"Aisle 18,"* I mutter to myself.

Again, another peculiar thing. *Aisle 18, Heir of Fortune, my initials, my necklace, my age.* What does this even mean? I don't understand, I am just very confused. I don't know what to do, so I just hopelessly walk down aisle 18 and make my way to the *"H"* shelf. I trace my fingertips along the bookshelf, feeling the hard spine of every single book. I abruptly stop when I see the bold *"H"* on the shelf.

I reach out and look at all the book spines, and I see just one: *"Heir of Fortune"*. I see about ten paperback copies, and then I see one hardcover copy. I grab the hardcover copy because it won't bother me nearly as much as a flimsy paperback copy of a book. I slowly open up the cover of the book as I hear the crisp awakening of this book, which is almost brand new. Maybe, just maybe, brand new. I can tell by the sound that this is a new book, freshly placed.

I walk up to the checkout counter and check the book, and I take about two minutes to fill out the paper slip confirming I've checked it out. I finally finished filling out the white paper slip, and I returned it to the librarian. I smile at her and make my way out of the library. I finally reached the lobby after walking for a few minutes, and I made my way out through the doors. I make it onto the street and head back to my apartment.

After the tiring walk, I take a deep breath and relax for a minute. I reach out for my apartment door knob and twist the key clockwise. The door unlocks, and I see what puts me in immediate shock. The mysterious man, sitting on my couch. *"Hello, Hellen. Nice to see you again."* He says in almost a mutter-like style. My eyes widen at the sight and I almost suck in all the air in the atmosphere. I am in utter shock.

"I like what you've done with the place, but seriously, we need to talk." He says professionally.

"Who are you?" I say interrogatively. "Why are you here? Where did you come from? How do you know who I am?" I say with almost every bit of panic in my body.

"I am your uncle, the Duke of England." He says proudly. My eyebrows rise, and I almost squint a little.

"How do you know who I am?" I say anxiously.

"I have known you ever since you were a young girl, Your parents sent you into adoption because your mother and father died in an assassination. With me being the Duke at the time, the royal court was left to me, and I became King. But I still have the title Duke of England. You have no siblings, and you are the next heir in the line. I can no longer uphold this position, I would like to hand it down to you. I know every single little thing about you: your birthday, name, age, height, weight, IQ, school grades, everything. Your parents' last wish was to make sure you weren't exploited as a young royal child. You're finally old enough to accept the throne of England, so I am handing it down to you. I am aware of your studies and your daily life. The royal code may affect this a little, but you'll still be able to continue your education."

I take a moment to consider everything, and I can hardly swallow it. It's like trying to swallow a peach seed or something of the sort. I ask him, "What about the strange clues since you seem to already know more about me than I do.".

"Mademoiselle Hellen is how I shall address you from here going forward. I can't even parallel the confusion you're probably experiencing at the moment. I set up every single little clue you found, knowing everything. I've been communicating with your step-parents about you since you were adopted. Letters, telegrams, calls, and occasionally in-person meetings. Does that explain well enough?" He says patiently. After all, I am still *very confused.*

I take a few minutes to attempt to understand everything, and after a couple of minutes, I finally make sense of it. Uncle is what I shall call him because he is family, has offered to make me a cup of tea, and I accepted. Tea sounds very pleasing after today. I asked him what I should do next, and he simply responded, "You move into the palace, attend the coronation ceremony, and continue like normal."

"Seriously?" I say, slightly shocked. "When do I move in?" I say.

"As soon as tomorrow, Mademoiselle Hellen." He says politely.

I can't imagine it. I have been being watched ever since I was a toddler up until now, and I am next in line for the throne. He also said the coronation ceremony was next week, but I think I will have trouble getting settled in. But it all makes sense now, the weird clues, everything falling hand-in-hand with each other.

Soon enough, it's evening. Uncle heads home, and I go to bed. I quickly fell asleep due to my exhaustion. My schedule will be a little different now that I am royal, but I choose to worry about the details later.

The week flew by, and before I knew it, I was attending the coronation ceremony. I arrive at the palace, and a group of five kind ladies show me the palace and present to me a lavish sage green silk dress. I simply love it. I can't believe this is my new home, it's crazy. I'm not used to this; my definition of home is Venice and my step-parents. But I guess now *I have to deal with it.*

I arrive at the ceremony, I take my seat on the stage, and I listen to my uncle's speech. By the time I have to approach the podium, I say a few words, and Uncle places the sparkling diamond and sapphire crown on my head. I can't believe it, and in a few months, a graduation cap as well. After a few other speeches, the ceremony came to an end, and I entered the palace.

It's hard for me to accept that I finally live here. I'm used to the busy streets of Venice now, it's the quiet halls of the palace.
A few months pass, and I'm the official Princess of England. I earned my education degree in History, and now I am studying for a doctorate. *All of this over a brown package.*

The Day My Life Changed Forever

by Cassie Thomas

The holy spirit has always been something I wanted . Every year I went to youth camp I tried to get filled with the holy ghost but I never got it. I even tried at winterfest but nothing. But this year at camp everything changed.

I wanted to be filled with the holy ghost so bad. No matter how hard I tried I never got filled with it. Saturday night at winterfest they had us say a prayer if we wanted to be filled so I said it but nothing happened. Everyone around me was getting filled but me. People all around me were feeling God's presence but I wasn't. I started to get really mad at God. I didn't understand why I didn't get filled with the holy ghost or why I felt like God was a million miles away.

I walked out that night at winterfest and I was so upset I was so mad at God. Everyone was so happy and full of joy. They were all talking about what had happened to them that night. When we got back to the motel, my room leader asked us about what had happened to us that night. She asked us if we had received something from God. When she asked me I said I didn't receive anything from God. Then she said I know You didn't get filled with the holy ghost but did you get a blessing from God. I didn't want to talk about that night. I was trying to hold back my tears. Yes I got a blessing from God. Great, I'm so glad to hear that. I had just lied to someone I had known for all my life. I felt so bad. I shouldn't have lied to her. I should have told her the truth.

It was finally June and it was time for youth camp. I was so excited for Wednesday night I had so much faith that I was going to get baptized in the holy ghost. And if I didn't get filled this time I would just try again. I was excited and scared. I couldn't wait for Wednesday night's church service.

It was finally Wednesday night and I was so excited. I couldn't wait for church service to start. Church started off like every night at youth camp. We walked down and stood in the front and did praise and worship. The west band led us in worship just like every night. That night I worshiped so hard I had tears rolling down my face. After that we went and sat down.That night we had a seat in the balcony. When we sat down the speaker came up and she started reading in the New Testament where they were filled for the first time.

Then she talked about how the Holy Spirit is your comforter and about a lot of other stuff. Then she told a story about when she got filled with the holy ghost and she told us if we wanted to be filled come down to the front and start to worship so that's what I did. I began to worship and started to cry so much my whole face was wet and I could barely see for all the tears in my eyes. One of my friends was laying on the floor. She had fallen out in the spirit.

I kept worshiping and everyone around me was receiving the holy ghost. I started to worry that I wasn't going to get it. Then I started to get chillies. And started to cry even more. Church started to come to an end and we only had a few minutes left. I started to sing along with the west as I was singing. I said a word I didn't know, a word I didn't understand. I spoke in tongues for the first time.

I was so happy I finally got filled with the holy ghost as I was walking out of church with my friend. My arms were swinging back and forth. I pulled my phone out and told my mom what had happened. Me and one of my friends went and got victory ice cream. That's what we call ice cream after church at youth camp. Ice cream tastes so much better when you get out of a church service like that. My mom finally text me back ''WOW you will never be the same.''

She was right. I haven't been the same since.

There's times know when I go in my room for hours. I turn on worship music and just sit there and pray and think God for everything he's done. Know when I start praying the holy spirit speaks through me. I say words I don't understand. I pray in the language of heaven. It is one of the most amazing things ever.

My life changed a lot that night. I got baptized in the holy ghost. And I realized that I needed to trust God's timing. All the years at camp and winterfest I tried to get filled with the holy ghost but I didn't. I was so mad at God. But now I realize that God had it planned for me to get filled with the holy spirit on June, 12, 2024.

A Legacy To Uphold

by Emma Dansbury

'*Even the lamp is starting to look different...*' Lacie thinks as her surroundings seemingly fade into the abyss. However, as if the world had simply blinked, everything begins to return to normal. Lacie's eyes flutter open. She hears the voice of silence creeping up on her. The world disappears again, but only for a fragment of time. She sits up, desperation clawing at her throat.

"Behind you." A faint voice whispers in Lacie's ear. She turns around slowly, unsure of herself. Yet the only eyes that greet her are those of her cat, Cleo. Cleo's tail swooshes back and forth as she nuzzles into Lacie's leg, her onyx eyes appearing almost...crimson?

Lacie's face contorts into an expression of curiosity as she takes a moment to really look at Cleo for the first time. She's tall, even for a Maine Coone. Her eyes glisten in the moonlight from the window, reflecting the speckles of light in the silhouette of the world that is her soul. Her fur is pitch black, with only a few outlying patches of white.

Lacie stands up slowly, to make sure everything is still real. She sneaks a glance at the lamp. '*Still there. Maybe I'm dreaming?*' After that, she attempts to forcefully shut her mind off. It works, but not for long. A dismal hum of the refrigerator drags her into the kitchen. With Cleo following suit, Lacie finds it difficult to not trip. However, she manages to get all the way to the fridge in one piece.

Her eyes hover over the pictures of her family clumsily taped to the refrigerator doors. She glances down at Cleo, then back up at the pictures. She notices something...off. Something familiar. In every single picture, the same pair of blackish red eyes and the same docked ear make themselves known. She looks down at Cleo once more, horrified. Cleo stares right back at her, impersonating the somber gaze of a human.

Once again, Lacie's eyes linger on the lamp. Still there. Her heart beats rapidly as she races to find the pictures in her scrapbook that she made of her whole family tree when she was little. She digs through boxes and boxes of books until she finds it. A thick, pink, glittery scrapbook titled, 'My Family!' in sparkling orange bubble letters. A sheer contrast to every single emotion she's currently feeling. She opens it carefully despite her shaky hands, and flips through each page with an abnormal amount of delicacy.

"There's not a single image without Cleo in it...some of these pictures are hundreds of years old..." she mutters to herself, intrigued. As if the words she had just uttered were some kind of spell, a billowing gust of wind suddenly shatters the windows. It swirls around her in a caliginous shadow.

In less than a second, her vision goes dull as her world fades to black. Except, her eyes are open. She *knows* they are. "What's happening..?" She voices aloud without realizing, however, all sound gets drowned out by the wind.

Minutes pass. The only thing she can hear is the same voice from earlier, yet she can't make out anything it's saying. The wind suddenly comes to a screeching halt.

"Lacie. Today is the day you have stumbled upon the legacy of your family. Young one, the only way to leave this dimension of eternal darkness is to take a picture with me. Everyone in your family has done it. Are you willing?" Says an unknown voice, yet somehow it's familiar. Lacie pauses for a while, but eventually speaks up, "Cleo...?"

The voice doesn't grace her with a response. However, instead it seemingly teleports her back to her living room. Cleo is sitting on her lap. She looks up at her, purring.

Without another complaint, Lacie pulls out her phone and snaps a quick picture of her and Cleo.

And just like that, the legacy lives on.

The Bee's

by B. D.

It was a summer afternoon in downtown California. My grandma and I just dropped my grandpa off at the airport. He was heading to New York for work. When we left my grandma asked if I wanted to go grab something to eat. Of course I said yes, I'm starving and going out to eat with my grandma is the best. I can order anything I want.

Grandma said "Once we get over the bridge back into town we will go grab some pizza."

"Sounds great," I said.

As we get to the top of the bridge we hit stop traffic. We sit there for ten minutes, when all of a sudden we see a whole bunch of bees.

We did not know what was happening, where did all these bees come from? There seems to be millions of bees swarming around. I was so scared I looked at my grandma and said " we need to get out of here I'm allergic to bees.

My grandma said " where is your epipen?"

" I don't have it with me," I replied.

The look on her face was turning white and had a scared look on it.

"What do we do grandma," I asked

She quickly dial nine one one the lady on answered said her name was pam.

Grandma said " We are on the bridge and what seems to be like millions of bees are swarming around. We need help. My grandson is allergic."

Pam said " Stay claim, do you have an epipen? "

Grandma said " No he doesn't have it with him."

Pam said " OK what I need yall to do is to close all the windows and shut all the vents. Stay calm. I have called for an ambulance and they should be there soon."

We asked Pam what was going on and why there were so many bees.

Pam said that there was a beekeeper moving her bees when she got into a wreck and the truck turned over and all the bees got out. They are doing their very best to get all the bees back in.

Thirty five minutes later and the bees were swarming and they landed on the car. One got in and it looked like one of the vents wasn't all the way closed and it sneaked in. Grandma told Pam what was happening she told us to stay still and don't move. If the bee gets scared it will sting us. The bee landed on my face. I tried so hard not to move then the bee got down under my nose it tickled and it made me sneeze. As soon as I sneezed the bee got scared and stung me. Grandma told Pam someone needs to hurry. My grandson got stung and I don't know what to do. My face started to swell and It was getting harder to breathe. I guess I passed out because when I came to I was in the ambulance on my way to the hospital.

My grandma said "we are never leaving the house without your epipen again!"

Haunted House

by Kayden Hixson

One day me and a couple of my friends and I decided it was a good idea to go explore this old run down motel at the end of the block. Me and my friends and I have always wanted to explore a supposed haunted motel. So we grabbed a bat and a cross and some ghost equipment and a couple of batteries for our flashlights then we headed towards the haunted motel.

We knew we had to be sneaky just in case. As we arrived we took one glance around and all we had already broken off the hinge. One of the balconies was only held on by a bent metal bar. There were vines running up the bricks of the old run down motel. In the distance we could hear dogs barking and howling. At that point we were getting a little scared and were thinking about heading back home but something about the motel kept making me want to go inside more and more. We had started to approach the building. We thought it was a dumb idea but we were tough enough to handle anything as long as we put our mind to it.

As we approach the entrance we hear something that sounds like footsteps. We walked in. I had one hand on my bat just in case something bad were to happen. We stepped in checking all directions making sure no one was there. We look around thinking about which direction we should go. I shined my flashlight down both of the hallways and did not see anything. I shined my flashlight down the third hallway. It looked like a black figure bolted 'at the end of the hallway. It scared me so bad it was like I was frozen in place. Both of my friends ran over asking me what happened all I could do was stand there frozen speechless. I sputtered about a black figure at the end of the hallway. My friends laughed like it was a joke and questioned whether or not I was still tuff..

As me and my friends started up the stairs we heard a door slam shut. We opened the door and looked around. Nothing was there. I noticed the bedroom door was locked. I tried to open the door but no matter how hard I pushed the door it wouldn't budge like something was pushed up against it so I kicked it open and nothing was there. I turned around and looked at my friends. They said what was behind it. I said nothing, they laughed and said let me see there was nothing there. It made my heart skipped like beats we slowly started backing up watching the door we starting walking down the hallway we see this one room it looked like someone busted the walls and all the glass in the room and there was no door guess they needed a door.

Ella

by Branson Hudson

Cinderella was coming home from her work at the school down the street. It doesn't pay a lot but it gets the bills paid. She parks in the driveway and walks out of her car. She reaches for her keys but she can't find them in her purse. She goes back to her car and she sees them in the locked car. She lets out a sigh.

Cinderella Walked back to the door and grabbed the spare under the welcome mat.

"Honey, I'm home!" Cinderella said, looking for her "prince charming"

"Christopher?" Cinderella starts looking around. She opens their bedroom door to see Christopher with another woman.

"Christopher!!!" Cinderella yelled with tears in her eyes.

"Honey, I can explain!" Christopher responded.

"Get out of my house Christopher!" Cinderella yelled.

"Fine!" Christopher Responded.

When Christopher and the other women left Cinderella just sat on her bed crying. A few months passed and Cinderella divorced Christopher. One day she was lying in her bed, tears in her eyes looking at the ceiling. She looked over at the trash can with her and Christopher's marriage photo. Cinderella wipes the tears out of her eyes and she grabs the photo and a lighter.

Cinderella walks out in her backyard and she burns the photo. After that she felt like she was a new woman. After a few days she dyed her hair and she changed her name to just "Ella". She looked out of the window and sighed. Ella knew her story wasn't over just yet. She went to the store and drained her ex husband's bank account from the card he left at her house.

Ella got her life back together. She becomes the principal at the school she was working at. One day when she was on a walk she tripped and fell and a guy helped her up.

"Woah are you ok?" He said.

"Yes, thank you." Ella responded. They lock eyes with each other for a few seconds.

"Have a good day, miss." The man said while walking away. Ella just stands there for a few seconds. When she came home she went to sleep. When she woke up she got ready for the day. Later in the day, she took another walk. After a few minutes, she saw the guy from the day before.

"Oh, hi again." He said.

"Hi," Ella responded.

"By the way, my name is Charles." The man said.

"My name's Ella," Ella responded.

"Here's my number so we can talk later." Charles said, handing a piece of paper with his number on it to Ella.

"Thanks." Ella took the paper.

"Well, good day to you." Charles said as he walked away. A few days pass and Charles and Ella have been talking a lot. After a few mounts they start dating. On a Saturday afternoon Ella was on her way to a date with Charles. When there, they had an amazing dinner at a restaurant.

"So how's the food?" Charles asks.

"It's amazing!" Ella responds.

"Ella," Charles says.

"Yes?" Ella respond

"Well I have been thinking and we have been dating for a long time now and..." Charles says while standing up. Then he gets on one knee.

"Will you marry me?" Charles asks.

"Yes!!" Ella responds, tears dripping down her cheek. A month later they had their wedding and it was beautiful.

"And Charles, do you take Ella to be your well-wedded wife?" The priest says.

"I do!" Charles responds.

"You may now kiss the bride!" After he said that Charles and Ella have a heartfelt kiss. Looks like Cinderella has a happy ending to her fairy tale after all.

The Three Little Skibidi's

by Chase Smith

Once upon a time there were three Little Skibidi's who were planning to build frat houses. The Little Skibidi's left their mother to be sigma and rizz up all the huzz. The only problem was to build a house, you needed the necessary supplies, so that you could live in it. Each one of these three little Skibidi's gathered supplies to build their houses.

The first Little Skibidi only bought drywall to build his house. This Little Skibidi was a slacker that only wanted to play video games. He put four sheets of drywall up for walls and a drywall roof. Then he immediately began doing nothing. After about three days of playing video games, the Big Bad Sigma showed up! He said Little Skipidi, little Skipidi let me in! He heard the stomping of the Big Bad Sigma and said no, not by the hairs on my low taper fade! Then the Big Bad Sigma reared back and reared back, and karate chopped his house down!

The first Little Skibidi hover-boarded to the second Little Skibidi's house after the Big Bad Sigma karate chopped his house down. The second Little Skibidi liked to party, so he made his house out of only red solo cups. The two Little Skibid's partied all night and were tired. Then the Big Bad Sigma continued down the block until he came across the red solo cup house with the two Little Skibidi's in it. He said, Little Skibidi's, Little Skibidi's let me in! The Little Skibidi's saw the Big Bad Sigma through the window and said not by the hairs on our low taper fades! Then the Big Bad Sigma reared back, and reared back, then karate chopped the red solo cup house!

The first and second Little Skibidi's hover-boarded over to the third Little Skibidi's house, after the Big Bad Sigma karate chopped the red solo cup house down. The third Little Skibidi was different from his two little brothers. The third Little Skibidi focused on important things when building his house, like the foundation and strong walls. This Little Skibidi spent many days building his house using galvanized steel squares. This Little Skibidi also planned for an intruder. The Big Bad Sigma kept walking down the road and found where the three Little Skibidi's were hiding. He said Little Skibidi's, Little Skibidi's let me in! The three Little Skibidi's saw his shadow under the door and said, not by the hair on my low taper fade! Then the Big Bad Sigma reared back, and reared back, and tried to karate chop the house down.

The third Little Skibidi's house did not fall like the others. So the Big Bad Sigma reared back, and reared back, and then karate chopped again, but the house didn't fall. This angered the Big Bad Sigma, so he reared back, and reared back, and then karate chopped the house once more. The Big Bad Sigma then got so angry that the house would not fall and said I'm coming in through the basement. Then the third Little Skibidi put a banana peel at the top of the stairs. The Big Bad Sigma broke into the house and ran up the stairs, but slipped on the banana peel and fell down the stairs breaking his neck. The three Little

Skibidis took the Big Bad Sigma to the hospital and lived happily ever knowing he was in prison with a broken neck.

Christmas Ban

by Jackson Hatcher

Mr President, you have recently placed a ban on Christmas, and I'm writing to tell you that this is complete foolishness. Banning Christmas is one of the worst ideas that you have had yet, many young boys and girls are now going to be miserable because of this. Which is why I propose that you remove this ban.

Firstly, Christmas itself just makes somebody happier. Research has been conducted, and it shows that people are happier when thinking about Christmas. In the text, "Why is Everyone so Happy During Christmastime?" The author states," Research has shown that thinking about Christmas or being exposed to topics centered around Christmas can positively affect brain activity. The mere thought of Christmas can cause various regions in the brain to light up, which generates an emotion commonly known as "Christmas cheer." This shows that you shouldn't ban Christmas because people are just generally happy when thinking about Christmas. If this ban were to stay up, people would be miserable, you don't want that for your nation, right?

Secondly, Christmas brings families together. Your whole family comes down to one place to meet up, talk, and exchange gifts. In the article,"10 Reasons We Celebrate Christmas,"

The author states," Christmas provides an opportunity for families to come together and strengthen bonds. Family gatherings, festive meals, and shared activities create moments of joy and connection. The holiday season encourages people to prioritize spending quality time with loved ones." This quote shows that Christmas brings families together and strengthens bonds. This is another reason why you should remove the ban on Christmas.

Finally, Christmastime even improves the economy. In the article," Christmas is a Great Holiday," the author states," Christmas significantly impacts the economy, driving retail and customer spending. Businesses and retailers experience a surge in sales during the holiday season. The Gift-giving holiday shopping tradition contributes to economic growth and job creation." This quote shows how Christmas spending can improve the economy of the nation. As a president, you would want this for your nation.

I see why you might have thought that this ban is a good idea. The First Amendment states that there shall be no law respecting the establishment of religion, and Christmas celebrates the birth of Jesus Christ, which makes it somewhat of a religious holiday in your sense. However, non-religious people can enjoy this holiday without believing in Christianity. Just because some people are not religious, doesn't mean they can't enjoy the happiness that Christmas brings. In the article," Should Christmas be abolished as a national public holiday?" The author states" There are those who emphasize Christian cultural aspects of Christmas Day rather than Christian religious beliefs." This quote shows that Christmas can be celebrated without it being religious.

In conclusion, I urge you to think about this ban on Christmas. This holiday is more than just a religious celebration, it is a time of joy and family. I ask you that you protect this cherished holiday, making sure that our freedom and respect are plentiful in this great nation. Thank you for your attention to this, and I'm hopeful that you preserve the spirit of Christmas for years to come.

The Letter

by Douglas Rudolph

S he found it in the back of her desk drawer. Seeing this envelope on her desk that had just been placed there on her birthday, she thought it was her cousin who had come over yesterday. Excitedly, she screamed, " Thanks for the letter, guys," expecting an answer to your welcome. She sat there waiting, only to be engulfed in silence. She thought it was weird that the elephant in the room was silence.

She was so weirded out that she went downstairs where she had heard her family's whispers. She stepped into the room and asked, " Who gave me this card?" eager to find out, but her mom said, "What are you talking about, honey?". She felt weird for two reasons: her family did not know she had gotten a card, and her mom never called her honey. She thought it couldn't have been possible for a random card to show up in the back of the desk drawer, but the one thing that she hadn't done yet was open it.

She ripped open the red envelope, and it had an overbearing smell of cinnamon, cloves, and pepper. She thought that was weird because that day, that is exactly what the whole house smelled like. Thinking it was just a coincidence, she opened the rest of the envelope and found a nicely designed letter with her name, Jamie, on it. The design was unusual with gates on it. She wanted to read it, but her mother called her to come outside. She went to put her shoes on and she was interrupted by a really loud bell, but the weirdest thing is her mom said "It's time!".

She noticed when her mom opened the door, she was blinded by whiteness everywhere. She fell back and tripped over her shoes when she saw that the people there were lined up waiting for something to happen. Then, she saw a godlike figure, it was Jesus himself giving everybody a welcome. Her jaw dropped and she ran right back into the house. As she was going back inside, she noticed that her mom was an angel with the most angelic and beautiful wings she had ever seen.

Noticing that everybody else was going into lines and waiting for their turn, she went to ask questions. "Am I dead? " she asked an old lady with really big oval glasses. She shrugged and went along in line. She noticed that when she had gotten into the line, she had a different shirt on with the words *father's fault*. What does father's fault mean? She went into a line with all the younger people and they all had the same words on their shirts: Father's fault. Those words gave her chills since her father was not in her life only a little of the time. She had her letter in her hand. Fueled with curiosity, she opened it and it read. " Hi, Jamie! You were my everything until your mother took it away, so I decided that if I can't have you then no one can. So I took it into my own hands and got rid of you!". With her father's name signed at the bottom of it. She put two plus two together and realized what her father had taken. Her father did it, he took her life away!

New City

by Bryson Couch

Has your life ever been flipped upside down? Well let me tell you a story that began in 2000...A rich guy, that is me, I had everything in life: money, and so much more. I didn't have to want for anything; had all I needed and more than I ever deserved could use in a lifetime. That was until one Sunday morning it was all taken away. My parents kicked me out and i was 21 of the mansion I grew up in, took all my fancy fast cars, and I didn't have a cent to my name. Then my life became my worst nightmare I ever had!

Hello, I am Alfredo and this is my life that should for you not to take anything for granted you may have to do things you would never dare. On a cold May Sunday morning and I heard a knock at the door and my mother answered it infront of her was the local police department officers. I was so nervous, my heart was beating so hard it felt like it was fixing to jump out of my chest as I heard hello mam' I am officer Knox with the New York city police department.

As I hear him tell my mother all about the street race whet a 1980 porsvhe 911 entered that night before. This wasn't the first time I had been pulled over caught and I should have listened when my mom said son one more time and all those cars will get sold. You will be left riding the public bus. I thought no way she would ever do that to me.

I could never be that close to strangers with all those germs! Little did I know that she would, and she did. All the friends that cheered me on as I raced down the streets those nights wouldn't answer for me to have somewhere to stay.

I walked and walked until I met the only person willing to help me; he was and he told me he was a homeless veteran . He had a sandwich he offered me. As all the thoughts of germs and who or where did this sandwich come from I felt my stomach seem like it was eating away at itself. He then offered me a warm place for a few hours on a public bus ride. I can't believe here I am, fifty strange people touching everything with all the dirty hands of everything they touched all day. Bus making stop after stop taking hours to get us just miles down the road.

Asking myself over and over how did I get here again. People looked like they haven't bathed in a while. This is where my life had led me. As I listened to this sixty year old veteran that had fought for our country explain his life I realized that I had fallen short of being the man I was meant to be. The man my parents had raised me to be. Where I went wrong was so clear they just wanted to keep me safe. I fell asleep for that short time on that bus wondering how Ican prove to my parents that I understand and in just one day I see that everything can change in just a blink of an eye.

Kendall
Allen

Trump As President

by Khloe Roddy

There is an election for the president you want to be in control of your country coming up so close, I decided it would be a great opportunity to compare and contrast the two presidential candidates we have running, Kamala Harris and Donald Trump. I think this is a great way to show you their pros and cons and hopefully will give you a clearer view of their vision. Who will you pick, Trump or Kamala? I am going to list their similarities and their differences to help you decide!

First off we have Donald Trump. He was born and raised in New York City. Even before being president he was a very smart and intelligent man. He was a real estate developer and businessman who owned and managed his hotels, casinos, golf courses, and resorts to name a few. He was also on the hit tv show The Apprentice, which was well known for his phrase "You're Fired.' He is our Republican nominee. His children are also walking in his footsteps becoming very well known and are also helping him campaign. He has many houses around the world, the most popular is his Mar A Lago resort in Palm

Beach, Florida. He was the president in 2017-2021. He was the 45th president. Trump reformed the U.S. tax code as well as negotiating the trade agreements with Mexico, Canada, China, Japan and South Korea. He also was the president when Covid would hit. Donald Trump gave the American people more tax credits as well as giving out stimulus checks and making sure if you lost your job during that time that you were still paid. He had good relationships with China and Russia unlike we do now. He is pro life. He is against violence, protecting the American people, and against the drug epidemic. He even helped get the Covid Vaccines for the American people.

Next we have Kamala Harris. She was the vice president from 2021 to present. She was the first woman African American vice president. She is married and has no children. The thing that shocks me the most is how the economy has gotten so much worse with Biden in office that some people are willing to vote for her when she was right there beside Biden this whole time and now she says are you ready for a change, vote for me. I feel she just says whatever the people want to hear to get their votes. If she was really for the people, why wouldn't she have done all this when she has been in office since 2021? She is a pro choice. I feel she stands with the riots when people are breaking into stores and stealing because she stated they were peaceful protesting when everything on the news and tv was showing it was not peaceful. She does not have the experience as compared to Donald Trump.

I hope everyone that can will get out and vote. I hope they truly do their research and do not just listen to friends, family or the news. You need to really get involved and see what each candidate really stands for, not just what is popular or cool. It is so important to vote. You can go to the website, "whitehouse.gov", and get facts about the candidates and what each one stands for. Go vote!

The Special Cat

by Braden Smith

It was just a normal day in my neighborhood and I decided that I was going to look through old pictures so I went down stairs and I asked my parents if I could go in the basement to look through old pictures and they said I could. I walked down the stairs with each step "CREEK CREEK CREEK" when I stepped on the basement floor I heard Little feet scurry across the floor. Then I look to my right and there it is the boxes of old pictures so I start to go through the box I pick up one that catches my eye "CREEK CREEK CREEK" I hear the stairs I ran behind a shelf but turns out it was just my mom.

My mom walks down the stairs and she says "Honey you there"

I reply " I'm right here mom.

She looks and i'm sitting there looking at a bunch of pictures that catch my eye my mom walks to me and asked "wy only looking at those specific picture"

I reply " because all of these have the same cat in them wy is that"

she said "I don't know let me see"

I hand them to her she looks and realises that they have that same cat turns out that cat has always followed them but I think there is more to it so I make it my mission to find out these things how old is the cat, why the cat is in all of these pictures.

First to figure out how old the cat is, the first thing I did was I asked my mom if I could take some of the picture with me so I could group up with my friends so we can figure out how old the cat is. So I told my friends to meet me at a secret hideout. When we all got there they all asked me why we were meeting up. You said it was important. I replied that we are now on a mission to find out how old this cat is then I showed them the pictures. So we looked through the pictures and we found out that the cat is about 300 years old judging based on how old the oldest picture we had.

Now to figure out why the cat is in all of these pictures, the first thing we did was ask my dad about it and he said that he thought the family was just lucky to have the same cat. Then we asked my mom and she told us that that cat is weird so she did not know anything about the cat. The last person we asked was my grandma and she said that the cat was a special heirloom for the entire family tree and it was just simply good luck For the family. So now we know how old it is and why it is in all of the pictures. By The Way I hate cats.

Should Kids Have Daily Chores?

by Aliya Smith

S hould kids have daily chores to do when they get home? I believe that kids should have daily chores. Because it will be helpful in the real world. Not only that but it will teach them how to be independent.

In the article, "Should Your Kids Do Chores? We Asked the Experts and TBH, Their Answer Might Surprise You" It states that "It teaches them the value of hard work." If kids don't do chores then they will not know how to do a lot of things. Then they might not ever know what hard work is. Also not to mention, in the real world you get a job but you also get paid. Like people say "hard work pays off." right?

Also if a kid has chores it will Benefit both the parent and the and the child according the text "10 Reasons Why Household Chores Are Important" states how "in many cases your child will be able to eventually do his or her chores completely independently," that's how that helps the child And it helps the adults not have to worry so much about doing so many chores.

Along with responsibility, because as everyone knows responsibility is a big deal and the real world and as a kid even. and in the article it states how "Kids who do chores learn responsibility and gain important life skills that will serve them well throughout their lives." Therefore the kids who do chores gain important life skills so it helps in the real world too, whether you believe it or not. and it also helps the siblings,mother,father. Not have to worry about so much.

Also I know a lot of kids who don't want to do chores but once they do chores and get recognition for it they feel a lot better about themselves. because they did something and it made him feel better because they did something and got recognized for it. Also, purpose is another big thing about yours. "Having responsibilities like chores provides one with a sense of both purpose and accomplishment."

"Preparation for Employment" Is another big piece for the Big World. As it will help children learn how to carry out household chores, whether that be doing the dishes, laundry, sweeping, mopping, and cleaning in general. Again according to the text "**10 Reasons Why Household Chores** Are Important" it says"Learning how to carry out household chores is an important precursor to employment." This helps as well because if you get a job you will be more organized and responsible.

I also think that anyone who gives you a job will recognise your ability to carry out tasks because you have learned to be responsible.

So, in conclusion, there are a million benefits to having chores. You will know how to be responsible, how to be held accountable for your actions, what doing hard work is like and how to do it. You will be more ready to join the real world and also how to lend a helping hand.

You will know how to take care of yourself, your household, and your pets. The ability to do what you have to at a job and do it the right way.

The Run That Changed My Life

by Jon Timmons

My name is Bill. I will tell you about an extraordinary thing that happened to me.

I walk about a mile on the campgrounds every day. Then I got to class, and this girl asked to go on a run tomorrow with me. I said yes because she was pretty, and I admitted that to myself but not to her. I'm scared of women.

The next morning, I got ready. I put on a sleeveless shirt and shorts, and I put on some cologne because I was trying to impress her—I'm not going to lie. So, I headed to the spot where we were going to meet up to run.

I see her standing there waiting in some shorts and a tank top. I was stunned because she was the quiet kid in my class, but wow, she looked good. So we started running, and she was able to keep up. We were almost done, and she stepped into a pothole and hurt her ankle, so I quickly picked her up and brought her to a tree that was shaded. I set her down under the tree and looked at her ankle to make sure it wasn't broken, and it was. I learned a lot from my dad because he was an E.M.T. I suddenly saw myself through her eyes, and I heard what she was thinking: "Wow, he's nice." After that.

I picked her up and went to my car, and I set her into the passenger seat, and I started off to the hospital because it was an awkward brake that needed to be fix, so we were just making small talk and laughing and listening to music and singing i park and go get a weel char for her and bring her into the hospital.

We were in there for about an hour. When we got into the room, she grabbed my hand because she was scared of doctors. The doctor walked into the room. She shakes my hand and shakes her hand and asks what happened, and I tell him what happened, and he looks at her ankle and says that if she would have waited, she would have lost her foot and told me to become a doctor jokingly. He informs her that she will need a cast. She tenses up and says ok.

We walk into the room were thay put the cast on and she is realy scared and i start telling her about the time when i broke my leg because i decided to jump off a bridge in to the water we thought it was deep but it wasent i landed on my leg braking my shin and femur. She lagged because it was stupid. I was glad she was laughing because it distracted her from the cast.

She had to be in a wheelchair or crutches, and since I had every class with her, I was her

wheelchair shofer.

Two months later, we started dating, and she is now my wife of 15 years. We still talk about the run, and I told her about me seeing myself.

The Aliens

by C. C.

The football game was normal.Georgia was playing Tennessee and then all the lights went out and then a person got taken.That person was me. I was so scared that my hands were shaking really badly And then after all of that I tried to jump out of the ship, which didn't go too well but there were also other people. I tried to get the military to be involved, which didn't work so well either but I had a good idea and those aliens look just like humans I mean just like humans barely distinguishable. It's almost like they were Transformers but they weren't. I would probably be even more scared but yet I somehow managed to escape and then they found me again. I'm not the one who would yell at people like that but I probably was yelling so loud at the aliens. They were trying to get them to get away from our planet but they really wouldn't so yeah to be completely honest those dang aliens have nothing to lose. I kept running and running and running and running and running and running and running we're like 3 hours I'm pretty sure I beat Olympic times cuz of how fast I was running but then I went back to the game and I continued watching it blending in with the crowd and then all the sudden the lights went out again and it took somebody else and I saw UFO leaving so this time they actually stop the game and I just got into my car and I was driving after them traffic was built up on the highway because the game was almost over and then...

Cliffhanger more UFOs are starting to show up. the military this time they actually showed up after being called they said that the only thing they could do is shoot an EMP, which would turn off their systems and then the aliens would have to get out and surrender but I was talking to the military guy and he was saying to me kid you need to get out of here I know you've been abducted and will test you later, but you need to get out of here now 2 hours later it was on the news cuz the newspaper people are curious, but they were also running for their lives the only thing everybody was doing was running. I asked myself why are there aliens why are there aliens the military kept fighting the aliens And that was the scariest day of my life not knowing what to do with my teenager self once all the aliens were gone I went back to my normal life still had a question to answer I kept thinking of all possible answers that could have been to answer it the question was did Bigfoot ask for the aliens and a fact check that my answer was do not trust Bigfoot when he's walking through the forest.

Robot War

by Carsen Groce

One day, in 2090, I was taking a ride in my jetpack. I was having so much fun until I saw a factory where they were making robots. They were making a lot of them. I wondered if they could take over the world, but I didn't think much about it.

So I went to my friend's house because they have a robot that does stuff for them and I asked my friend if he got that robot from the factory. He said "Yeah I did why do you ask", I said, "No it's nothing, I was just wondering if you did".

After that, I went home to where out of nowhere my parents had brought back a robot and I was so happy about it. Where I could not sleep because I was so glad that we got a robot. So the next day came around and my friend came to my house in his floating car I hopped in and took me to where all my friends were hanging out. When I got there and my friend hopped out and got inside, then we started to play Fortnite.

The news comes on and tells us to go inside and stay because the robots are taking control. But I didn't want to stay, so I went outside and took my friend's car, and drove to the factory. All I saw was a lot of robots in the factory and they were angry. As I was leaving the factory, I saw more robots and they didn't look angry, so then I went over there and asked them what they were doing. They said, "We are planning to stop the evil robots." I said, "Do you all have a leader because I will," they all said yes, and the next thing I knew I was in their army of robots and planning the next attack on the evil robots.

When we were planning the attack, we saw robots getting lined up on the line because the evil robots were going to take the first attack. As the battle went longer in the attack, we were able to push them off and we were able to push them back a lot to the point where they had to retreat. But we didn't push them because we had lost too many robots on our side and they also lost a lot so we waited until they least expected it. In the middle of the night, we took our chances and attacked them. I sent robot-controlled airplanes with bombs, and the air defenses didn't see us because the plane was so high in the sky until another plane started to shoot at our plane, and it began to go down, and we crashed. I was saved by some of my robots, and I went on to live and we won the war, and because we dropped the bombs on the factory. They could not make more robots again, so that is how me and my other robots saved the world.

All Seeing Roots

by Michael Eaker

It started as an ordinary afternoon stroll across campus, the kind of walk I often take to clear my mind between classes. The autumn air and golden leaves crunched under my feet as I wandered off the main path towards a quiet grove near the old library. I had passed the cluster of trees countless times but never really paid attention to them until today.

Something about the tree in the center of the Grove: The roots twisted over the ground like old vines and as I reached out my fingers brushed against the rough bark. At that moment, a strange sensation jolted through my head like a static shock but with a deeper tingling at the edge of my consciousness. I stumbled back, shaking my head, and then I heard it.

At first, it was just a whisper, but then the words sharpened. They weren't coming from my surroundings; they were coming from people walking past on the main path girl with a red backpack thinking about how she forgot her roommate's birthday, a professor rushing to a lecture worried about an argument he had with his wife this morning. Every thought flickered in my mind as if it were my own. I gripped the tree for balance, overwhelmed by the flood of unspoken words.

I could sense people's thoughts if they were talking to me. It was a weird sensation, like I could read minds. This was crazy. I stepped away from the tree, and then everything went quiet. I couldn't hear anything; it was all really confusing. Maybe I was going crazy, but I could just be imagining things.

I heard the bell ring; it was time to get to class, so I ran to class, trying not to be late, but it was impossible. I was on the other side of the camp. A hall monitor stopped me and gave me a tardy pass. I finally made it to class. We were learning about all kinds of things, but my head couldn't stop thinking about that tree.

As soon as class ended, Ii went to the tree, and all its power was gone almost like someone absorbed its powers, and no one was around, so how could the power of the tree go mising maybe a super hero or a villains trying to take over the world or maybe just my imagination.

So I went to my next class, sat there, and finished my test and assignments. I went down to the cafeteria and told my friends, and we ate are food. We went to the library, and no one believed me so i showed them the tree with a scar on it, but they still didn't believe me. They just thought it was odd i entirely gave up thinking im crazy

The Mirror That Changed Everything

by Jonah Cecil

One day I went to an old store and they had a lot of old stuff like bowls and cups also like makeup and perfume and big mirrors for makeup. I decided to get a mirror just because I did not have one in my house since I moved out of my parents house. They haven't been talking to me recently but I still wanted one because I alway had one in my parents house but not in mine. It also kinda gave me a memory of my old house. I bought it for a low price for thirty bucks, the store owner said that the previous owners had said there was something wrong with it. Like the reflection would not always move like them but, of course I did not believe them because I thought it was ridiculous because reflections always move with you. I grabbed it and put it in the back of my car. Luckily it fit because it was very big. It was a long way mirror the ones that stood up.

When I got home I ran inside with the mirror because water was falling hard on my head. As soon as I got inside I closed and locked the door behind me and I went to my bedroom. I set the mirror right inside my room. I went to go take off my jacket and shoes and got some sweat pants and a comfy shirt. I was home at last and it was getting late so I went to my room and went to my bathroom to brush my teeth while I was standing in the mirror. I noticed my reflection was not possible. I thought my reflection was taking a second to do what I did. I did not mind it thinking it was my mind playing tricks on me like always like last time I went camping with some friends we told scary stories and that night I started imagining things.

So I shrugged it off thinking it was playing with me again just because I heard what the owner said.Little did I know I was going to wake up and,Like a brand new person I had the best sleep i've had in years.I was thinking that this mirror brought good luck somehow but I think it did.I went to my bathroom and like always I brushed my teeth then my hair both with different brushes you know like always after I got done with that I got dressed real fancy and I headed out to go to work I work at a fashion store I randomly got a call from. MY MOM! I haven't talked to her in years. I fumbled the phone while bringing it out of my pocket. I answered mom.hello?

"Hello, are you there?" she yelled into the phone yes i'm here I answered. "I need your help now!" She once again yelled it into the phone. Okay mom is this a prank she hung up the phone. I rushed to unlock my phone. I dialed her number RING. She didn't answer on the first ring before it could ring a second time

she answered "hello darling" my mother said she sounded fine like nothing happened.

What was that I asked, she sounded confused, "what do you mean honey?"You sounded like you were frightened earlier when you called me. "Oh that was nothing dear but we were wondering if we could come over to your house. We have nothing better to do and I haven't seen you since."

She didnt finish her sentence weirdly enough. Yea I agree we haven't seen each other for a while. Ok i'll clean the house y'all can come around one or two in the afternoon."That sounds fine we will see you then.

"Wow, that was weird. I got off my shift and I went to the store to pick up some food to make while they came over. When I got home it was twelve already and I started cleaning up the house. By the time I was done cleaning the house it was almost two I rushed to get food done and as soon as I got it done the doorbell rang. I opened the door and they looked super pale. Are you ok I asked? "We are fine, why do you ask?" never mind.Come in they walked in and sat down at the table."Honey we are not hung thank you but no maybe tomorrow. What do you mean tomorrow "DIdn't we say we were staying the night?" No."Sorry my love if you don't want us to we will just leave?"No its ok yall can stay ok thank you after we got done with dinner we all said goodnight to each other I went to my room and brushed my teeth then went to bed in the middle of the night I woke up I looked straight and saw there was a reflection of me in the mirror.

I Was On A Train

by Hayden Hogue

This is the story of how I found the love of my life, when I was at one of the lowest points of my life

I was on a train one morning at 9:46 Am specifically in the New York subways. It can get very crazy busy so I went early, thinking it wouldn't be busy. It was confusingly busy. I don't know why but this morning felt off. So I headed to my office.

I worked for a banking company. Nothing too special, just a regular office with phone calls 24/7. I don't really know why it was busy this early, usually it gets busy around 10:30 - 11:00. But I didn't mind because I am used to this, So I got on the subway, and sat by this lady. She was a pretty elderly woman, but on the other side of me was this dude. He was very frail, very skinny, very pale. I don't know how to describe him, but he was very off, he didn't seem like the typical guy, but I sat down. It was like a five minute ride. It didn't feel that long. I was waiting on the train for people to get off then I would be the last one. some people got off and there were people about to get on then I got up and saw this brown paper bag....

I didn't want to pick it up but what if there was an explosive, a gun, or it could just be a little gift with something cute in it. So I took it, I was fast walking, I was very curious about what was in this bag. It was definitely worn out, like it was meant for a specific person, like it was a rush to give this person a brown paper bag, I got to my office, and it was a ring....

It didn't make any sense it wasn't in a box it wasn't in anything just the beat up wrinkled brown paper bag my first thought was I need to find this guy but I don't know, it seemed like it was meant for me, like that gut feeling that you always have if something was for you, or that thing was suppose to happen to you. But you're not sure, it's very mysterious. you're not sure, like is this a sign I don't know. But I need to find this guy. I need to be sure It was an actual diamond. So the thoughts going through my mind now are, "I need to keep this safe" and "I need to find this guy".

After work, I went to this gas station. And I went in and this guy is behind this register. I said "you look familiar" but i didn't want to assume and sound like a total weirdo. And he said "you're the girl on the train. Right?" I immediately said "is the ring yours?" He said "what ring?" I said "the one in the beat up crinkled brown paper bag" He had a stunned look on his face he said "YES!" with an anxious look on his face I said "I took it right after you left the train. I didn't see you around so I kept it safe."

He looked so excited I gave it to him and he looked so sad he said, "I was looking for it but assumed it was still on the train, it messed my whole day up because it was my great grandmothers she sadly passed a few weeks ago and she said "spoil the next lady you find, and when you are determine she's the one get down on that knee and use my ring pass it on." This story brought me to tears. I said "she will always look over your shoulder and know who the one is."

Few years later we got married and were expecting and that's how I found the love of my life and will continue to love him even when we pass on.

The Rebellion of Euphoria

by Evan Williams

Have you wondered what life would be like in the modern day if monsters and powers exist? I have created a fantasy world that takes place in the modern day with futuristic technology with mystical powers and dinosaurs. The land is called Euphoria and is as big as Pangea. No other continents exist. It's like Narnia but larger.

In this world, there exists a prophecy that speaks of a future that speaks of a time when Euphoria will be threatened by a great darkness, and the balance will be maintained only if a great hero will fight back. It says he will arrive in 1964 from beyond the sky.

I decided to repurpose this story because I decided I didn't like how the last story went and decided to do a darker version of the story

<u>Chapter 1: the beginning.</u>

Call me Ishmael. Just kidding, you're not reading Moby Dick. But onto the real story. The year was 1964, everything was way more simple than it is now. Monsters and dinosaurs played and pranced in fields and forests, the people mainly hung out in the city, the dark overlord,

Malice, plotted while looking over the city in his conspicuous, dark castle that is 1/10 miles (528 feet) away from the city. The world would change when a newcomer arrived.

At 3:33 pm on Wednesday 1964, a white, spherical ship had come to Earth and landed in Euphoria. Once it landed, everyone had surrounded it and were in awe. It was the top story on the news. The Cyan, circular door on top of the ship opened and revealed a man in a completely white suit with a black visor with Cyan eyes and antenna with a white ball on top of it. His chest has a Cyan circle on it. The fingers are made of black rubber. His entire army is white with Cyan circles on the palms of his hand.

The people ran back to the city to hide in their homes. He entered the city and watched the people run into the buildings. His memory was foggy and forgetting what his mission was. A young man went up to him and asked why he was there as people from inside the buildings were warning the kid to stay away from the strange newcomer. "I...I don't...know..." said the man, with the voice of a 12 year old.

A man, behind the newcomer, punched the man in white in the back of his head. Since it was made of metal, it hurt his knuckles. The visor on the armored man turned into static as he fell to the ground. Once it was black with blue eyes, he remembered his name and personality but very little of his mission.

"I think I was supposed to vanquish something but I'm not too sure." he said as he got back up to answer the kids question.

The kid told the people of the city that he knows his intentions, everyone came out of their homes and buildings. They asked him to describe the thing he came to vanquish.

"I think he wears a black top hat that has feelings and is alive, black tuxedo with red pupils and red bowtie and black hair."

"You mean Malice?" a man in the crowd said.

"Who?" said the newcomer, 333.

"The man in that large, black castle with the red glass eye on it." said a woman in the crowd. 333 flew up to a high point to see the tower. He flew back down to the crowd. He bonded with the people and saved them from the attacks from the monsters and villains.

A soldier is walking to the top room of the castle. He knocks on the door to the top room. A voice from inside the room says "Enter." The soldier opens the door and walks up to the man in black. The man in black is looking out of his large window in the shape of an eye. "I have just gotten word about the man from the ship." said the soldier, Mason.

Malice walks towards Mason and asks "Is he here to join me or to oppose me?" "Well, he's here to defeat you." said Mason. Malice grinned a sharp, toothy grin. "Well, I guess I shall kill him before he does the same to me." Malice said. His hat, Merlin, snickered.

<u>Chapter 2: What's going on now?</u>

The entire land is now enslaved after Malice and some of the other villains decided to work together. The skies are crimson with black, thunderous clouds. Malice is one of the two main rulers. The other is his wife, Pricilla. What they didn't know is that a group of people are plotting a rebellion, underground. Over the years, Malice's design has changed.

He now has black pupils and red iris', an amulet that looks like his stained glass window, a black cape with a velvet inside, and boots with claws on them. He also has a daughter he named Mida he made as an Ai. He also made what he calls "The Ultimate Deity" he named Mollo and a robot he named Monty. This is the day the prophecy speaks of. The day of endless darkness.

Underground, a 2,400 square foot base with walls that are twenty five feet tall was built in case this happens. This list of people plotted their revolution: Charlotte, Anthony, Chi-Chi Mota, Eden, Shogiro Mota, The Prankster, Audrie, TooToo, and Nite.

(Seven of the nine people on this list have powers while the other two have no powers. The powers of these people will be shown later in the story. Also, Eden and Shogiro are married. But Eden is Chi-Chi's step father. She's twentyfour. Charlotte also has a two year old, with a singular eye, named Ada. Since Charlotte has no powers, she has to stay at the base.)

But before they could do that, they needed one person. But unfortunately, he was captured in Malice's prisons. Tomorrow, he will be publicly executed in the courtyard. In the prison, a sentinel is walking around and guarding the prison cells. 333 sits in his cell and waits for the dreaded next day. But time felt slower than usual and he waited for someone to rescue him.

Chapter 3: Execution Day.

"Hey, pal, time to get up." A super soldier said as the titanium cell door slammed open. 333 failed to stand up and felt uneasy.

"Stop messing around and follow me." The soldier said as he grabbed 333 by his arm. They went out to Malice's courtyard and 333 was put on a stone block. His arms were tied behind his back and his legs were also tied together. Malice sat next to Pricilla and Mida. He stood up and began to say his speech.

"Dear soldiers and monsters in the audience, today we will all watch the execution of my enemy who has been ruining everything I planned for years. But now, he has lost and is now hopeless. Let his execution be a lesson to all who will rise against me and defy me. When he is executed, we feast on his corpse as our royal dinner and wring the blood from his veins for us to drink!" He sat back down and watched as the executionist walked up to 333 and grabbed the large axe. 333 took a deep breath and closed his eyes and waited for it to happen. Before the axe hit his neck, the executionist caught on fire and ran off the stage. 333 opened his eyes and looked to his right.

It was a tall woman in a purple dress. It was Shogiro Mota.

"People in the crowd, kill them!!" Malice said as he stood up and pointed toward the two. Shogiro Mota grabbed 333 and turned into a dragon and flew away.

"I forgot she could do that." Malice said as he bowed his head in disappointment.

"Well, everyone get back to work!" Pricilla yelled as she got up and walked away

Chapter 4: Back At The Base.

They flew back to the underground base and hurried to open the door quickly so they wouldn't be seen. The door leads to an elevator that also leads to the base. The base had four bedrooms, three bathrooms, two kitchens, and an entertainment room with a table that turns into their planning table. The people in the entertainment room looked at the elevator door open and saw 333 was back.

"Guys! She brought him back!" Charlotte said as she got up and hugged him. Everyone rushed out of the room they were in to see if it was true. They cheered the second they saw him.

"It's been so long since we've seen each other!"Chi-Chi said as she let go of 333.

"What happened to your suit?" Anthony asked as he looked 333 up and down.

"They took it off when I got captured." 333 said.

"Luckily, we went through your house and grabbed all of your spare suits and weapons before they searched it." Nite said as he went over to a wall and pressed a button on a shelf. The shelf moved and led to a room full of suits and weapons.

"Great! Now we just need to make our plan and fight back against Malice." 333 said as he walked over to the room full of his spare suits.

"We thought we should use most of the suits in that room to distract Mal's army while some of us go face off with Malice." Nite said as he leaned against the wall.

"Hmm...I think I got a plan!" 333 said as he walked out of the room with his suit on. They all sat down at the table and listened to 333's plan.

"So, what's our plan?" Eden asked.

"Do we use any part of my plan?" Nite also asked.

"Yes, we do. Also, Anthony, do you remember when I talked you into leaving Malice's child soldier part of his army?" 333 said.

"Yes, I'm glad you did," Anthony said.

"We get all of Mal's child soldiers to rebel against Malice with us." 333 said.

"Shogiro, if I'm correct, can you manipulate the other dragons?" 333 asked.

"Yes, but only when I'm in my dragon form. I am a dragon warrior afterall!" She said, "Chi-Chi can't because she's not a dragon warrior yet. She can turn into a dragon, though."

"I can turn into a giant coconut crab." Audrie said.

"I'm sad because this is the only line of dialogue I'll get. I wish I had more." TooToo said.

"We should all use our powers against Malice's army and talk the children out of killing us and rebel against Mal. Me, Shogi, TooToo, Audrie, Eden, and Anthony stand outside the castle and transform before **we** fight his army. The rest of you will go and fight Malice, head on. " The Prankster said.

"Agreed." Everyone else said.

"Alright, let me turn on the suits and we get the swords, guns, and everything else and we're ready to go. I almost forgot that Anthony kept his soldier outfit and made it bigger so it can still fit him. He can use that."

Chapter 5: Malice's Dark Future Plans.

In Malice's throne room, Malice overlooks the ruined city in front of his dark castle on his large throne. His three dark giant pets laid asleep. Mida walks up to him.

"Father, what do we plan to do when we fully take over Earth?" she asked as she looked up at Malice. Monty walks over to her and gives her the answer.

"Simple, we travel to other worlds, galaxies, and universes and take them over and become the most powerful army in all of the multiverse." Malice looks over at Monty.

"Correct, we just need to make sure that we eradicate that roach before he gets any ideas on how to rebel against us." Malice grinned. Merlin jumped off of Malice's head and walked toward the suckled human arm that was laying on a desk that just so happened to be in that room. Pricilla walked into the room and pet Merlin.

"Fragile, little things, humans are. Shall we rule over them as gods or play them as our own puppets?" She asked.

"Both, dear. But we are left with one last question—when do we unleash **her**?" Malice said.

"What does thou mean?" Pricilla asked as she walked closer to Malice.

"I forgot to show you **her**. What I mean by **her** is something I've been working on for the past five years."

"She is almost complete, she is at 98% at this very moment, Father." Mida said.

"Do you think she will be and stay loyal when she awakens?" Pricilla asked.

"She will. She was made to obey us. She was made by Father." Mida said. Malice walks over to her.

"You've always had faith in your sister. She is the final piece to our grand design!" Malice said as he put his hand on her head. She smiled. Malice looked over at Pricilla.

"I think I have security camera footage on the lab in the bottom floor. I can show you the footage of **her**." Malice said.

"Sure." Pricilla said back to him. Merlin got the tablet off of the desk and brought it over to Pricilla. He turned it on and it showed a large being in a capsule filled with water. **Her** face was covered by her large, red feathered wings. The only things that were on **her** head that weren't covered were her six, red horns. **Her** body was entirely grey and **her** legs were completely black. **Her** black tail covered her waist.

"What is **her** name?" Pricilla asked.

"**Her** code name is M0110. **Her** real name is Mollo." Mida said. Mollo moved the wings from **her** head.

"She's awoken." Malice said.

"Where is **her** mouth?" Pricilla asked.

"She was designed not to have one. She needs no nutrients, nor food." Malice said. A soldier ran into the room.

"Lord Malice! We have gotten word that 333 is heading our way with reinforcements!" He said as he was catching his breath. Malice's sharp grin quickly faded into a frown.

"Uurgh! Of course he ruins everything the day I finally win!" Malice said. "Send out the sentinels! Everyone else, get ready for battle!" He yelled. Before anyone could react, the stained glass window shattered.

"It's him!" Mida said. 333 looked at all four of them before he got into a fighting position. Nite and Chi-Chi were behind him.

"I take Malice, Nite takes Pricilla, and Chi-Chi takes Monty." 333 instructed. The battle began.

Chapter 6: The final battle.

Shogiro Mota and the others stood outside Malice's castle and began to transform (besides Anthony, he just made sure the gun on his armor was full). Obviously, Shogiro turned into a dragon, The Prankster turned into a giant Jack-In-The-Box with a boxing glove and wind-up jaw as arms, Audrie turned into a giant Coconut Crab, Eden grew antlers, his head was surrounded by fire, and grew wings, Too Too just becomes larger. Yeah.

"When I say three, we run and start attacking." Too Too said, "One...Two...Three!!!" She yelled as she flew into battle

Malice's army rushed out of the castle and began attacking. The sentinels flew onto the battlefield.

"I've had experience fighting one of these." Anthony said to the others before he ran into Malice's castle and into the room the child soldiers were kept in. Shogiro called for all of the remaining dragons in the land to aid her in battle. They fought hard. The Prankster was damaged a lot for some reason. Shogi made it out with no scratches. Too Too was able to outsmart the sentinels. Audrie snapped the heads off of the sentinels. Actually, it was pretty easy. The people they were fighting were men with guns. They had a giant Coconut Crab and dragons. The battle at the top of the tower began, too. The three dark giants woke up and formed into a large monster and jumped to the battlefield. Malice transformed into an enormous cobra and slithered to the top of the castle. 333 flew to the top and pulled his sword from his back. Malice spewed fire at 333. 333 landed on Malice's scaly body and started piercing through it. The dragons started flying in and fighting against the army and sentinels. Monty also ran away because he's afraid of confrontation for some reason.

Inside the castle, Anthony rushed to the room with the child soldiers. I wanna make this short because I'm getting tired. He gets their help and they start attacking Malice's army. Mida used her magnetism powers to create giant, robotic arms to counteract Chi-Chi's dragon form. Nite controlled shadows and was up against Pricilla. Pricilla turned into a large vampire bat. Nite turned into his fright form. We all know they beat Pricilla and Mida. But what's going on with 333 and Mal? Malice returned to his normal form after one of his fangs got broken by 333's unbreakable sword. A thunderous cloud struck 333 and supercharged him. He punched Malice into the dark giants and they collapsed onto the battlefield. Mida got up from the ground after being beaten by Chi-Chi.

"Enjoy this victory for now, our final monster has yet to awaken. And I think it's about time she does." Mida says as the capsule opens. In Malice's lab, Mollo awakens and punches the glass capsule. The water from the capsule spills out more as she punches the capsule more. She steps out and stretches. She flies out from the lab and looks down at the battlefield. Multiple dead soldiers on Malice's side had been split in half, eaten, or stabbed. Maybe even missing.

Mollo creates a staff from complete stone and sets it on fire. A red smoke surrounded the fallen body of the dark giants. Limbs protruded from the body and transformed into Malice's true form. Malice used to be a Grand Titan and split into five separate beings. Three of them were the dark giants, another one was Merlin. When they collided with each other, they turned back into their true form. 333 looked at the 754 foot monster Malice had become. Malice looked toward 333 and smacked 333 so fast and hard, he died...333's body flew onto that battlefield, lifeless. Just for good measure, Malice stomped on 333's lifeless body.

All of his friends started to cry. Malice, Mida, and Pricilla laughed. Malice had one, again. But now, he's more powerful than ever. He looked over at Mollo.

"Mollo, I am your creator. Do you know what your job is?" Malice said.

"Yes, I will follow every command you tell me."

Chapter 7: The Hero's great return.

333 woke up in a white void. He had no idea where he was. A large eye opened and stared at him. 333 screamed.

"I'm sorry, is this not what you were expecting?" the eye said, "Here, let me turn into something more...fitting." The eye grew the same size as 333 and turned into something more adorable.

"I'm Quoraz! You're in your purgatory! But since you are one of the greatest heroes in the land, you get a second chance. You will gain amazing powers to help you regain Euphoria!" Quoraz said. He placed his hand on 333's forehead. 333 disappeared. Malice's foot was still on 333's dead body. A yellow and blue light appeared from the bottom of his foot.

"What was that?!" Malice said as he looked at his foot. His foot began to lift up. 333 was lifting Malice's large foot off of him. 333's friends just watched as this was happening. They wiped their tears away. He flew up to Malice's head and stared at him.

"Even when you die, you still find a way to come back!" Malice said, "Mollo, my first command is for you to defeat him!"

"Yes, Father." She said, She flew towards 333 and prepared to pierce him with her flaming, stone staff. 333 counteracted her attack by summoning his own sword from matter. The others on the battlefield decided to give 333 the upperhand. Shogi told the dragons to attack Mollo. Their swords clashed multiple times while 333 never said a word while this happened. Mollo got distracted by the dragons and was pierced by 333's sword. She fell to the ground, dead. Malice looked at her dead body. He took a step back. 333 flew toward Malice and just stared at him. 333 pulled out his sword and pierced Malice through his head.

Chapter 8: Malice's defeat and the finale.

Malice returned to his human form. 333 flew back down to the ground.

"Eden, do it." 333 said with an echoey voice.

"What are you talking about?" Malice asked. A red hand appeared from behind Malice, Mida, and Pricilla and dragged them all into a random dimension. 333 returned to his regular form. Everyone ran towards and hugged him. They cheered for him. They rebuilt the entire city, freed everyone from the Prisons. 333's business was finally done and he can finally rest after all evil in Euphoria is gone. What is the first thing he's going to do? Celebrate of course! For the first time in Euphoria, it was at peace.

But what dimension did Malice, Mida, and Pricilla get sent to? It was a dimension that was like Euphoria, but they had no powers. Every person in that dimension was an exact copy of everyone who lived in Euphoria.

The End

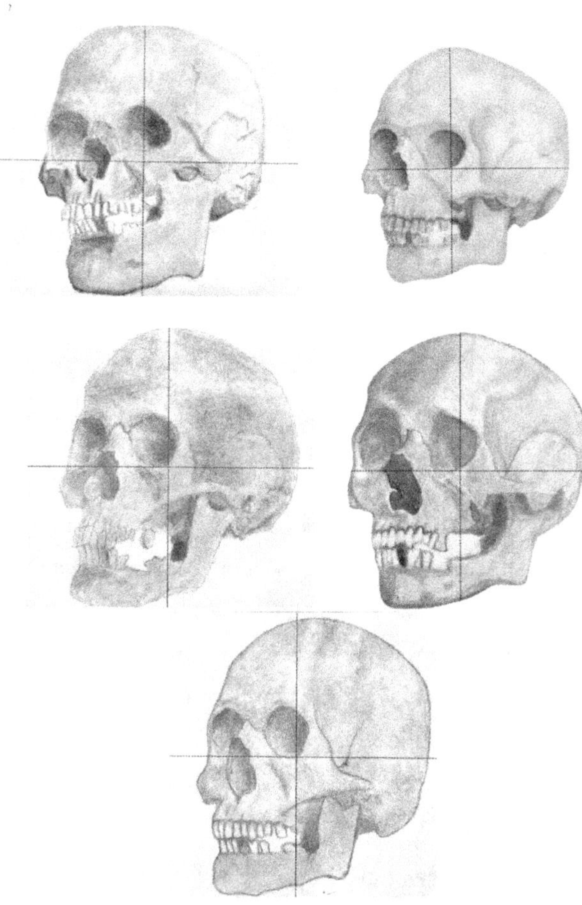

"Value Study: Human Skulls" by Sydney Turner, Trinity Shipley, Lex Hixson, Hayden Hogue, & Harper Imami

Something Was Going On

by A. S.

The sun has risen. My alarm is going off and I needed to get up so I can get ready for my day at school. This morning it was very hard for me to get up and get moving to get ready for school. I could not figure out what it was. I went to my closet to get clothes.

But the clothes that I was going to wear today were suddenly wrinkled. They weren't the night before so I was very very confused. Maybe something was happening and I just didn't realize it yet. They're already had been a weird morning since it had tooken a lot just to get up out of bed. Normally it doesn't take that long for me to get up. I was so confused and lost in my thoughts.

Once I had gotten dressed and ready I went downstairs to tell my mom what had happened. she was also very confused. things like this just don't happen all the time it's rare cases and normally that means that something has gone on and I haven't realized it yet. shortly after I've eaten and everything my mom says it's time to go to school Anna. I go get in the car but everything seems normal again. I had about 5 minutes until I got to school. so that 5 minutes I spent reading my book that I was very very interested in.

I fell asleep and my face was laying in my book. but we had arrived at school once I noticed. There's this beautiful tree but I never noticed before. I reach over to my mom and I say "Mom have you ever seen that beautiful big tree before?" but she didn't answer so I wave good-bye to her and said I love you. but I noticed that I could see what she was thinking when we were by that tree together. I remember in my mind thinking why is she worried About stuff that's not even realistic. then I realized right there under that tree I could read people's minds. maybe that's what was running through my head this morning.

This was so weird because nothing like this had ever happened before.

"What's going on, are you okay?" Kenlie said, sounding concerned.

"Oh yes everything is okay but can I show you something?" I say back.

" Sure lets go" Kenlie says with excitement.

Off we go. I take her to this tree and that feeling comes back to me. that feeling of knowing what she was thinking. I finally had figured it out this tree was making me able to read people's minds. I soon begin to question her about what she was thinking to see if she was going to actually tell me what she was thinking. but sure enough she had told me what she was actually thinking. I guess the special tree that I had never noticed showed me that I could read people's minds whenever I was near it. Okay all done.

The Secret
Shadow

by Millie Trundle

A week of horror. My family and I never get out of the house. We are like that one boring family everyone talks about. The one week we decided to branch out turned out to be haunted. It all started with an idea from my grandma. She is a really quiet person, you never hear from her. The one time I heard from her was just about a strawberry pie. All this was besides the point,but we agreed to stay in her mansion. The one every kid is scared of on Third Street No one goes beyond the gate, even while doing tricks or treating. All the dim lights and brick siding make your bones shive

As I packed up, my stomach hurt more and more. This is just grandma's house we are talking about, right? I can't let myself get into my head. I put on a cute sweatshirt that she had got me for my birthday. I hope this can bring peace to whatever species lies within the house. As we got in the car, you could tell mom was timid, no one said a word the whole way down the street. We had to speak to a secretary just to get through the gate. The driveway led us through a maze, a creepy one, too. As I saw the house from a distance, I could see Puffy, the dog who never dies. That thing has been limping around for over 20 years now. That bark could tell you otherwise though. I took a very deep breath and stepped out of the car with a smile on my face. Here we go, into the house.

As Puffy nibbled on my toes while I walked through the doorway, I heard a loud, repeating bang. Sounded like someone was getting whipped, grandma was the only one who lived in the mysterious place. She walked over and greeted me with a side hug. I knew something was off as the television was playing Barbie. Lord knows grandma is the driest person of her kind. She pointed up the stairs and muttered

"You're staying up there, sweetie --- take your bags."

" sweety?" I said in my head. This is already turning out bad. I'm on the second floor.

As I walked in the room, the banging was louder. I saw a shadow of a person in the bathroom, but everyone was downstairs... Why does this have to happen to me? I'm already scared of the dark, more less what lies in it. I picked up my bag and went towards the bathroom slowly. The shadow seemed to be dancing near the toilet. I tried to make peace, maybe it's friendly. I yelled "HII" but the shadow disappeared. It's hard to go to sleep when something is lurking in your myths. I tried shoving my head in the pillow, watching **Dance Moms**, and even praying over the room. I was exhausted, I was starting to fall asleep, and suddenly, the shower turned on. I ignored it, thinking mom wanted to use the big shower. Then I woke up, it was morning. I walked into the bathroom to see the shadow, scrubbing his head with MY lofa. As soon as I opened the window the shower turned off and my soap fell off the shelf. I stepped on a spoon and screamed. Who leaves a spoon in the bathroom. I know I didn't .

I walked down the spiral staircase and heard a sound so annoying that I decided to walk outside. The vents were screeching as air came out. I stepped outside to prevent the dog from waking. Every step I took on the porch the more I sunk in on the rotted wood. I almost threw up looking at all the wet mud around the flower bed. I was walking toward the mailbox. I saw a dog walking by, but most dogs are walked by their owner. This one was walking their owner. The shadow appeared on the dog, but it didn't match. I knew it had been following me through the house.

I decided to play a little game with this sneaky shadow. I got flower and baking soda to start baking. The shadow was dancing in the flower and making a mess. I started filming on my baby brother's tablet. No one would believe grandma's house could actually be haunted. I gained a friend with the shadow, it seemed nice. I was no longer scared to walk through her creepy dungeon.

The Audible

by Cannin Smith

It was the 5A California State Championship game, The Stockton Tigers vs The Bakersfield Drillers. The starting quarterback for the Tigers was Bobby Bullard, a highly recruited five-star senior. Stockton was favored to win by four points, and become state champions for the first time in school history.

The Tigers were the undefeated one seed in the playoff bracket. The Drillers had two losses on the year and were the sixth seed. Bakersfield won the coin toss and elected to defer, which meant that Stockton would get the ball first. The opening kickoff went out of the back of the endzone for a touchback.

Stockton would get the ball at the twenty five yard line to start their opening drive. Stockton started off hot, scoring in just four plays in one minute and thirty seven seconds. It was seven to nothing, Tigers. Bakersfield ended up scoring on a long, seventeen play drive that took up nearly eight minutes. The game was now tied, seven to seven. No one ended up scoring again in the first half, so the score stayed tied at seven going into halftime.

Bakersfield got the ball to start out the second half, but the drought continued. The Drillers went three and out. The ball was now in the hands of the number one ranked pocket passer in the class of 2034,

Bobby Bullard. Stockton drove the ball down the field play after play, but it would all be for nothing as it was intercepted by the Drillers in the red zone. Bakersfield couldn't capitalize on the turnover though, and was forced to punt. Then, the drought started back up with punt after punt, up until there was less than three and half minutes left in the fourth. Stockton had the ball in Driller territory, right at the forty nine yard line. Stockton ran short pass after short pass, getting it all the way to the Driller seven. Then Stockton hit pay dirt with a seven yard passing touchdown by Bobby Bullard. It was now fourteen to seven, Stockton with the lead late. Bakersfield struck back in just one play, with a seventy five yard touchdown to make it thirteen to fourteen with an extra point on the way. It was right through the middle. It was now tied at fourteen with less than two minutes left to go.

The Tigers went with a read option to start off the drive, Bullard kept the ball but got lit up behind the line of scrimmage, Bullard wasn't getting up, holding his knee in pain. Then, Stockton had no choice but to put in Fred Figglehorn, also a senior quarterback, but more of a dual threat than Bobby. Figglehorn jogged out into the huddle, calling a speed option to the left on second down. Fred took the snap, and faked the pitch to his running back, keeping it for himself. He shed off one tackle and hit a burst, and was brought down by the safety for a huge gain of thirty three. The ball was now at the Bakersfield forty two, with fifty seven seconds on the clock after the Tigers burned their second timeout. Figglehorn took the snap and found an open receiver across the middle to the twenty eight before being brought down. Stockton ran hurry up offense and found another man open on the sideline to get down to the five yard line, but the receiver was tackled in bounds, so the Tigers had to use their last timeout with just three seconds left on the clock. Figglehorn called in half back dive, but when the offense lined up, Figglehorn read blitz.

He called audible on the play, changing it to a quick out to the tight end. Figglehorn took the snap, took a three step drop and delivered a strike into the endzone. It was hauled in by the tight end! Touchdown Tigers! Fred Figglehorn won the game for Stockton, and there were tons of scouts at the game.

A scout for the USC Trojans met with Figglehorn right after the game, offering him to come visit the campus. Figglehorn accepted and would later be offered a scholarship just a week and a half later. He would be immediately committed. Fred went on to win the Heisman Trophy and was selected in the first round of the NFL Draft by the Denver Broncos. He signed a huge contract and was financially set for life, as he went on to be a Hall of Fame quarterback.

The Depths
by S. W.

W inter, 1582

First layer Scyphozia.

"Why did I ever enlist in this, all because I had talents above others," I say from behind my mask.

"Well, your connection to the song is special, and not to forget your exoskeleton.

And to be fair you chose to do this so the Celtor incident doesn't repeat. The Etrean man says with a sense of hope in his voice.

"Alright, I guess you're right. By the way, my name is Vyke." The mask moves with every word.

"Well I'm Roland, so Vyke how about we grab some jobs to do." The scaled Etrean replies

This guy sure is eager to be in the depths and how did he know I'm different?

But anyways, Thresher extermination, a daunting task, and why not Gigamed regicide, it'll be easy.

"I've got the jobs you ready to set out," I yell up to the furnace on the second floor.

"Yeah sure lemme just buy a repair kit just in case."

"I'll be waiting outside just come find me" I don't feel right about this. Even though I've fought these things a thousand times eac

"Alright, I'm here." Roland looks the most anxious I've seen him since I've met him

"So uh, what are we after." He asked as we were walking out of Castle Lights border.

"We've got to hunt two threshers, a Megalodaunt, and a king gigamed. "

"And um, what are those exactly?" How fresh is this guy to being a diver.

"Well a megalodaunt is like a shark that stood up but triple the size and with two big arms and some huge legs with dangerous coral they can shoot like spines out of their backs.

Threshers are big crocodiles with sharp claws. And king gigameds are big jellyfish."

Speak of the devil my stolen Ignition Union pager starts to beep at me

"Something is near us take cover and look around." taking my dark steel greatsword off of my back

"It's the megalodaunt," Roland says unsheathing his Heroblade of Ice, which I've never seen in person before only heard rumors.

An ear-piercing roar rings between my ears. Conjuring my usage of iron sing to form a metal sword to surf on into battle.

The megalodaunt folds over showing us its back of coral immediately sending hundreds of coral spines toward us, I throw my sword up in defense blocking most of the spines, Roland doesn't react as fast though getting pierced by the majority of them.

Jumping off my metal sword board, into a heavy swing into the thing's abdomen almost cleaving it in two. It swats me off into a nearby coral tree. In my daze I see Roland picking himself up and forming Ice out of his sword through his Frostdraw, turning his hero blade into a red-ice Kanabo

And he slams it into the Megalodaunt's leg. The ice of the kanabo (A massive Japanese bat with steel semi-circles on the sides) melts back into a sword in just enough time for him to weave out of the wave of a kick.

Conjuring a domain of ice around himself and the Megalodaunt. Sharpened pillars of ice pierce the fish, now down for the count. The stolen pager plays a fanfare and says the bounty is done.

"Are you alright," Roland says rushing over to my fully injured body.

"It'll be fine, I just need to get back to Castle Light and can split the rewards."

"There is no way I'm fighting other monsters in my state"

"Yeah you um, have seen much better days. Maybe try taking a break at the surface for a bit, buy a condo in the isle of Vigils."

(AUTHOR NOTE: Any words you seen that are monsters are completely made up.)

Deep In The Woods

by Sydney Thomas

"Should we hide in the woods?" Sarah says with a slight hint of laughter in her voice

"I don't know. Some bad things have happened in these woods," I said anxiously.

"Come on, that story in the newspaper was so fake," Sarah said casually as if nothing wrong had happened.

"Fine, but if they don't find us in twenty minutes, we're going back to the house," I said worriedly.

"Okay, let's go!" Sarah said excitedly with a little squeal.

As we walked into the woods, a cold, eerie feeling washed over me. The sound of a stick snapping under my foot startled me, causing me to let out a little squeal. Annoyed, Sarah just looked at me and rolled her eyes. However, I was terrified. I felt my heart beating in my chest from the paranoia of thinking that a tall figure might be hovering behind me, but every time I looked back, nothing was there.

Strange.

Eventually, we found a spot with trees surrounding us. A couple of rocks lay there lifelessly in between the four trees. We sat down with the leaves crunching beneath us, and a cold breath of harsh winds blew against my neck.

"I'm scared, Sarah. I don't know about this," I said anxiously.

"You're fine. Stop being a big baby about this," Sarah said accusingly as if I was acting like a baby...which I wasn't.

I could feel the sweat dripping down my face as I sat there scared to death when, suddenly, I heard the cry of a coyote. My heart sank to the bottom of the Atlantic Ocean and was currently sitting on the Titanic. "*And that's how the story started,*" I anticipated with dread.

After a second's thought, I looked over at Sarah and said with panic, "We can't stay here anymore. Did you not hear that?!"

"You're so paranoid- and it's for no reason at all," Sarah said, still clearly annoyed at me.

"Some kids got murdered in these exact woods after hearing a coyote's howls!" I exclaimed in a stage of distress.

"That was all made up, idiot. Can't you just get over that?" Sarah said with increasing irritability.

"No, I can't get killed!" I said, hoping I could get out of those woods.

"Fine! Then I'll stay right here, and you have fun being a loser," Sarah said as if everything was gonna be okay.

Deep down inside, I knew that Sarah and I had never been that close. Truthfully, we were only friends, or should I say acquaintances, because of our mutual friend Topanga. It is not like I expected any more understanding from her. As I sat next to her, I knew that she could hear my every breath.

With as much courage as I could muster, I stood up and decided to walk out of the dark cold woods. That cold, eerie feeling I had felt earlier had come back but ten times stronger. Every step I took was like one step closer to the safe zone in a game. Then I heard the coyote's shrieking scream again. This time, I looked back and from a distance, it was right behind Sarah. *My soul left my body.* I just stood there blank. From the quick glimpse I caught, it was not a coyote. It was tall and skinny but not like a human. No, it was too skinny to be a human. It looked like it had claws.... and its eyes were glowing straight at me.

I turned around and sprinted to the end of the woods. We were about half a mile into the woods when I began thanking God that I was on the track team. I looked back once, and all I could see was that the tall figure had moved in front of Sarah. It towered over her. However, all I could think about was every man for himself.

While darting out of the woods, I didn't even look across the highway. I just ran straight to Topanga's house. When I arrived, she was sitting there with her little sister.

"Where have you been? Where's Sarah?" Topanga said, sounding concerned.

"Um, so do you know the story in the newspaper about the girls in those woods?" I replied, trying to calm myself, knowing full well that Sarah was more than likely dead.

"Yeah, why?" Topanga said, starting to sound even more worried.

"I told Sarah we shouldn't go in there, but she insisted that we did. When we were sitting back there in those creepy woods, I told her that it didn't feel right and that I was leaving. I heard a coyote scream and when I looked back, it wasn't a coyote. It was a tall, skinny figure standing over Sarah. I sprinted back here and didn't look back." I tried not to break down and bawl in front of Topanga.

"Wait what!" Topanga said with fear in her eyes.

"Yeah, and I don't know if Sarah came out of the woods yet," I said, hearing a slight cry and whimper in my voice.

"Should we tell my mom?" Topanga said with a shaky voice and tears of fear in her eyes...

"I think that's best. I feel so guilty, Topanga. I just want us to find Sarah and get her back," I said as I started crying.

When we told Topanga's mom, she called the cops, but they said they were really busy that night and couldn't check it out until the morning. Topanga and I just sat there staring at the deep dark eerie woods.

Sarah never came out of those woods. *EVER.* It's like her body just disappeared off the face of existence. I still wonder what happened to her, but it's in the past. I simply try not to think about it, but it still haunts me to this day. Needless to say, I've never gone into the woods alone or with someone since that night.

The Bunny Man

by A. M.

C hapter 1

There's a bridge you can't go anywhere near, because that's where the bunny man lives. He's armed with a bat, boxing gloves, or anything that's in his hammerspace. I swear this thing is like a cartoon, so you can't do anything to him. Trust us we tried everything, heck my friend tried to fight and the bunny threw a vault at him! But as Easter comes near, we see hope, because the Easter bunny has a chance to stop him. And if he doesn't we don't know what we are going to do. He's our last hope.

Because tanks don't do anything, bombs don't do anything and it was the same thing with robots or magic. Heck even Santa couldn't do anything! Jack Skellington couldn't either! So the Easter bunny is the only holiday character left to fight him, and the only one that has a chance. Because he has ended as many people as the Bunny Man, and he only comes out once a year. But the Easter Bunny is less durable, we found that out today because the bunny got run over by a bus! The bus was the one that broke, but when the easter bunny got run over by a truck, the truck and the bunny got hurt. But the difference was that the truck was unfixable and the easter bunny only got knocked out, and he broke his arm. But when the bunny man got run over by a bus, he just stood up and walked it off. Then he started fighting the people in the bus! But besides that, they're pretty evenly matched, but the Easter Bunny is stronger and more powerful. Because the bunny man wasn't able to lift a truck, but the Easter Bunny lifted one the same day he got his arm broken, and he flipped a tank! And the easter bunny not only has the hammerspace like the bunny man, but the Easter bunny also has magic. Well in two days they fight so let's see if the Bunny Man's durability can handle the Easter Bunny's power.

Chapter 2

Well today, the Bunny Man sent a message to the Easter Bunny. He wrote "Come and get me Easter Bunny" on his bridge. We saw this at 3:00am, then we just went back to bed. But then when we woke up he had written on a skyscraper "No one fight me, or try to stop me from killing this other bunny. Well he's actually a rabbit sent from the easter bunny" And this was the only time the Easter Bunny did something before Easter. But before they fight, we have to try to weaken him first. So we made the perfect clone of the truck that broke the easter bunny's arm.

Because there might be something special about that truck, we fired it up and drove into the Bunny Man's bridge. The bunny looked up at the truck and it hit him. The truck broke, but the Bunny Man didn't, he got right back up and fought the war robot in there. Then we sent another thing there, a whole gang of war robot's, and a brute. Which is just a war robot but bigger and stronger but that did nothing too. But we did the same thing to the easter bunny last year, and it didn't work for the both of them, but it did hurt the Easter Bunny. We needed to hope and pray that the Easter Bunny is able to kill this guy.

Chapter 3

At the start of the day it was pure chaos, any other easter riots and everything like that came up, because the Easter Bunny is coming soon, at 6:00pm. But way more people today tried to fight the Bunny Man. They were dressed up in creepy, cute, and unsettling bunny costumes, but with his iconic bat in hand, he tore through them like paper. The clock hits 6:00pm, it's dark, and the Easter Bunny comes into town. He starts killing and terrorizing the town like normal. Then he makes it to the city, and he sees the bridge, and walks toward it. Killing anyone that gets in his way but then he's stopped by a bunch of bunny man supporters, he kills them with his bare hands. He steals one of the bats with barbed wire and nails on it, and walks onto the bridge. As the Bunny Man turns around, he gets hit in the face with the Easter Bunny's bat, and the Bunny Man starts bleeding out of his nose.

The bunny man hits him back with his bat, which knocks the Easter Bunny back and sends him flying in the sky. He lands on the ground, with birds flying around his head. He pulls out some boxing gloves, and drops his bat and puts them on. The Bunny Man does the same thing, drops his bat and puts on some boxing gloves. The Easter Bunny just teleports in front of the Bunny Man, and punches him right in the face with stars flying around his head. A bump appears on his head, and the Bunny Man is knocked out for a few minutes.

In those few minutes it starts to rain, and soon the Easter Bunny thinks he has won, and turns to walk away but the Bunny Man gets up! The bump disappears, the stars fly away, he takes off his gloves, grabs his bat, then a vault from a bank appears out of nowhere. And he hits it with his bat towards the Easter Bunny and he doesn't miss.

And then the easter bunny picks it up weakened. Holding his arm, and starts bleeding out of his nose, and has a black eye. Then takes off his arm and uses magic to chain up the bunny man then grabs his bat and the bunny man and starts hitting him with both of the bats.

After a while the bunny mans bat breaks, and then the bunny breaks the chains, and with one more swing of the easter bunny's bat, it knocks him out cold and then the easter bunny's bats breaks but filled with adrenaline the bunny man gets up starts swinging at the easter bunny and he hits most of his punches but with one punch from easter bunny to the face the bunny man falls to ground died and the easter bunny walks away with a broken arm bleed out of his head , and a couple of brain injuries and several broken and missing ribs and falls to ground asleep and the next day gone.

The end

Will People Be There?

by McKenzie Weber

Hi, my name is Kate. I'm 33 years old, and I've been stuck in my house ,living with my parents. I've never walked out to the outside world, but yet today, It's the middle of summer So according to my friends it's great and pretty. I am very scared to go to the outside world considering my parents have brought me virtually everywhere reality except to see the actual outside world. I've seen almost every store in the United States but never trees and living things. I've started taking pictures of insects off cameras because my dream job is a marine biologist.

but yet I'm now 33 and just leaving out. I've decided to move to New York, where the best marine biology courses can be taken. I'm going to get an apartment, but first, I have to overcome my fears. I took three steps out of the house, bringing boxes to the truck where I was walking on grass. I live in Lexington, Kentucky and travel 21 hours by flight. never been in a car, never done anything, this is going to be a big change.

going to the city of lights is my dream. I've always had Vision boards with it. but there was all of my stuff packed up. My mom and my dad were crying. I had my pet lizard, frog fish, and dog with me, named Luna, Jerry, Fred, and Mario.

My first drive was with my dad. He was driving. My mom was in the front seat, and I was in the back seat with all of my pets. Since I have never been out of the house, I do not know how to drive. I don't even know how a car works. I'm going to be a part of the plan. I'm sitting in the back of the car, we are going so fast I was getting really scared. but yet the trees were green and beautiful, they were nothing like I've ever seen. photos cannot tell you how pretty it was.

When I got to my flight, everything was perfect. I fell asleep for about 15 hours. The other was that I was paying attention to my pets and walking and feeding them. I did have a layover for about an hour to finish the rest of my flight. but here I was getting into a rental car to my first apartment, where I'd never been out of my country or my house. I was so scared and devastated.

There was in my first apartment all of my pets. The first thing I did was set up my kitchen, then my pets, then the living room, etc. I didn't sleep for about 3 days just because of how nervous I was, but since I was new to the apartment, I did not have much food. I had to conquer my fear and go to the grocery store all by myself. I called my mom for a little bit of confidence but realized I'm an adult now, and I do not need her. I hung up instantly and texted her, saying I was sorry and that I didn't mean to call. went downstairs, bought a train ticket and walked to the train station.

I got on the train. it was really fun and really scary; people looked at me like I was nuts, that gut-retching feeling in my stomach while sitting there. I was super scared but conquered my fear. I got my groceries and got my next train ticket. It went back. That wasn't too bad. The next day, I looked into Driving School, got scared, and walked back off. went back to my taxi supposedly they call it traffic but I wouldn't know there's so much of it you barely can even own your car you have to write taxes everywhere you go the rent is ridiculous but it's so much fun. I had to get back on the train to go to school the next day, and again, everybody was staring at me.

I tried everything I tried to go into different spots. I tried walking around. I tried to hold on to one of those bars. Everyone still looked at me and stared. I did not understand what was going on. awkward silence fell among all of us. Okay, v I'm hopefully done

The Three Little Pigs

by Alex Lovelady

I am going to tell you a story about softball while relating it to the classical fairytale of "The Three Little Pigs". Once upon a time I was about to go to my first practice with my new softball team. I was looking forward to this season because my two best friends, Sarah and Olivia, were playing on the team with me. We all came from different elementary schools so we had been looking forward to the day that we would all get to play together on the same team. Practice went well and we really liked our coach. The season started and as we went on throughout the season none of us were getting any play time. We were all really bummed about this, it was almost like the game of softball was a big bad wolf trying to eat us up. We decided we needed to make some changes and try to get more playing time. Especially since our big championship game was coming up.

Even though Sarah was one of my best friends, she was really lazy and seemed like she didn't really care that she was not getting any play time. She never paid attention in practice and never wanted to practice with us at home. She would goof off in practice and try to distract Olivia and I from paying attention. She reminded me of the first little pig who built his house with straw that eventually got blown down by the big bad wolf because he didn't want to put the hard work in to build a strong house. She eventually got upset about not getting play time and just stopped trying.

Olivia started practicing a little more after school and would pay attention at school practice. She also seemed like she didn't really care though to get better at the game and get more playing time though. She would always want to stop practicing outside of school shortly after we just got started. She would complain about practice being too hard or taking up too much of her free time. Even though she did put in some effort she also did not get any more play time since the season first started. Just like in the "Three Little Pigs" her house, since it was only built with sticks was blown down by the big bad wolf as well and she stopped putting in the extra effort altogether too.

After the first few games of me not getting any play time, I sat down with my parents and talked with them about how I could get more playing time. I decided to really pay attention in practice and try my hardest at every drill we did. I also started practicing at home with my dad every day after school. My parents saw the hard work that I was putting in and even got private softball lessons for me to get better. It wasn't easy and sometimes there were days that I didn't want to put in the extra effort but I knew that I wanted to play. So I kept trying my hardest and putting in the work. My dad said that I was like the third little pig, who spent all day building his house out of bricks so that when the big bad wolf came he wasn't able to blow my house down. As we had a few more games, I started to get more and more play time. Sarah and Olivia noticed this and asked me if we could all practice together at my house after school. We all started putting in the hard work at practice and paying attention to the coach and putting in our best effort. I worked with Sarah and Olivia on some of the drills and skills that I was learning in my private softball lessons. Just like the two brother pigs ran to the third pigs house after blowing their houses down, they came to me when they realized that the work I was putting in was getting me more play time.

The Drawer

by Jaise Boyd

She found it in the back of a desk drawer. It was a liquid, a lot of it. She didn't want to touch it further than the slight tap of discovery. Although it intrigues her further as she looks at it, what exactly is it? It had absorbed into her skin, which worried her. She wanted to try and ask someone else about it, but there weren't many options she could choose from. She decides to investigate what this strange liquid is.

She figures that she has to go in alone. Where does she start first, though? The library? Yeah, the library would probably be the best place to find information on this unknown liquid.

She started walking to the library to check out some books on different liquids., Iit was yellow, wasn't it? Yeah, yellow.

She asks the librarian, "Excuse me, are there any books on liquids? I need some information about a yellow one, but I don't know what it is."

The librarian tells her, "Oh? Of course! Just over there in the science section."

Celeste says ecstatically, "Thank you so much!"

The librarian says, "You're welcome! Come to me if you need anything else."

She says, "Alright, I will."

She heads for the science section in search of any books with information about the unknown liquid.

She searched for about thirty minutes trying to find a book on anything that might help her. After her searching, she found a few books that seemed like they could help her, so she went to the librarian to check the books out.

The librarian asks, "Did you find everything alright ma'am?"

She says, "Yes, I did find everything I was looking for."

The librarian asks, "Okay, that's good, what's the name for it?"

"Celeste Knapp."

The librarian says, "Alright Celeste, have a good day!"

"You too!"

Celeste goes home with her books and plans to look for whatever that yellow liquid is.

"Alright, let's see, could it be fluorine? No...doesn't look the same."

She searches diligently for whatever strange liquid she's trying to find.

None of the books seemed to hold what she was looking for. Eventually, she found one page that had what she needed. She started reading through the page to see if it matched the liquid in her drawer.

"Alright, so I think it's isoamyl nitrite, but what is that?"

Celeste decides to go back to the library to ask about it.

Celeste walks into the library and asks the librarian, "Are there any books with isoamyl nitrite in them? I think that's what I need."

The librarian tells her, "Oh yeah, I can show you where to find one."

Celeste is led to the library section holding the book with Isoamyl nitrite in it.

"Here it is! Would you like to check it out?"

Celeste says, "Yes please."

She checks out the book and goes home.

"So, Isoamyl nitrite, what exactly is it?"

She reads through the book and finds a heading telling what it is.

"Highly flammable? Doesn't that drawer have a lighter in it? Oh crap, I need to get that out of there!"

Celeste quickly ran home, dashed over to the drawer, and rushed to grab the lighter out of the drawer. It wasn't the best idea, she accidentally set off a spark.

The drawer went up in flames, quickly spreading to the walls. As the house set ablaze, the quick flame caused Celeste to lose her vision, she couldn't react to the growing fire. Celeste couldn't make it out in time.

School Should Only Meet Four Days A Week

by J. N.

A four day school week would be more beneficial to students and staff, instead of a regular five day school week. It creates a more flexible schedule for teachers and students, especially students involved in extracurricular activities. It gives teachers more time to plan lessons and grade assignments. It also gives students more time to complete homework assignments as well.

Paragraph four of the article, **"School Should Change From 5 Days a Week to 4"** written by Makiya Mack says, "Lastly, a four-day school week allows for greater flexibility in scheduling. The additional day off can be utilized for various purposes, such as extracurricular activities, community service, or internships. This offers students the opportunity to explore their interests outside of the traditional classroom setting and develop valuable skills that can contribute to their personal and academic growth." By creating a shorter school week, students would be able to spend more time doing the things they enjoy, while also being able to rest. Giving students more time to complete homework would allow students more time to study. If this was the case students would also put more effort into their academics.

Not only would it benefit the students, but it would also benefit the teachers. In paragraph three of **"School Should Change From 5 Days a Week to 4"** the author says, "By having an extra day off, educators have more time for professional development, lesson planning, and collaboration with their colleagues. This can lead to increased job satisfaction and a more energized teaching staff, ultimately benefiting the quality of education provided to students." Giving teachers more time to create lesson plans would add to the quality of the students' learning experience. Teachers would be able to spend more time creating each lesson, which would expand the students' knowledge of each subject. Giving teachers an extra day to grade assignments would also reduce stress, leading to a happier educational environment.

Paragraph four of, **"School Should Change From 5 Days a Week to 4"** also says, "A four-day school week can lead to cost savings for school districts. With one less day of operation, schools can reduce expenses related to transportation, utilities, and other operational costs. This can free up resources that can be redirected toward other educational programs or initiatives, enhancing the overall educational experience for students." This means that supplies would be used more sparingly, which would also mean that teachers would not have to spend nearly as much on school supplies. The money saved could be used to improve campus, quality of teachers supplies and equipment, and even giving students a fun experience to look back on.

Although there are many benefits to shortening the school week, of course not everyone agrees. Paragraph four of **"Why Five Days a Week"** by Baan Dek says, "Consistency helps children feel at ease and slowly gain confidence in the world around them. Not only do they get a chance to practice new skills, they increasingly start to develop independence in their everyday lives." I agree that it is important for young children to learn independence, but consuming the majority of their week with schooling limits their ability to explore their own interests. More students would be able to excel in things outside of their school work.

A four day school week would be more beneficial to students and staff instead of a regular five day school week. This is because it would allow students to find and enjoy their own hobbies and interests, all while teachers can create more quality learning opportunities for their students.

"Pumpkins" by Doouglas Rudolph, Trinity Shipley, Alyssa Reavley, Branson Hudson, & Abigaile Green

My Perspective

by Avery Bates

The day when my perspective changed on the way I see God, will be a day I never forget. I used to be a skeptic, wondering if he was really able to do all the things the bible said he could. Now I am 100% a believer in God based on the events that happened to me.

About 11 years ago I lived with my biological mom (Lauren). My parents have been divorced for a long time and somehow my mom got custody of me. Living with my mom, we rarely went to church and when we did it was very boring. We went to Dallas bay I think and i never liked it. I had no friends over there and i didn't really learn anything. To be fair I never really knew what to expect because I never had anyone even try to tell me who God even was.

In 2015 I got taken away from my mom and went to live with my dad and stepmom. It was very hard because living with my biological mom I was surrounded by drugs, alcohol, sex, smoking and all that. Living with my biological mom I was constantly surrounded by sin. After I started living with my dad we tried several different churches until we found the one we all loved, Sale Creek Church Of God. When we first started going I was in the kids class called One Way. One way was the class for second grade to sixth grade. I learned a lot in that class because our youth pastor (Mrs.Alisa) was very encouraging and loving and made interacting fun.

For my first month going I was super scared of going to the class because I didn't know anyone, but soon enough I started making friends who also came out to be my step cousins. Chloe Goins, my cousin and also one of my best friends, became my first ever friend at my church. We stuck like glue ever since. Anytime we are together we laugh so hard we are either crying or peeing. Ava Moore, Khaylee Escobar, and Anslee Parker came to our church a little while after me but we became super close friends not only through school but also through our church.

Yes, I went to church but I was still skeptical of the concept of God. I had never had a firsthand experience with the Holy Ghost so I didn't really know what to think. All that changed in March of 2024.

In march of 2024 our youth group went to winterfest 2024. Winterfest is a fellowship mission to get closer to God in many different ways. It was a saturday night service and we were just getting into our worship time. I wasn't really feeling anything in my gut yet but then the worship group started singing a certain song, "trust in God" by Elevation Worship. Something just tugged at my heart when they sang the part "I sought the lord, and he heard, and he answered." When I heard those lyrics I dropped to my knees and started praying. I was crying and praying so hard that I fell out (i don't know how to describe it but it's when you, like pass out, but it's from the Holy Ghost). When I woke up I had a whole group of people around me, praying. I never felt so loved and valued. My youth group is the best I could ever ask for and I wouldn't be this close to God without my church family.

That night was the best night of my life, not only because it was my first experience with God but it was confirmation that God is actually real. Ever since that day, I have become a whole different person and it was for the better. I love that I found God and my church family. I'm now constantly praying, reading my bible, going to church, and trying to spread God's word to others.

Public Transportation

by Jaden Gross

One day there was a couple named Jeffrey Higolbottom and Susan Higolbottom. They were like any other regular couple, but one day they got into a car crash and lost all their money from hospital bills. Since they were both in the hospital, no one could pay the rent money, they were broke and living on the street with nowhere to go.

So Jeffrey decided he would apply for jobs once he started to feel better. Jeffrey decided to go and try to work at Arby's. It didn't work out, he got fired for being too smelly, and he scared off all of the customers. So then he tried to get a job at Wendy's and he got approved, so now he has a steady job and all he has to do is clean after closing so no one will see him at all. But he has no way around. So what will he do, go buy a bike?

NO! He is gonna take public transportation. As he was taking public transportation one day, he got jumped and robbed so he never took public transportation again.

After this day, he started walking to work every day, and after work, he decided to go to a free open gym and start boxing, so if something were to ever happen like that again, he could defend himself. After a few weeks of going to the gym after work, he started to notice progress, and one day after work, he was at the gym working out and boxing, he saw the guys who jumped him, so he decided to get revenge. So he walked up to the first one and hit him super hard in the stomach, the guy fell on the ground, and the other guy ran over and Jeffery did the same thing to that guy.

Now that he got his revenge he started to use public transportation again but now he had a steady pace at his job he could start trying to move into an apartment with Susan Higgolbottom but Jeffery doesn't know that Susan went to the courthouse and filed for a divorce and in the mail he got a paper saying that he had court on February 25th he was curious but he still went and as he got there he saw his "wife" Susan and was curious on why she was there and they went into court at the same time and as the judge said to sign the divorce papers he started bawling crying.

After that day he kept going to the gym more and more by week and after a year he was jacked but he felt like he needed to stop working at Wendy's so he decided to gamble play after play he kept losing money so he just went to the casino to play some blackjack and he won 10,000 dollars after the casino he went back home and decided it was destiny to gamble more so he got on and bet half of the money he won at blackjack and won... 100,000 dollars and now Susan is still homeless while Jeffery is winning big.

Rusty

by Hayden Gentry

I wake up in the middle of the night to a loud bang outside my house. I get up groggily and I slip on my shoes, I step out of the house towards the woods. I slowly walk to the forest, KLANG KLANG KLANG! The loud bangs startled me, and I let out a small squeak. "H-Hello?" I yell out into the wooded atmosphere. "Who's there?!" I say nervously. BEEP BEEP BEEP! I see a rusted figure in the corner of my eye. "A robot?" The robot limps closer. The robot speaks in a broken voice "Power insufficient, please charge... R-run..."

A bright purple laser zips past my head when I hear those words. I see the shiny silver androids in the distance, grab the rusted robot, and dash out of the forest. I scream at the top of my lungs as I toss the rusted robot into the back of my truck. I turn the key and the engine sputters. "Start you old piece of $&!%!" I yell as the robots march closer. I eventually get it to start and I slam on the accelerator driving into the open road. I drive to my dad's worn-down workshop, once I get inside I slam the door shut locking it behind me.

I grab some tools and I work to repair the rusted robot, a couple of hours later I install a new battery in the robot and it springs to life. "New friend?! NEW FRIEND!" the robot yells as it shakes my hand vigorously. "Shhh! Be quiet!" I exclaim. The robots from before begin to break down the door. The rusted robot pushes me to the side "I got this" The rusted robot holds his arm up as his hand morphs into a laser blaster, it tries to fire but instead of a bright laser the only thing that comes out is a brown puff of dust. "Uh oh..." We both say. "Run!" We both dash out the back door dodging the incoming laser fire.

A laser hits me but luckily my book "Jam Sessions" by Jerry Harwood blocks the laser."Dang it! That was my favorite book!" I yell as I look back and I see the rusted robot dominating the other robots. The robots lay on the floor sparks flying off of them with the rusted robot standing over them. "You couldn't have done that earlier?!" I yell as I walk towards the robot. "Hey, I never got your name..." I ask. The robot quickly replies. "Experiment - 93600371." I look at him confused. "Yeah, I'll just call you... Rusty!" The robot nods. I suddenly pull out a wrench and I fix up his blaster hand. Right as I fix it up another swarm of robots march towards us. I dash towards them quickly taking some of them apart while Rusty fires his brand new blaster at them. "Woo hoo! This thing is amazing!" He yells. Right as he speaks all the robots gang up on me and beat me up. "NO!" Rusty screams, and fires a powerful blast destroying all robots in the immediate vicinity including him. He made the ultimate sacrifice.

The End

Last Christmas

by Khaylee Escobar

L ast Christmas I was a different person. I took everything for granted, and I thought that Christmas was all about the gifts and Jesus's birthday. However, as important as those are, the truth is that it isn't all just about them. It's also about spending time with your family and friends, which is something that I wished I would have realized a long time ago.

Sadly, I had a lot to learn about myself. I was so stuck up and self-absorbed in my life that I had never really thought of the people who were around me, that is, except for my boyfriend. To be honest, I had the worst attitude in my family, and I was always hating on the people who loved me the most. As far as Christmas was concerned, my main priority was the presents. Everything was simply just all about me. I struggled with many things. It wasn't just things about me; it was just about everyone.

A few months ago, I was admitted to this facility because of my behavior, and I had no idea how long I would be there.. When it dawned on me that I might have to spend Christmas there, it made me really sad. I was really struggling, and I felt like my life was over. It was then that I realized that Christmas isn't just all about the presents; it's also about the people you spend your time with on Christmas day.

Fortunately, I was able to go home on November 7, 2024. When I got there, I hugged my family and friends so hard. I had missed them so much, and I knew then how much they meant to me. It was then that I also knew that I had finally changed. I could have changed for the better or for the worst, but under those circumstances, I can definitely say that I changed for the better.

When I stop and think about what Christmas would have been like if I had stayed in the facility, I understand now the importance of family and friends. After being so far away from them during that time, I knew that I had to change my attitude for them and never take them for granted again. I had to do whatever it took to become a better person.

Although I still struggle to enjoy what Christmas is all about, I now have a better understanding of the purpose of Christmas, and my attitude about it has definitely changed. Instead of being so self-centered and focusing on the presents that I will get, I realize what I have to be grateful for on a beautiful Christmas day. I now have an attitude of praise, and I'm thankful for God because he has helped me become the person I am today. He has helped me change my life, and he has clearly turned it around.

There are many ways I think that I have changed. Most of all I think I have changed the way I view things. I used to view things in such a negative way, but now I have started to realize that the world isn't that bad when you walk with the right attitude and the right people, especially at Christmas.

Jesse's Life

by E. C.

Meet Jesse Pinkman, a youth who was a straight-A student . One day he started hanging out with the wrong group of kids who were very bad influences. After a while, his grades started to slip, he started staying out late, and not coming home or going to school. His mom starts to wonder why he was acting differently. Once he finally got home his mom decides to have a talk with him about why he's been acting like this. Jesse decides to tell his mom a little about what has been happening and what he has been doing.

Jesse is one of those kids who can be peer-pressured into doing anything. So one night he and some of his friends started to do very bad drugs, something that he should never do. Once this had happened Jesse started spiraling out of control, spending all his money on various drugs. His parents started to notice that he was always on some sort of drugs, so they decided to kick him out and throw all this stuff out.

Now Jesse was on the streets and had no one to turn to, he is living in a tent and only has the clothes on his back. He started asking his friends and some lawbreakers to lend him money so he could feed his addiction, which left him in debt to people who would do anything to get their money. He tries to go back to his parents but when they open the door and see his face, they slam the door immediately. The same friends that got him hooked on drugs got sober and left him all alone on the streets. Everyone he borrowed money from came asking for their money back. When they didn't get it, they took his clothes, tent, and food.

Jesse ended up finding a shelter to stay at for a few days to get out of the weather, there was a bad storm coming. While he was there he met a man named Robert. Robert had once been in Jesse's shoes and lost everything because of drugs. Thanks to him, Jesse opened his eyes and realized this lifestyle wasn't how he wanted to live. The shelter workers had hookups with a few recovery places and were able to get Jesse into a program. While going through rehab, he started making changes in his life that were for the better. He reached out to his mom and told her about what he had been through and that he was finally clean and asked her to come visit him. The next visitation she was there. She was so proud of him for his progress! Jesse completed the rehab program and was moved to a halfway house where he was able to get a job. After several months, Jesse was able to move out into his own apartment and moved up in his job, with a pay raise. Jesse never turned back to drugs, found a woman he fell in love with, and had a family with her. Life was good after all.

My Path To God
by Jordyn Sneed

Today I will be talking about how I got closer to the lord, and what he's done for me. I wasn't always close to the lord and I wasn't a good christian. I was in a rough spot before I found the lord and I'm grateful that I found him. Finding the lord was a great feeling, and I hope other people get to experience it too.

Seeing my friends being so close to the Lord made me want to have a relationship with him because I saw the good things that he did in their lives. I know not being close to the Lord made things harder in life because you dont know he's in control, and that made me worry more before I had a relationship with him, and I had a bunch of anxiety built up, and none of my friends had that feeling, so that's when I knew I should go to church to build a relationship and get to know him and know how he wants me to live my life.

I started to go to church, and started a relationship with the Lord. I started trusting him, and not worrying as much. I could've worried less but that's a part of creating the relationship. When I walked into that church, I immediately felt like I belonged there. I felt comfortable and supported in the church and that they wanted to help me. The first time I ever went to the church they did small groups, and they said to flip to a certain verse and I flipped there first because I had tabs and it's easy to flip to the chapters. I said I was there and they asked me to read the verse and I did, it didn't feel awkward, or uncomfortable. I felt like I was welcomed there.

Now I study the bible every other night. I'm a nicer human being and I treat others the way I want to be treated. I do what God wants me to do, most of the time. Not every christian is perfect. I go to church every wednesday and worship the Lord and learn about him, and I go on sundays sometimes too. I got closer to my friends and god helped me build a stronger friendship with them, he helped me realize to higher my standards and don't settle for less, And always follow god's path and sometimes you just need to let go of some things.

I was not a good christian and I didnt even know who the Lord was but now I am a good christian and I follow the path he has for me because I started going to church to learn about him, and have a happier life. I'm so grateful that I found the Lord and I know he'll always be there for me. I wish I would've realized it sooner. I hope everyone has the experience with the Lord like I did, and realize the Lord has everything planned for us. I wish I would've realized it sooner. I hope everyone has the experience with the Lord like I did, and realize the Lord has everything planned for us.

Secrets Don't Last Forever

by Vada Turner

My breath was shallow and sharp, my mind was racing, searching for something to say. My heart quickened, I found myself on my knees, begging for her not to look in the back of my desk drawer. The world was spinning, and I noticed the shaky state of my hands. I felt the tears well up in my eyes, they begged to fall.

I felt my heart drop when I saw it...In her hands. My mind raced with the words. She found it in the back of the desk drawer. I watched as her eyes widened and flicked to the heavy jewelry on my wrist. I jumped to my feet and I started to back up, she found it. The world spun faster, everything was out of place, my mind was in ruins. I was at a loss for words. I had nothing to say for myself, I was caught.

"Trix, what is this?" She said as she held up the knife.

"That is nothing, okay just drop it!" I screamed the anger overcoming me in a moment.

"It clearly isn't nothing, if you're getting so pressed, Trix." She said and I felt the anger take over in her eyes. I look I had never gotten before. It broke me.

"I said it's nothing, what is so hard to understand about that!" I screamed and threw my hands in the air.

"I have a question, Trix, I want an answer." She said walking towards me.

"Yeah and what is your question, you psychopath." I said and I felt the words bitter on my tongue.

"Do you hurt yourself with this knife?" I saw all the anger and disappointment leave her eyes, replaced with concern and sadness.

Lie,Lie, LIE, LIE My mind screamed at me.

"No of course not, why would I do that?" I said, and I was acting like I was offended. "Who in their right mind would hurt themselves?" I said and I scoffed.

"Trix, don't lie to me, this is serious." She said as she laid the knife down.

"Oh, so now you're calling me a liar, you know what, I'm tired of getting belittled by you everyday." I felt the anger boil and grow. "I am so done with your constant nagging." I grabbed my purse and I stormed off leaving her, *my mother*, alone.

I walked down the street to Novs (that's short for Nova). I knocked on the door, and I saw her standing there with her hair in a bun at the nape of her neck. She is wearing these little shorts, they are low rise. Her shirt exposing her belly button ring.

"Hey Trix, what's up?" She said as she opened the door and welcomed me inside.

"Nothing much. I was gonna head down to the Pens (short for Penny) wanna come with? I asked her, I didn't want to be alone right now.

"Yeah, Of course I do. Just let me grab my bag." She said and I watched as she walked off to her room.

I stood there and I waited for her. I fidget with the bracelets on my wrist, the undeniable feeling of guilt. I didn't mean to lash out at my mother. I just didn't want her to know my secret.

"Okay let's go, Trix Trix." She said and I wrapped my arm around hers and we skipped off to the house, giggling.

"Let's go have some fun, Novs!" I said as I skipped with her, she was the only person that I could be truly happy with, but I couldn't tell her about my secret. I swore to myself that I would never tell anyone.

Novs and I made it to Pens, and I saw a group of teenage boys there, and they looked to be about 16, we were all 14, except for Pens, she is 15. One of the boys was standing with their arms around Pen's waist, pulling her in and kissing her in a messy kiss. The other boys were messing with each other, Novs and I decided which one we wanted to approach and "talk". We were just gonna get messed up and makeout with them. That's what always happens at Pen's house.

The boys were tall, and one had Dark brown hair, with blue eyes that complemented his complexion, the other one had Black hair, with brown eyes. I went for the one with blue eyes, and Novs went for the one with brown eyes. Pen's motions us all inside and she went and grabbed the "stuff", basically the alcohol from her parents room. I had some cigarettes in my purse, I had stolen them from my mom, she didn't notice at all. She is so stupid, god, I just want to forget what happened today. We drank, and the boy with blue eyes motioned to me, he wanted me to follow him. I smiled and grabbed my drink, waving to Novs, as he took my hand, and led me off somewhere.

Blue eyes and I wandered off into the back yard, it was surrounded by trees. He pinned me to the wall, and carefully took the drink from my hand.

"Close your eyes, sweetheart." He said and I stupidly listened, I wasn't in the right mind, I was drunk.

I closed my eyes with a nod of my head. I giggled, I heard a rustling but I didn't pay it much mind.

"Open your eyes, blondie." He said, and I opened my eyes looking up at him.

"Open your mouth for me." I listened, and his finger traveled under my chin, tipping my head back. He started to pour the drink into my mouth, it was bitter, and tasted funny.

"Swallow it for me." I listened, I kept my eyes locked on his as he poured this drink down my throat, I swallowed.

The drink was gone, and he tossed the bottle to the ground, pinning me to the wall, and catching my mouth in a hard embrace, his tongue slipped its way in my mouth, my arms found my way around his shoulders, his arms around my waist.

Suddenly I didn't feel so good, my head was spinning, and his hands were all over me. My vision blurred, and my thoughts were clouded, blank. He picked me up and pushed my back against the wall. I wanted him to stop, I didn't like this anymore. I pulled away, and he looked at me with a harsh look.

"Why did you pull away?" He said in a harsh tone, I felt a shiver travel up my back.

"I don't want to do this anymore. I don't feel good." I said and I tried to get down, but I was trapped.

"Oh, you're not going anywhere, not till I'm down with you." He chuckles, and I feel the world go in and out in waves.

"Put me down, now!" I screamed and I hit my head on his, he screamed.

"You're a psychopath!" He grabbed me by the throat, and it got even harder to breathe. "You will pay for that you little." he choked me and the world went out again.

"Let me go, now!" I choked out the words, as I hit his head harder and he dropped me, my knees hit the ground, and I let out a cry of pain. I got up and I ran back inside.

"Novs we need to go, now." I looked at her my legs shaking, my knees bloody, and the boy behind me.

"Come on, Novs!" I grabbed her hand as I ran out of the house and I looked back to see the blue-eyed boy holding up his middle finger and Pens, yelling at him to get back inside the house.

"Omg, Trix what happened to you!?" She asked, stopping by a tree.

"I-I don't know, I think he might have spiked my drink, he started to choke me and it hurt. I hit him hard on the head, I ran." I said my speech slurred.

I watched as her expression softened and she looked more concerned.

"Trix, let's get you home, we'll just say that you hit your head, okay?" I don't know why, but I felt mad, I felt like she was pitying me. Novs treated me like I was a child.

"Novs, I don't need your help, much less your pity, I will walk myself home. Thank you." I walked off pushing away Novs, and my heart hurt a little.

I walked the rest of the way home, my knees bruised and covered in dry blood. I made it home, and my mother was draped over the couch with her boyfriend beside her. With an alcohol bottle in her hand, she was asleep.

I walked into my room, closing and locking the door behind me, I saw the knife laying on the desk, she didn't think to move it, take it. The thoughts overtook my mind, all the anger I had bottled inside, overflowing, like boiled water. I grabbed the knife, removing my bracelet. I violently dragged the knife across my wrist, till the skin was stained with the blood of my sins. I sobbed, I felt my head spinning, and my heart racing. I didn't want to do this, but I am just so mad all the time, and it is the only thing that helps with the anger. The anger I get from watching my mom with her boyfriend, leaving my dad behind.

My dad and my mom got divorced when I was 10, and ever since my mom has just stopped caring about what I did. I spend my days away from this hell hole. I avoid her, I stay in my room all day. While she sits back and watches my dad live his perfect life with his new girlfriend, and his new family, leaving me here to rot with my mother and her boyfriend. I am so sick and tired of it, I want this to end.

Suddenly I heard a knock on my door and it was my mom. I jump to my feet and I hide the knife, covering my wrist with the sleeve of my shirt.

"Trix, are you in there, we need to talk now." She spoke and I know she knew, I don't want her to know.

"No mom, go away, I am trying to sleep. I don't need you to keep me up all night." I pushed her away, like I do with everyone I love.

"No Trix, this is serious, *I need to take a look at your wrist.*" She said and she started to move the door handle.

"Mom, what no! You're not looking at my wrist, you have no reason to!" I screamed and my heart rate quickened and I got scared.

"Trix, open this f-cking door, right now." She said and I stared at my secret. I had a flashback.

I am suddenly 2 months younger than I am now, I'am on the couch with my mom, and we are having the best time. I had Novs over, we had just become friends. I had started to distance myself from my other friends, I hung out with the "popular girls". I was a sweet girl, one who would've never treated her mother like this. This is all Novs fault, she turned me into this druggie girl, who sneaks out, and drinks and smokes.

I hate this life I have created by believing I had to fit into the same social construct as everyone else.

My mothers voice brings me back, and I unlock the door. I am just so tired of who I have become, I fall into my mothers arms, and I break down. I hold my mother close to me, and I melt into her hold. I am just so tired of fighting. I want to stop all the hurting, and pain.

"Mom, I have a secret to tell you." I said as I buried my head into her chest.

"I am here for you, Trix." She said and I felt her tighten her hold on me, it felt comforting. I told her everything, I showed her my wrist, I watched as the tears formed in her eyes, as her eyes danced across my marks, clinging onto the blood smeared by my shirt.

"Mom, I just want to stop hurting, I am so tired of it." I said, I hugged her and held her close.

"I will help you, baby, I want you to know, I am always here to support you. I love you Trix, you're my baby girl, I don't want to see you hurt ever.

We hugged and I fell asleep in her arms, my heart was warm, and I didn't feel as anger for the first time in a while. I hope I will get better, I never want to feel this way ever again.

This is a lesson on how secrets don't always last forever. To past me, I want you to know that we are so much happier and healthier. Dad comes to visit more often, he doesn't know about "the secret" but some things are better left unsaid.

AUTHOR'S NOTE: This is not a personal story, just something inspired.

Willow

by Layla Maggio

Leaves, blowing in the wind,
The beauty they bring will never end.
As they sway and sway,
The little birds come and go away.

Green; glowing in the sun,
Dancing and having so much fun.
As they sway and sway,
The little bugs come and go away.

Branches drooping down way, way low,
They sit and watch as the waters flow.
As they sway and sway,
The little squirrels come and go away.

Brown; so thin and light,
They always shine oh so bright.
As they sway and sway,
The little sun comes and goes away.

Back In Time

by Graci Harrison

"Wake up, sleepyhead!"

I hear my mom say out loud to me. I looked at her and asked her why she had to wake me up at the crack of the sun.

"What do you mean, Izzy? It's 9:45?" Mom says.

My clock was off by three hours. "That's weird," I say. My younger brother must have played a prank on me. I hear slight footsteps outside my door, and the next second, my younger brother Gabe opens the door. " I knew it was you !" I say. You set back my clock!"

"No, I swear it wasn't me. I just came in here to see why you were sleeping in so late!" My annoying brother says.

The door slams behind him. Who was it then? I don't have time for this, I need to get my day started. I walk down the stairs, I think to myself maybe I'm just being crazy, I'm probably just hungry. Feeling disoriented, I stumble over to the breakfast table, a warm breakfast waiting for me.

As I'm putting my pancakes into my mouth, I hear my dad say, "Love you guys! I'm off to work. I have a very important meeting with my coworkers today". But didn't you have that meeting 3 days ago?

"No, Izzy, I have it today".

But never mind that I'm starving. I finish my breakfast within minutes, stuffing down every bit of food on my plate, not a crumb left over. I hear my grandma calling for me, Her name is Jan; ultimately, we all call her Nanny, though.

"Izzy dear, I need to show you something in the attic, very important, very important," she repeats.

I follow her upstairs, and then comes the attic ladder. I thought I hadn't been up there before, but my nanny reminds me.

" When you were a toddler, oh how gorgeous you were with eyes as bright as the sun and bluer than the sky itself." "You used to play up here all the time. Here, I'll show you!"

I see a little light as I climb into the attic from the little circle window. I pass by old boxes filled with baby clothes and old baby toys. I'm hit with a terrible stench of dust and- actually just dust, it covers the whole airspace. And then I see a little play corner with my baby picture on the wall. It still has so many toys, and a little bunny stuffed animal.

"Mr snuggles!" Nanny says.

What?

"Mr snuggles," she repeated, "the bunny".

Oh, I say, and without saying anything, nanny opens a compartment behind my picture, tears in my eyes as I see a picture of me as a newborn, my aunt holding me for the last time... I took it to my room, and after that, I didn't say anything else to my grandma. My mom told me, when I was 8, about the story of my Aunt Grace. When I was born, Aunt Grace was right beside me, but she had cancer. She was only gonna live a couple more weeks, but she chose to spend her last moments with me and my mom. Aunt Grace passed away 2 weeks after I was born. I was way too young to remember anything, but I know what happens at funerals. I walked outside my room for the first time in about 3 hours. I think I may have fallen asleep, but something doesn't feel right. Breakfast on the table, mom?

"Oh honey you're awake, breakfast is ready!'

But you already served breakfa-.

"I'm off to work! I have a very important meeting with my coworkers". Dad says.

Dad, but you left 4 hours ago?

"Oh, it seems a bit early to leave for work then. I t's 9:45 now, I say perfect timing!" Dad says.

The door slowly but surely shuts behind him. "Hungry, Izzy?"

"No, thank you, Mom," I say. I go to my room, almost slamming the door behind me. Wha- what is happening? I I- I'm going crazy, I don't even know how to feel. I started to put two and two together. First, my clock goes back 3 hours, then the new morning turns into 3 days ago, and now! It's back in 3 hours. I notice a tear run down my cheek, holding my picture tight. Wait- I turn the picture frame around and feel a little bump on the back, I haven't noticed it before. Almost like a little pocket, I use my fingers to grab a chain out of the back of the frame. A locket looks like, as I open it up, it's the same picture, the last time she ever saw me... in a heart shape. Engraved on the back, it reveals the words "When the time feels right, hold it tight". A small tear from my cheek falls down fast onto the locket, but time feels slow, almost like nothing. Before my mind can process what to do next, I see a small glowing light come from my backyard., I look out my window and see rays of sunlight shining through my fence and onto A Hole. Whe- where did that come from? I wrap my locket around my neck and slam open my door. MOM!

"Izzy with a scream like that, I would think by the time I'm here you'd be lying on the ground almost dead. What happened, though, honey?

The hole in the backyard!

"Izzy, there's no hole., maybe you should take a nap;, you might need it".

I- she doesn't believe me. What if she can't even see it? Enough is enough. I sneak out my back door, almost a few feet away from the hole, not intending to go in, and I trip on a stick. Right then and there, I fell in. All I can hear is a faint "tick tock, tick tock" as it repeatedly does it. I screamed and screamed, with nothing else left to do. Ahhhhhhhhhhhhhh- bam, I hit the ground, I think? Im- wait my house?? But it looks all the same. How is this even possible? A million things were racing through my mind: holes, falling in, landing here. I go with my absolute last ditch decision to walk inside. It's gonna be all normal, I hope, I hope. As I stride into the house, things are most definitely not normal, the kitchen is different, the living room, the bathroom even. Everything! Wait, my locket is gone! No, no, no, I repeat to myself, this can't be happening. Caught by surprise, I saw two people walk into the kitchen where I was. I freaked out and backed into the table behind me. The table rattles; now I know I'm gonna be discovered, but wait. "Oh, Emily, the air vent is blowing air out too much again; the table's even rattling now." Emily, what is my mom's name? And that voice sounds like a nanny's! Another person walks down the stairs. I couldn't make out their face, but already assuming no one could see me, I walked around freely. As soon as I walk closer to her, she yells, " Mom, I'll be there in a bit!' " Ok, Grace", she replies. I can't help myself by saying Aunt Grace? Expecting the worst outcome, she says a few words.

"Izzy!" " I knew you were gonna be here, I just didn't know when! Come with me."

Without letting even a few words leave my mouth, I'm dragged up to what looks to be my old room, but what I assume is now my aunt Grace's room.

"I know this all seems weird, but I can explain everything."

Ok, then let me get this straight, nanny is down in the kitchen with my mom Emily, and you- your aunt Grace but my age? But what about my watch? That's where it all started.

"Oh yeah, sorry I did that," she replies. "I wanted to start off slowly, giving you hints".

But the days are all mixed up! Again she replies,

"That was me too".

But the locket?

"I told your nanny to give it to you on this exact date, well, in your time, and she remembered."

Why, though? What was your motive here?

" I created the locket to bring you back to me when you were old enough. I only had a few moments with you when you were born, and I can't miss anything now. You'll be able to go home, but remember, I'm the only one that can see you".

The only words I can pull out of my mouth after so many things happening in just very few minutes were, I miss you. Tears are going down my face; the only thing I wanna do is hug and catch up. After an hour of talking, even Aunt Grace said it herself,

"It's time for you to go home".

I know, I know.

"Alright, where's the locket?"

I don't know. I was wearing it when I fell into the hole, and it just disappeared!

"Think, Izzy, where could it be?"

I- I, wait, follow me Aunt Grace! I sprint down the hallway and open the latch to the attic. As I climb up the stairs, I think to myself, it has to be there, it has to be. Sure enough, in that little corner with the circular window, there's an empty picture frame on the wall. I carefully placed it down and opened the compartment behind it.. Sure enough, there it was, the locket, with the rays of sunshine hitting it just right to show its glow.

"Come on," Aunt Grace says.

We reach the backyard, knowing what happens next. I hug Aunt Grace tight, I love you I say. And sure enough, she says the same thing back. "When the time is right, hold it tight". I clench my locket carefully, and there it is: the big hole., I have no fear this time; I just jump in. And soon enough, I'm home. My mom noticed me right away, "did you take the nap I suggested Izzy?" Well I guess you could say, I got the time I needed.

My Meaningful Encounter

by Emma Goulart

I have had many memorable encounters when meeting people for the first time, but this time it was different. I didn't know that talking to someone or the first time could affect me the way that it did. This person inspired me in so many ways, and changed my perspective on many things. They showed me the importance of finding your faith and committing to it, which is something that everyone needs to hear.

Last summer my family and I started going to church a few times but we never felt connected to the church or anything. This was because the current pastor wasn't what we were looking for, so we started thinking about trying other churches. We went for one more Sunday to give it one last chance, when the pastor announced he was retiring. Of course we were sad that he was leaving, but we took this as a sign to stay for another week.

The time came when the new pastor arrived, which he was only there until we found someone new, but we were still excited to give him a chance. He preached and after the service he came and talked to my family and said that he noticed us in the back. This surprised us because we usually sit in the back quietly, but for some reason he noticed us. We told him how much we enjoyed his preaching and he told us he loved the church but can't stay because of his job. Every week after that we started coming to church and our temporary pastor started to notice. I had a very good relationship with him and we would make jokes together and talk every week. I ended up being very comfortable around him and I started to forget that he was only temporary.

During the service he started mentioning baptism and making important decisions in your life, and listening to him encouraged my brother and I to talk to him. We were pretty nervous because we haven't really thought about baptism before this, but for some reason I felt like I had to talk to him about it. After the service we walked up to him and asked if that was a good idea. We had a pretty long conversation about the importance of baptism, and he encouraged us to get baptised. He said that we seemed very faithful and he set the time for next Sunday. We were really scared but he told us that this was the best decision we would ever make, and we wouldn't regret it. He prayed over us, gave us hugs, then he explained what we would need to wear, when we would need to arrive, and any other things we needed to know.

This was definitely the biggest decision I have ever made in my faith and it was all because of him. If he didn't come to our church and talk to my family then we probably wouldn't have gone back. We realized that he was the sign from God that we have been looking for. He encouraged me to start going to church more and I started to feel excited at the thought of learning about God. At the time I didn't have a relationship with God and I didnt know much about him, but over a short amount of time that changed. He also made the thought of baptism achievable and we wouldn't have made that commitment if he wasn't there to encourage us.

At the time he might not have realized it, but just him showing up to church made an impact on my family and I. Taking the time to talk to us and show us that he cares for us can make a huge difference! My small encounter with him made me realize one of the most important things in my life, so don't forget that first impressions do matter!

The Close Call

by Madalyn Jones

I ran my hand along the uneven surface of the table. Devon and I have been running the warehouse for a while now. It's just a "perk" of being together I guess. It's not fun if you're caught, but sure is fun in the meantime. I walked over to Devon, he turned at the sound of my ridiculous stilettos and smiled.

"What are you doing up so late?" He said smiling, I laughed walking behind him to fix the printer which clearly says out of ink.

"So you want me to put ink in this? Or let you struggle?" He laughed at my remark and opened the ink slot.

"You were trying to take this apart?" I announced surprised, he has never worked with printers, CLEARLY.

"Well it wasn't working, and the last batch we printed and processed was not passable." He turned to me with a sigh.

"How much was the batch?" I was scared of the obviously expensive mistake.

"Well…. We made 1,000,000 and the cost.. 100,000" I winced at the huge loss, he looked ashamed.

"Well crap!" I exclaimed.

"It's fine, we'll just have to work more, and teach you how to change the ink." I joked at him.

He bent down and held my heels in one hand.

"Devon!" I giggled and shook my head. He guided me to sit on the bed.

"Violet, I will." He said offended at my independence. I took the heels out of his hands. I slipped them on while he sat unamused. Ari burst through the door.

"Oh my gosh!!" I dropped my heels.

"Excuse you!" Devon stood up and stalked toward him.

"I told you Mr. Ari to not under any circumstances burst into this room!! You have scared Violet and me as well. Leave Ari." He stated coldly while walking to the door he just burst into.

"But s-sir." Ari spoke wearily. A very tall, strong, well taken care of man walks in. I stood after I put on my heels. Devon the 6,5 man that he is, towers over me.

"Violet please exit the room." Devon said while taking my hand.

"Why? He seems tiny compared to you!! I can handle myself." I spoke looking up to him. Devon has dark brown hair, blue eyes and a stocky build. I stretch onto my tiptoes and brush the stray hair out of his eyes.

"I can handle myself." I said in a soft voice and strutted to the closet. I picked out Devon's outfit for the masquerade ball at one in the morning. I'm not sure what it is with criminals and late nights anyway. I walked out with the jet black suit and lay it on the bed.

"Who was that?" I spoke in a quiet tone. I look up and the lights are off.

"An old friend of mine from high school." He was picking up the suit.

"You don't seem so happy about that, Love." I said taking it from his hand.

"I am just not an enthusiastic person." He muttered with a sigh, he assures me out the door and takes the suit.

"I'll meet you outside princess." He closes the door. I walk down the stairs astonished, and a little upset. *How could he act like that!* I'm wearing a black matte dress that puddles the floor, with black stilettos and my hair is pinned back while being curled on the ends. The car pulls up and I see Devon walk down the stairs.

"Nice of you to join us, Mr Castro." The driver commented politely, I took his hand and pulled him inside the van.

"What's up with you today? Ever since that man showed up you've been different!" I said annoyed. He lets out a long sigh.

"He's my brother and he had a fiasco." He drags a hand down his face.

"His assistant drew a prototype of a 'software' that can spot fake money. So therefore, we could be busted." My jaw dropped and I stiffened.

"What exactly do you mean 'caught'." I said, twisting to face him.

"We have had this business for long enough that we should have already done the 'dirty' work such as buying us some time from the law." I said as I rested my head on his shoulder.

"This means we have to relocate, Princess." He squeaked weakly, I just stared at him. *This whole operation can't just be MOVED!*
"The printers can't be moved!" I declared annoyed, he looked at me and we made eye contact.

"Princess, you have to trust me. I've been doing this my whole life." He said and picked up his phone.

"When we get to the ball, we meet the people and leave" He spoke sternly, I smiled.

"You're so funny when you're angry!" I said giggling, he gave me a cold glare.

We walked inside hand in hand, and were immediately greeted by hundreds of people. I give Devon a glass of champagne.

"Sir, why are you so pretty?" I said in a mocking tone while smiling. He smiles while shaking his head.

"Miss I have a beautiful girlfriend named Violet that has blond hair, brown eyes, and short." He said smiling while taking my hand to make me spin.

"I am not short" I whin while losing my balance. I squeal as he picks me up with one hand.

"DEVON!!" I scream while he throws me over his shoulder.

"Are you okay?" He said laughing, he set me down on my feet and the room was surprisingly still. He was beaming down at me,

"Y-yes!" I yelled laughing, I looked up to meet his eyes.

"Let's stick to our plan." We walked into the crowd.

I open the door to the van and my stilettos hit the ground. I walk to the front door and Devon follows. I see a cop inside and I look at Devon.

"Well this is our luck!" I open the door, I stroll in and start to take off my heels ignoring the cops in the room. Devon looks confused and he takes off his suit jacket.

"Hello, why are you here?" I said straightening to look at them.

"Well quite a long story, my friend's daughter drew a prototype that can spot fake money and we have suspicion that you guys are printing illegal money." Devon grits his teeth as the cops explain. I smile and walk over to the drawer to take a recorder out.

"Here this will record therefore if I lie you can use it against me in court. However the only way I can explain to you is if my boyfriend and I talk first.You guys have to exit the house while we do so." I said while twirling my hair around my finger.

"I suppose that would be ok" The short one speaked, they exit in line.

"What now!" He yelled annoyedly, I smiled.

"We're now Vincent and Evelyn. I'm twenty-one and you're twenty four (we're actually twenty six and twenty eight), you work for a paper company and I'm a writer." I said and took a seat on the kitchen stool.

"So we're gonna lie?" He spoke amusedly, I rolled my eyes.

"Got a better plan?" I declared annoyed, I stood up and looked him in the eyes.

"I'm not going to jail Devon" I stated sternly and opened the door to let them in. I gave him a quick kiss and took the recorder.

"My boyfriend's name is Vincent Jackson and my name is Evelyn Moore. He works in a paper factory, he's twenty four, I'm twenty one and I'm a writer. That's why there is a warehouse of printers and paper. We have been together for three years, and we have dated one time before." I said with a straight face, and the cops looked amused.

"Any questions?" I announced, smiling to myself and twiddling my fingers.

"How long have you been working at your jobs Miss? Parents' names? Name of one of your books? How long have you been living here?" The two cops spoke in unison.

"I have been working as a writer for seven months, and Vincent has been working there for three years. Therefore my book isn't done yet and we can't give you anything related to our parents. My parents passed away when I was young and he was adopted. We have lived here about five years because we took a break between our relationship." I replied smoothly and I grabbed the recorder.

"I think we're done here officer." I said looking officially over it.

"Besides it's four o'clock in the morning and you were in my house when I returned home. That's illegal sir." I said and started to laugh.

"Have a nice night" Devon snorts while they walk out with their heads down. I close the door behind them.

"Good job Evelyn" He said with a laugh.

www.ingramcontent.com/pod-product-compliance
Lightning Source LLC
Chambersburg PA
CBHW071141180726
48291CB00007B/2290

ANY OLD
DIAMONDS

KJ CHARLES

Any Old Diamonds

Published by KJC Books

Edited by Veronica Vega
Cover art by Vic Grey
Cover design by Lexiconic Design
Print layout by eB Format

ISBN: 978-1-912688-08-1

I'll sing you three-O
Green grow the rushes-O
What is your three-O?
Three, three, the rivals
Two, two, the lily-white boys
Clothèd all in green-O
One is one and all alone
And evermore shall be so

Green Grow The Rushes-O, British folk song

Chapter One

London, 1895

How ought one dress to hire a thief?

Alec woke up with the question in his mind and couldn't let it go. He couldn't answer it either, no matter that his options were exceedingly limited. A lounge suit would presumably be best, for informality, but should he wear a colourful waistcoat, to indicate his divergence from sober respectability, or a plain one to avoid attracting attention?

He mused on that throughout breakfast and decided on his muted maroon silk waistcoat, but was immediately struck with uncertainty. Was a lounge suit right after all, considering they were meeting in, of all places, a box at the music hall? Ought he wear evening dress? The Grand Cirque was of the better class of music hall, and he would normally wear evening dress to take a private box, but what if the men he was to meet were clad as he imagined thieves to be, in rough fustian, perhaps with neckcloths pulled up over their mouths? No, that was ridiculous, and he'd been assured the criminals would look like gentlemen, but in *that* case...

Round and round it went in his head the whole day, a maddening litany. Alec knew perfectly well that he was fretting in order not to consider any of the larger questions, such as *What the devil are you doing?*

He didn't, couldn't think about that. He'd been driven to this extremity by the slow-building fury of years and the grief and anguish of the last six months. He wasn't going to back out now.

He spent the day completing a picture of Hyde Park in bloom for the *Illustrated London News*, because when he drew he didn't think so much. When evening finally came, he put on the grey lounge suit, tried all four of his waistcoats, discovered the maroon one had a spot on it, changed into evening dress, took it off again, and realised that after all this, he was going to be late.

"Alec, you dunderhead," he said aloud to the man in the speckled mirror. He hurried on the lounge suit, no time to play the fool now, hesitated for a painful second between a darker grey waistcoat and the bright green and gold one he hadn't worn for six long months of mourning, glanced at the cheap clock on the mantel, and grabbed the green. It suited him, at least. He only just remembered to snatch up the flimsy ticket on the way out.

It was a warm June, too warm to run, but he couldn't afford hansom cab fare so he hurried instead, while telling himself he needn't be on time to the minute. Punctuality was the politeness of princes, but did that apply when one was meeting criminals?

Holborn was its usual chaos. He picked his way through the crowds, past flower-stalls and shouting newspaper-boys proclaiming the last edition, and approached the Grand Cirque feeling unpleasantly sweaty for more reason than the thick heat. Christ, was he going to do this? Really? Was he going to keep an assignation and solicit a crime?

And if he turned around and walked away, what the devil would he do next?

That was the great unanswerable question, the one he'd stuck on during every sleepless night. If he didn't act, what *would* he do, today or tomorrow or for the rest of his life? If he missed this chance, would there be another, and would he have the nerve to take it, having refused the fence once already? He had a feeling he knew the answer to that one.

It's now or never.

He squared his shoulders, fished the ticket out of his pocket, and walked up to the doorman, feeling appallingly self-conscious and rather as if a policeman's heavy hand might descend on his shoulder at any moment. He hated that feeling, one with which he was all too familiar, albeit not for the current reasons. It would be so much nicer if he were risking arrest on the usual grounds, if the men he was going to meet were...well, quite different from what he expected them to be.

Music-hall misbehaviour à trois was a charming fantasy that distracted him up the several steep flights of stairs and shivered into nothing as he made his way to the indicated box.

He knocked. "Come in," a voice called, so he did.

The performance was already in full swing below, the noise of five men singing in close harmony and the groans of an unimpressed crowd blasting up. The smoky gaslight—no electrification here— cast a yellowish glow over the dark red walls and gilt decorations and left the box mostly in shadow. The box, and the two men waiting in it.

"Sit down," one of them said. "Mr. Pyne?"

Alec nodded. "Yes. That's me."

"Remind me whence you had our names."

He sounded very educated, with a university man's drawl. Alec blinked. "Er, I don't have your names. A chap named Holcomb told me you were the people I needed."

"We may be," the man said. "The question is whether we need you."

Alec's eyes were adjusting now and he was able to take a look at the pair. They both seemed a few years older than himself, thirty to thirty-five, perhaps. Well but casually dressed, Alec noted, and felt relieved he hadn't opted for his black tailcoat. The one who'd done the talking had a curling moustache, thick chestnut hair with a notable wave, and eyes that might prove to be blue in daylight. The other man had dark brown hair, darker eyes, and a substantial moustache and beard. Alec restrained the impulse to put his hand to his own naked face. More fellows were shaving now, particularly the fashionable sorts, but as far as many people were concerned, failure to grow a respectable moustache remained an indictment of one's virility.

The two men opposite him looked virile enough. The moustachioed speaker was strikingly big: broad, sturdy, and giving the impression he would tower over Alec when they stood. His bearded companion was of more usual proportions, lean and long-limbed in the way of hunting men. Both of them looked capable, confident, and not at all like the rapscallions of Alec's imagination. They looked more like soldiers. Or police officers.

"Uh," he said. "I don't know what Mr. Holcomb told you."

"Don't you?" Moustache said. "Pal of yours, is he?"

"An acquaintance. Not really even that. A friend of a friend said he might be the man to put me in touch with, uh, someone like you."

"I do hope Holcomb is sure of his friends." That was Beard, speaking at last. His voice was deeper than Alec had expected, not as aggressively upper-class as his partner's. "He told us you had a worthwhile proposition for the Lilywhite Boys. Why don't you tell us what that might be?"

"Uh," Alec said again, seized with urgent panic now he was on the verge of commitment. "Um. I don't wish to be rude but how do I know...?" He let that tail off in the hope that someone would interrupt him. They didn't.

"How do you know what?" enquired Moustache after a painful silence. He lifted a hand and counted on the fingers. "That we're the Lilywhite Boys and not, say, masquerading police officers, or friends of your pal playing a joke? That we'll keep your request private and not demand a large sum to forget about it? That we can do what you want, that you can trust us to make a deal, that you won't end up in chokey?"

"Well, yes," Alec said. "All of that."

"You don't."

"Oh."

"We can't really offer guarantees," Beard said. "Let alone contracts."

"You don't know who we are, and we don't know who you are," Moustache added. "For all we know, Mr. Alec Pyne, you might be a police officer yourself."

"I'm not."

"I dare say, but I'm not taking your word for it."

"Well, what do we do then?" Alec said, baffled.

Moustache smiled suddenly. He had a charming smile: the kind, Alec rather thought, that he'd often been told was charming and had learned to use accordingly. "We'll just have to rub along. Did Holcomb tell you an important fact about us?"

"He said if I played straight with you, you'd play straight with me," Alec said. "And then he added, 'They've got their own idea of straight, mind you.'"

Beard gave a crack of laughter. Moustache grinned. "Yes, that's about right. If you don't play straight with us, we'll resent it, and you'll regret it. Got that, Mr. Pyne?"

"Noted."

"Good. My name is Templeton Lane, and my colleague is Jerry Crozier." Beard—Crozier—lifted two fingers to his brow. "Now, why don't you tell us what it is you have for us, and we'll tell you if we're interested. And if we're not, or if our interest doesn't suit you, we'll all forget about this conversation and enjoy the show."

Alec took a deep breath. He thought of George, of Cara and Annabel, of Mother, and a small near-empty church, and the smell of squashed holly berries.

He said, "I want you to rob the Duke of Ilvar."

Crozier's eyebrows shot up. Lane's mouth curved. "Do you. How intriguing. Any particular reason?"

"He's rich."

"That's a good reason," Crozier said. "Is this a general suggestion for larceny, or have you anything more substantial to add?"

The close harmony singers stopped their warbling, to some applause. Alec hadn't really been aware of them but now the lower background noise made him feel self-conscious. He leaned in. Crozier's brows tilted, angling upward to the middle of his forehead as if silently repeating the question. Alec had never had that sort of eyebrow control, and envied those who did. Mind you, apparently it gave one wrinkles and one wouldn't want those; it was bad enough he'd turned twenty-eight and had already found suspiciously grey hairs among the blond at his temples.

Oh God, he was terrified.

"You look like a conspirator," Crozier said. "And one that's about to be sick, as well. Sit back, you're making me twitch."

Alec recoiled. Lane sighed. "Don't mind him. He's never got over the army." He flickered a glance over the side of the box, to the stage. "The dancing girls are about to come on. I assure you, nobody will be looking up here, or able to eavesdrop. You mentioned the Duke of Ilvar."

"A name to conjure with," Crozier said drily.

There was a roar of applause from below as the dancing troupe pranced on to the stage. Alec glanced over, made himself look back. "He's very rich. I suppose you know that."

"Immensely," Crozier said. "And much of his wealth is hung around the neck of his Duchess, who has one of the greatest collections of jewels outside royal hands as testament to his affection."

"Such affection," Lane added soulfully. "His devotion is legendary, and there has never been a breath of scandal against her name. Aside from notoriously cuckolding her first husband with the Duke, of course, but they married afterwards, so who am I to quibble."

Alec looked between them uncertainly. "Yes. Well. Ilvar is spending a king's ransom on a diamond parure—a matching set of jewellery—"

"We know what a parure is." Crozier spoke quite gently, without emphasis, but the words still jarred Alec, because these men, these well-spoken well-groomed men-about-town, were professional jewel thieves. It was hard to keep that in mind.

"Yes. Of course. Uh..."

"The diamond parure?"

"Earrings, a magnificent necklace, a bracelet. Matched stones of the finest quality. He commissioned it over a year ago to be a gift for her on the twentieth anniversary of their wedding. It cost eleven thousand pounds."

Lane whistled. Crozier's mobile brows twitched up.

"And that's what you want?"

"I'd think it would be what you want too," Alec said. "No?"

"Oh, unquestionably," Crozier said. "The difficulty would be getting it. Her collection is kept at the extremely remote Castle Speight which is heavily staffed at all times and equipped with the most up-to-date model of safe—a Chatwood, cursed hard to drill, with a Bramah lock, famously unpickable. Moreover, lacking the endearing carelessness of those born to the upper classes, the Duchess takes a great deal of care when travelling that her jewel case is constantly guarded. And the castle is never thrown open to visitors. It makes a fellow's job quite impossible."

Alec's mouth was hanging open. "How do you know all that?"

"Because we've considered the Ilvars and given them up as a bad job," Lane said. "They are perhaps the worst target in the British aristocracy. Or are we wrong?"

"I don't know about that. I—" Alec had planned this, rehearsed it, but the words stuck in his throat. "I, uh. I could get you into the house. Into Castle Speight."

There was a pause. The music blared, the dancers' feet thundered on the stage, the audience whooped, yet Alec's breath seemed far too audible in his own ears.

"Could you," Crozier said at last. "In what capacity?"

"There'll be a grand event there in August, for their wedding anniversary. A dinner. It'll be the first one they've held there in years, they don't usually entertain in that way. The Duchess will have all her most magnificent jewels and the parure will be presented. There'll be all sorts of guards, security, but—but you know how to, to—"

"Steal things?" Crozier said. "Yes, we do."

"Well, I'll be attending," Alec said. "And if you can come with me—"

"Noted. First question, Mr. Pyne: what terms do you have in mind for this?"

"Terms?"

"Do you simply want to see the Ilvars robbed on principle? Are you hoping to settle a grudge? Or are you looking for a cut of the loot?"

Alec felt his cheeks flush. "The latter. I, er, don't know what you usually..." He loathed negotiation at the best of times. "Fifty fifty?" It came out as a question despite his best intentions.

Crozier's brows angled again, one up, one down. Alec was becoming fascinated with that. "Ambitious of you, if we're doing the work and taking the risk."

"You couldn't get in there without me, though. And there's risk for me too."

"Which brings me to the next question," Lane said. "How will you be in a position to get us in?"

"I'll be able to." Alec didn't want to go into this. It was too hot in here, too smoky. He could feel the sweat beading on the back of his neck. "If I get you in as a guest, can you—"

"How long for?" Crozier interrupted.

Alec blinked. "How long do you need?"

"How long is a piece of string? We need time to assess the lie of the land. I don't intend to hold the room up at gunpoint, in a mask, like one of those dreadful Americans. We prefer to plan a little better than that."

"Specifically, we prefer to be a long way away from the scene of the crime when the police are called," Crozier added. "Ideally having ensured a solid alibi for our accomplices."

"Oh."

Lane winked at him. "We're called the Lilywhite Boys for a reason, old chap. Few arrests, no convictions."

"Well, that's...good," Alec managed.

"It is good," Crozier agreed, "and it's achievable given a bit of planning time. Again: do your powers stretch to that?"

Alec took a deep breath. "I could get you there a few days before the dinner. There will be a house party before the grand ball; I dare say I could add you to that. You, uh, you would need to present yourselves as gentlemen."

"Entirely achievable," Lane assured him. "And that raises the final and most crucial question: how is it that you, Mr. Pyne, are going to be present at the notoriously inhospitable Castle Speight on this touching family occasion?"

Alec's mouth was completely dry now. The performance had changed again while they were talking; he hadn't noticed it, except to become vaguely aware of a comedian's shrill Scottish-accented voice buzzing in his ear, waves of laughter.

He licked his lips. "I'm acquainted with him. The Duke of Ilvar. I can get you in. That's all you need to know for now."

Crozier and Lane exchanged glances, a flicker of a look. Crozier sat back. Lane steepled his hands, flexing them slowly. "Lord Alexander Greville de Keppel Pyne-ffoulkes, with a small f. Or even two small fs, when you think about it. Third child of the Duke by his first wife, deceased. By trade an illustrator for the picture papers as Alec Pyne. I can't blame you for shortening that mouthful."

"What—"

"We don't go into situations blind, Mr. Pyne, or should that be Lord Alexander. We knew who you were within twelve hours of you seeking this meeting. It is our habit to look ahead."

"Give me six hours to chop down a tree and I will spend the first four sharpening the axe," Crozier said in a tone of quotation. "We keep our axes sharp, Lord Alexander."

"Alec. Or Pyne. I don't go by the title."

"Why not?"

"I don't think that's any business of yours."

Lane leaned forward and tapped him on the knee. "Alec, old pal? If you want us to come to your father's house as your friend and rob him in his own home—to pose as your guest and clean out your stepmother's drawers—it *is* our business. No lies, no surprises. You work with us in full or you don't work with us at all."

"That is an option," Crozier added calmly. "We'd far rather you change your mind now than later. No hard feelings and all that. But if you go ahead, no finer feelings either. We would be very upset if you committed our time and then decided you couldn't go ahead with stealing from your own father."

Blood surged into Alec's cheeks. "It isn't like that!"

"We don't care," Crozier said, with terrible simplicity. "You're in or you're out. And if you're in, there will be no middle ground, no secrets, no sudden surges of decency in the third act. Either you're going to help us steal from your father and split the proceeds, or we'll shake hands now and watch the show."

"Actually, we're going to watch the show anyway," Lane said, and pointed to the stage, where a woman was coming on to wild applause. "Miss Christiana."

"About time. We're actually here for her," Crozier informed Alec. "You have a think."

On which they both turned to the performance. Alec sat, stunned. He'd imagined a lot of ways in which this conversation, this conspiracy might go; he hadn't pictured admitting his treacherous intent and then having that dreadful confession put to one side in favour of a music-hall act.

And a female impersonator to boot, he realised, as he heard the light tenor. The singer was painted for the stage but not to excess, and wore a wig with cascading dark ringlets and a high-necked dress suitable for a governess. The respectable appearance was doubtless deliberate, because she was singing "I'd Just Like to Know," a minor sensation of innuendo that required the performer to deliver the filthiest possible implications with total innocence.

The Lilywhite Boys hadn't been joking about being here for Miss Christiana, either, because they were both watching intently. Lane started laughing almost at once, a deep and infectious sound. Crozier's response was more restrained but his smile widened at the more outrageous lines, into a sharp-angled expression that was frankly wicked.

Miss Christiana would perform perhaps three or four songs, and then the Lilywhite Boys would turn back and demand a decision.

Alec had come here to set up a robbery, but he hadn't quite let himself think of it in the bare terms the thieves had used, the ones the newspapers would use if or when this went wrong. *Planned to steal from his own father, abusing his position as a son and the hospitality of Castle Speight...*

But his father had stolen from him, from all his children. He had stolen their birthright and the lives of luxury a duke's offspring might expect, and far, far more than that. Alec had no position as a son except on his father's humiliating terms, which made him feel hot and sick to consider. Castle Speight's hospitality was a joke, and not one that would draw the roars of laughter now echoing around the hall.

If the only way to get to the Duke of Ilvar was through the Duchess, and the only way to get to her was through her hoarded jewels, he'd bloody do it, whatever it took. And if that made him a villain, so be it. He wasn't going to abide by *Honour thy father*; he needn't trouble himself with *Thou shall not steal* either.

He'd be a criminal. That was what you were when you conspired to commit a crime, even if you didn't lift a finger yourself. A criminal like Crozier and Lane, both of whom seemed to be quite happy watching Miss Christiana sing, and laughing at the punchlines. They weren't racked with guilt, and nor should Alec be, because this would be revenge—for loss, for a lifetime of contempt, for the life Cara should have had and the one Annabel ought to have and the strain in George's eyes. Revenge because he'd finally accepted that he couldn't wait for fate or natural justice or God's will to punish the Duke and Duchess. It was down to him.

Miss Christiana had left the stage while he was lost in thought. The Lilywhite Boys were both watching him.

"You look as though you've decided," Crozier said. "Last chance: if you want to forget this conversation ever happened, it can be done without consequences. After this, we aren't open to changes of heart. If you say no now, you won't see us again. If you say yes, we'll be the best of friends." He smiled. It wasn't the most reassuring smile Alec had ever seen.

"I've decided. I want you to do it. To rob my father."

Lane and Crozier exchanged a swift look. Lane nodded. "In that case, thirty seventy. In our favour."

"Fine."

Crozier's brows flicked up. "Then we have a deal. Are you going to tell us why you're doing this?"

"Well, the money—" Crozier's eyes narrowed sceptically, as well they might. Alec scowled. "And because he's a terrible person and he deserves something terrible to happen to him."

"Well, that's us," Lane said. "We happen to people, don't we, Jerry?"

"Better than having people happen to us. When's the house party?"

"The grand dinner will be on the seventh of August, at Castle Speight," Alec said.

"So we have two months." Lane looked at Crozier, questioning. Crozier shot a glance at Alec, then lifted a single finger like a man bidding at an auction. Lane opened his hands. Crozier tilted a brow.

"All right, then," Lane said, for all the world as though that had been a conversation. "Jerry will be your new best pal and eventual guest. You won't be seeing me for some time after this, if all goes well. If you let Jerry down you'll see me when you least expect it, and not pleasantly, but I'm sure that's an unnecessary warning. Have fun, gentlemen."

He stood, proving to be as sizeable as Alec had feared. "Catch up tomorrow, Jerry. Pyne." He nodded at Alec, took up his hat and coat, and left.

Alec blinked after him then looked back at Crozier. "What did he mean by that, about seeing him?"

"That if you run to the police, now or later, you might be able to inform on me but Templeton will be at large and resentful. To illustrate that, a certain gentleman recently put pressure on our fence—receiver of stolen goods, you know—to pay him protection money. In the ensuing discussion, Templeton dropped one of the gentleman's henchmen out of a second-floor window. We look after one another."

"Out of a *window?* But—was he hurt?"

"He strained his shoulder a little. Oh, you mean the droppee? Yes. He was." Crozier's smile was satanic. "Don't play silly buggers with us. We play it better."

Alec swallowed. "I won't. I mean, I've made up my mind."

"Good. Right, then. If I'm coming to your family event as a friend, we should strike up that friendship. Where do you like to drink?"

"What?"

"If we're to be sufficient pals for me to attend your parents' wedding anniversary celebrations—"

"Father's," Alec said. "She is not my mother."

Crozier's eyes hooded but he didn't comment. "If we're to be sufficient pals for this, I shall need to strike up acquaintance with you, enough that you will have a plausible story should things go south. So where do you drink?"

Alec's mind went blank. Where he actually liked to drink was a quiet, unobtrusive public house called the Jack and Knave that catered for a very particular clientele. He had no intention of sharing that titbit, whatever the Lilywhite Boys said about secrets. "I go to the Stratton Club sometimes, the journalists' club. Or the Sketch. It's a sort of place for artists."

"I can't draw, and I prefer to avoid journalists for obvious reasons. Anywhere else?"

"Not often. I can't afford much in the way of night-life. I just go to the pub, really."

"Lord Alexander Greville de Keppel Pyne-ffoulkes just goes to the pub?"

14

"Alec. And yes, actually, I do."

"Well, that's no bloody good," Crozier said. "How about the Criterion Bar?"

Alec woke up the next morning with a sense of impending doom. He lay in his narrow bed for a brief moment, feeling the worry without being able to identify the cause, and then he remembered.

"Oh, shit," he said aloud.

He'd done it. He'd actually done it, he'd contacted the criminals and made the devil's bargain. He was part of a conspiracy to commit burglary. It was terrifying, and shameful, and yet he could feel that same golden thread of excitement running through the very real fear as he had the first time he'd followed a man down a dark alley with unlawful intent.

This wasn't the same thing, but perhaps it wasn't a mile away, because Alec didn't believe he was truly doing anything wrong in seeking male embraces, and he also felt a deep sense of justification at what he planned to do to the Duke and Duchess. The world would not agree, and his brother and sister would not like any of what was to come, but that couldn't be helped. The smouldering resentment he'd carried so long had caught into flame, and it would be his guiding light.

It, and the Lilywhite Boys. He was, he thought, probably glad that it was Crozier who would be his "new best pal". Lane had made him uncomfortable, even if Alec couldn't put his finger on why: it was something about the very charming smile he wore on his frank, open face while his eyes ran calculations. Crozier seemed a little more...Alec couldn't think of a better word than 'straightforward' even though that was wrong. Unambiguously dangerous, perhaps. Templeton Lane smiled and smiled and was a villain; Crozier didn't bother to smile.

Alec was to meet him in the Long Bar at the Criterion this evening. *I'll strike up a conversation,* Crozier had said. *Follow my lead. Feel free to be charmed.*

That seemed an extremely unlikely outcome, and Alec had no confidence he could sham it. He'd pointed that out as politely as he could, terrified he might ruin the entire scheme before it started by going bright red and stammering. If the Lilywhite Boys were depending on Alec seeming happy and relaxed in their company, they'd be in trouble. He'd said as much, but Crozier hadn't seemed concerned.

"Let them do their job," he told himself, and got out of bed to face the day, propelled by one positive realisation: he would have to go through this meeting and discover more about what was expected of him before he spoke to his siblings. He was not looking forward to the latter conversation at all.

Alec wore evening dress that night. It was, after all, the Criterion Bar. He checked his appearance in the mirror and was reasonably pleased with the results. The grey among the blond hair at his temples was only perceptible under close inspection; his nose was a little marked by the spectacles he used for close work but that couldn't be helped. He looked really rather well, considering; it helped that his evening dress was expensive and not greatly used, and that he had put on a little weight recently, filling out after the months around Cara's death when he'd barely been able to choke down a mouthful for rage, horror, and grief. He wouldn't stand out for good or ill, and that was all he asked.

He took an omnibus to Piccadilly, self-conscious in his smart clothing among labourers and clerks, and strolled into the Criterion Bar with all the insouciance he could muster. He hadn't been here for a couple of years and the tiled interior was more magnificent than he remembered, the mirrors bright under the electric lights. When he'd come here before he'd probably been drunk.

He ordered a whisky and soda and took a seat at a small table, sitting back and looking casually around in the manner of a gentleman awaiting a friend. It was something he'd done hundreds of times without thinking twice, but now he was absurdly aware of himself, as though he were somehow the object of everyone's gaze. He picked up his glass and sipped the drink in a manner that felt ludicrously wooden. If a stage actor handled a glass that clumsily Alec would have felt inclined to boo, yet he couldn't help it; his fingers felt stiff and sausagelike.

He must look like a bad narrative painting of a man waiting for a friend. He glanced around, wondering if he'd recognise anyone, imagined he saw pity or mockery in the few looks thrown his lonely way, knocked back the whisky and soda in the hope of a bit of Dutch courage, and rashly ordered another. He was actually startled when someone leaned over his table to address him.

"I say, sir, is this seat taken?"

Alec looked up and blinked.

It was Crozier. Or at least— No, it was Crozier, but he'd shaved. The beard had been trimmed into a sharp goatee, revealing a firm jawline, the moustache thinned to a neat line. It was a striking style that gave his narrow face distinction. *Mephistopheles*, Alec thought again. He wore evening dress as well cut as Alec's own, and his brown hair was sleeked back. He looked every inch the man about town with a bright red carnation in his buttonhole, and he was regarding Alec with an expression of courteous inquiry.

"Uh. Yes, certainly," Alec managed. "I mean, no, it's not."

"You aren't waiting for anyone?" Crozier suggested.

"No. Yes, actually, yes I am, I was, but he's late. If he's coming at all. So you might as well." Alec attempted a casual wave at the chair opposite and nearly knocked over his glass. The last time he'd been this tongue-tied about inviting a man to take a seat, he'd been panting in a back room within the hour, hot breath in his ear. He felt a momentary wish that his lawbreaking was going in that direction now.

Not that Crozier was quite so handsome as that previous man had been. He was a little more than medium height, though his sinewy build probably made him look taller than he was. Mid-brown hair, skin that was neither interestingly pale nor notably darkened by nature or sun. Not an unattractive face, of the sort Alec would sketch for the background of an army or clubland scene, and the dark brown eyes under his sharply defined brows were striking, but the goatee would be the main thing most people remembered. If he were a politician, the caricaturists would bless him for the goatee and curse him if he shaved. If the police asked for a description of 'the man who stole the jewels', the goatee was what they'd get.

He was looking at Crozier as he would a subject, and, he realised, Crozier was looking back.

"I do beg your pardon. Have we met before?"

"What?" Alec had a momentary panic—he couldn't have got it wrong, could he? This was surely the man from last night?—and then realised that Crozier must be playing his part of a stranger, in which case Alec had indeed been gaping at him in a way that merited the enquiry. "Uh, no, I don't think so. I'm sorry, was I staring?"

"Perhaps a little." Crozier's mouth curved, very slightly.

"I beg your pardon. I'm an artist," Alec explained, tongue taking over since his brain seemed not to be much use. "An illustrator for the papers. I'm always on the lookout for faces."

"How intriguing. Specific faces, or are you a snapper-up of unconsidered features for later use?" Crozier's brows slanted comically. "Good heavens, I trust you don't work for the *Illustrated Police News*. I'd hate to hear I had the looks for a murderer."

That was very nearly too close to the bone. Alec wasn't sure what to say for a second; Crozier went on with barely a break. "So do you acquire faces from among your acquaintance when you aren't drawing from life? It never occurred to me to wonder before, but now I think about those great crowd scenes and coming up with all the different people..."

"It is tempting to use friends," Alec admitted.

"Ah, but do you use enemies? Allot some tiresome bore's face to a pickpocket or a dubious bookmaker? I would."

"Also tempting, but I prefer not to have actions launched against me."

"Good point." Crozier was smiling properly now, the amusement reaching his eyes. "I'm fascinated. Do you specialise in any particular sort of illustration? Exotic scenes, courtroom incident?"

Alec found himself answering with a peculiar sense of familiarity. He was pretending to strike up an acquaintance with a charming stranger, yet it felt awfully like he was doing just that in reality. As though he were making light conversation, taking the other man's measure, wondering what sort of fellow he might be.

And, still, looking at him. Crozier's most distinctive feature was the pair of remarkably mobile eyebrows which gave visual punctuation to his speech, and their dancing movement was another thing you couldn't convey in a police sketch. They combined with his apparently habitual half smile to give Alec the impression that he was being laughed either at or with. He wasn't confident which.

"So are the illustrated papers your primary interest?" Crozier asked. "That is, do you illustrate books, say, or otherwise exhibit?"

"I'd love to illustrate more books," Alec said, instantly forgetting everything else. "Especially for children. This is a glorious time for illustration—the publishing techniques are improving hand over fist, and the public are coming to expect far higher standards. I'm being considered for a new edition of Shakespeare at the moment, as it happens. I don't know if I'll get the work, but it's nice to be in the running."

"I should say so. That calls for a drink." Crozier raised his hand with the sort of calm assurance Alec could never manage, and a waiter appeared within a few seconds. "Two glasses of champagne, thank you."

"That's, uh—"

"My pleasure," Crozier said. "Why books for children particularly?"

Answering that took several moments, in which the champagne came in two glittering glasses. Crozier raised his and inclined it to Alec's. They tapped the crystal together with a delicate *ting*.

"To art," Crozier said. "In all its forms."

"To art," Alec managed. The whisky and soda had gone to his head already; the champagne prickled against his lips.

They talked on: about Alec's current work on the *Graphic* and the *Illustrated*, and then about newspapers and the latest scandals. Crozier volunteered a couple of stories that made Alec choke on his champagne laughing, and grinned, and waved his hand for the waiter again.

"Dinner," Crozier said, several glasses later. It was past ten already, and Alec discovered abruptly that he was starving. "Join me? They do an adequate table here."

That was a gross understatement. Alec followed him, floating on a cloud of champagne and conversation, through to the restaurant. There Crozier recommended the rognons de veau and the sole, which was a relief since, between the small type, lack of spectacles, and the alcohol, Alec found the menu somewhat challenging to interpret. He gulped about half a bottle of Vichy water, and found himself more able to keep up his end of the rambling conversation. This soon veered into theatrical tastes.

"Are you a great lover of the music hall?" Alec asked.

"Not much." Crozier caught his blink, and shrugged. "My interest in Miss Christiana lies entirely in the fact that she's a friend's sweetheart so I was required to tell him she was wonderful in convincing detail. As an artist, you're doubtless familiar with the obligation."

"Oh." Alec assimilated *a friend's sweetheart* and *him*. "Yes, indeed, with exhibitions and so on."

"What I do enjoy, and I dare say I should be ashamed of this, is the melodrama," Crozier said, eyebrows sliding up to indicate his own absurdity. "I like nothing more than a thoroughly idiotic hero, a vapid heroine, a lost will, a stalwart comic man to find it, and a villain with a proper blood-chilling laugh. All of that accompanied by a suitably dramatic scene in which someone leaps off a cliff or a train is trundled across the stage to the heroine's peril."

Alec clapped his hands. "Yes! So long as the villain expires with suitable drama. Staggering, with a hand pressed to his brow, and a speech of repentance that explains all his machinations and tells the hero where the treasure is hidden."

"Oh, no, not repentance. I like the villain to be villainous to the end. He should curse the hero's goodness with his last breath and die seething in his own frustrated criminality. It's only fair."

"You wouldn't consider a change of heart on your deathbed?"

"No decent villain dies in bed," Crozier pointed out. "He expires in the toils of his own plot, on the steps of his grand house or run through by the hero's blade. And no, certainly not. If I were inclined to repentance, and I'm not, I'd want to start now. To do it on one's deathbed is to be sorry because one has been caught, and that surely doesn't count."

"You're not inclined to repentance?" Alec repeated. "What, ever?"

"Never." Crozier's eyes glimmered dark in the electric light and the glitter of glass and silverware and mirrors. "I'm not sorry."

"For what?"

"Anything." Crozier tilted his head, eyes hooding slightly, gaze roaming over Alec's face. "Except missed opportunities. I regret those, but that's a different matter, isn't it?"

"Mmm." Alec didn't want to think about his own missed opportunities now, the what-ifs and if-onlies. "I don't suppose you have many of those, do you?"

Crozier's smile widened a fraction. It looked a little bit dangerous, and it made Alec's toes curl delightfully. "Not many. They're such a waste. And so often what one wants is there for the taking, if one only makes the effort to reach for it."

Alec swallowed. He wondered, very much wondered, if he dared inch his foot forward and nudge Crozier's shoe with his own, to see how he reacted. He had an idea that he oughtn't, and for a moment couldn't quite remember why.

Oh, yes. It was because Crozier was a thief, and this—this dinner, this companionship, the smile in his eyes—was all a lie.

The thought struck harder than it should have. He didn't say anything, but something changed in Crozier's expression, his eyes losing their laughter, as if he'd read something on Alec's face that he didn't like. It occurred to Alec that his companion might in fact look rather ugly in some lights, or in some moods.

"In any case," Crozier said. "We've gone on rather late, haven't we?" He summoned the bill, again with that magical flick of his fingers, and they sat in a silence that was all the more notable because conversation had been so easy. Alec had a heavy feeling in his stomach that wasn't only the drink. He was unpleasantly aware that he'd be in a serious hole if he'd somehow failed a test and was asked to pay his share.

He wasn't. Crozier pulled out a well-stuffed wallet as the bill was produced, left what must have been a generous pourboire given the waiter's bow, and nodded to Alec. "Come on, old chap, let's see you home. I think you're ready to call it a night, aren't you?"

Alec very much was. The drink caught up with him as he stood, and he felt Crozier's steadying hand under his elbow, firm and warm. "Let's get you in a cab. I shall pop in and see how you're getting on tomorrow."

He steered Alec outside as he spoke, past the doorman. The cool night air felt like a bucket of water to the face, clearing his head as Crozier summoned a hansom cab and gave the man the address, then held the door open for Alec. "An absolute pleasure making your acquaintance. I'll see you later."

"Yes, see you tomorrow, old man," Alec managed, and clambered in. The door slammed, the cab lurched off, and he shut his eyes and concentrated on his breathing.

Dammit, dammit, dammit. How had he managed to forget what he was there for? What sort of bloody fool was he? Suppose he'd actually nudged Crozier's foot or made his interest clear? Christ, suppose Crozier had detected it anyway, and had been tempting him to reveal himself? The jewel thief, the unrepentant criminal would have had Alec in the palm of his hand from then on.

Or suppose Crozier had actually been flirting with him. Suppose he'd decided Alec was there for the taking, and he'd been the one to nudge Alec's foot, and they'd finished the night in one of Piccadilly's dark alleys, as could so very nearly have happened. Alec put his hands over his face and groaned aloud.

When he arrived home, the cabbie told him the fare had been paid already, at which point Alec realised that he'd never told Crozier his address, but the man had known it anyway.

He did not sleep well that night.

Chapter Two

The next day, Alec went to the Turkish bath. It seemed like the only possible solution to a rotten bad head and a stomach filled with a sour stew of fear. He soaked and steamed and was impersonally pummelled by powerful hands, until both the worries and the alcohol had been temporarily driven away. He dozed afterwards for an hour, and woke feeling hungry, human, and newly determined.

He'd made his deal with the devil and there was no point fretting now. Last night had been about striking up a friendship with a charming and plausible man in public. Crozier was, it transpired, very good at being charming and plausible; Alec had been charmed. He surely didn't need to worry about that hint of possible flirtation: the way Crozier had spoken of the music-hall travesty singer didn't suggest a man who feared or hated effeminacy. He'd probably ended the night simply because he'd seen Alec was drunk enough to forget his role. There was no need to worry.

He told himself all that until he nearly believed it, then went back home to try to get some work done. He had the top floor room, with a skylight; it was a very decent space that allowed for a good-sized table and to hide his bed behind a folding screen. It wasn't a grand house or a fashionable location—Mincing Lane, on the wrong side of Eastcheap—but it was clean, and he could afford it on his earnings with no help from his brother, let alone his father.

Sometimes he felt proud of that achievement and his independence; sometimes he remembered that he was Lord Alexander Pyne-ffoulkes, slaving with inky fingers to keep the rent paid and his editors happy, and he felt like overturning the table and sending his pens and pots flying to the floor.

Not today. He had plenty of work to do, including providing a sample for a collection of fairy-tales. The publisher had given him a list of the stories to be included; when he saw "The Town Musicians of Bremen", with its dastardly gang of thieves, he laughed out loud. He sketched out a very nice composition—a dark rustic hovel with a low fire; a sinister robber recoiling in terror from the snapping dog and hissing cat as a cock crowed on the rafters—and was fiddling with the robber's eyebrows to achieve an impression of movement when there was a knock on the door.

"Mr Pyne, sir?" It was his landlady. "Visitor for you. A Mr. Jerry, he says."

"Oh. Please send him up. Thank you, Mrs. Barzowski, you're very kind."

Mrs. Barzowski knew he was a lord in disguise, and it had taken all the charm of which he was capable, plus dire warnings about speculative burglary, to persuade her not to spread the news throughout the house and to all her neighbours. She insisted on the *sir* and on bringing messages in person, and called him "Lord Alexander" in private as though to do so was a great privilege. She believed him to have been wrongly done out of an inheritance, which was true in its way, and that he would one day come into a title of his own, which wasn't. Alec had tried to disabuse her of that conviction, but it hadn't taken, so he accepted the advantages it brought and made sure his rent was always paid on time.

Crozier made it up the stairs a few minutes later. Alec heard him speaking to Mrs. Barzowski on the landing, smooth tone clear though the words were indistinguishable, and could imagine her bobbing in response. She doubtless thought him a gentleman, or perhaps a lawyer arriving with news of Alec's elevation to a non-existent coronet.

Crozier rapped on the door and entered, taking off his hat. He wore a light tan coat with a waistcoat in a darker brown, and a gold watch chain. He looked like a gentleman about town, significantly superior to Alec in his shirtsleeves.

"Spectacles?" Crozier asked.

Alec hastily removed them. "I use them for close work."

"Very reasonable. How's your head?"

"Better for a Turkish bath. I don't often drink much."

"So I gathered." Crozier's tone had his usual light hint of something between amusement and mockery. "Best to be careful in the near future, then. Still, we achieved what we intended. May I sit?"

Alec had one armchair, by the small grate. He indicated it and dragged over the chair he used for work. "Would you like tea?"

"Let's not trouble your landlady. That's a lot of stairs."

"It is. I need the light up here."

"It must be cold in winter."

Alec felt vaguely criticised. "Yes, and hot in summer. Do take your coat off if you're warm."

"I shall," Crozier said, suiting the action to the word. "Why does Lord Alexander Pyne-ffoulkes live in an attic?"

Alec opened his mouth. Nothing came out for a moment. He wanted to say "None of your business", knew he couldn't, but didn't have anything else to offer.

"Let me rephrase that," Crozier went on. "Do you understand what we did last night and what we'll be doing now?"

"Probably not."

"I shall pursue your acquaintance, so that you will have good reason to invite your new best friend to a family party. Hence, if I am caught or even suspected when your stepmother's jewels go missing, you will be seen as a dupe rather than an accomplice."

"Why does that matter to you?" Alec demanded.

"Because if you're arrested I'm quite sure you'll give me up to the police. Therefore I don't want you arrested. My presence in your life has to be plausible, and so does your attendance at a celebration of the Duke and Duchess of Ilvar's marriage. Understand? You can't just walk into your estranged father's house with a stranger and have the jewels go missing."

"I understand that very well. I was going to talk to my siblings tomorrow."

"You're going to talk to me first." Crozier spoke quite pleasantly but Alec felt a prickle on his skin. "I want to know all about the Pyne-ffoulkes family, all about your charming father and delightful stepmother, and very much all about why you live in an attic working for your bread while your sister Lady Caroline lies in something near a pauper's grave."

Alec couldn't breathe. He sat, mouth open, staring at this damned intrusive impertinent bastard with pure hate boiling up inside him, and Crozier shook his head. "Can you illustrate a book, or a story, without a brief? I need the brief. I need to know what not to say; I need to know how to tell your story and who is going to raise questions and how we answer them before they're asked. I can't help you if I don't know the situation."

"Of course your main interest lies in helping me," Alec said bitterly.

Crozier gave him a look. "My interest lies in helping myself to the Duchess's diamond parure and getting away clean. Is that not what you asked for?"

"Yes, well, that's very sensible." Alec knew he was being absurd, but shame and resentment were overwhelming all common sense. "I'm sure you'd be quite ready to give over your family history for profit. Forgive me if I'm not."

"As if you've anything to tell me that's worse than my history," Crozier said. "Do you imagine I'll be shocked by anything you have to say? Do you think I care?"

Alec snorted. "At least you're honest."

"That's precisely what I'm not. Consider me the antithesis of a Romish priest. I take confession, I keep your silence, but instead of absolution I give you vengeance. That's what you're after, isn't it? Some way to get through the armoury of wealth and title, to hit the Duke where it hurts."

That was savagely accurate. Alec rose, needing to move, needing not to see Crozier's face or anyone's. He went to the skylight, staring out over the rooftops, took a few deep breaths.

"My father met Mrs. Clayton when I was six. Clayton was my father's estate manager at Castle Speight. He came from a good family that had had a crash. His wife had no birth, a little money, not much beauty, or so I'm told. Apparently she had something, though, because my father was obsessed with her from their first meeting and their affair became public extremely quickly. My mother was unwell. She had had a terrible time when Annabel, my younger sister, was born, and never really recovered. So my father—it wasn't surprising for him to take a mistress, but he didn't even try to be discreet. And then, you see, Mother died, and my father told Clayton to petition for divorce so he could marry Mrs. Clayton. Ordered him to. Mother hadn't been dead six months. Father was still wearing mourning."

Crozier didn't say anything. The glass of the skylight was grimy. Alec rubbed at it with his thumb but the muck was on the outside; he couldn't reach it to clean it off.

"Clayton wouldn't do it," he went on. "The local story is, he told my father in the street, 'You've made her your whore but you'll never make her your wife.' Everyone knew he was being cuckolded by his employer, and I suppose preventing them from marrying was his revenge. He didn't keep his grievances private, though: he spoke quite wildly about my father ruining his marriage and destroying his happiness. They say he was drinking too much. And then he was found dead, in the grounds, some little way from his cottage, with his gun by his side."

"Considerate of him to do it outside."

"Oh, no, it wasn't suicide," Alec said sardonically. "The coroner said so, because of the missing ring."

"What's that?" Crozier enquired, perking up.

"A very fine antique emerald ring he always wore. It was a family heirloom, to be passed to his son or returned to the next heir, his brother, if he died without issue. The ring was about all the Claytons had left from their crash, and it wasn't on his body when it was discovered. That allowed the coroner to float a theory of a poacher shooting him, whether by accident or on purpose, and robbing the corpse. So the verdict was death by misadventure."

"What a remarkable conclusion."

Alec snorted. "My father is the richest, most powerful man in three counties. Of course the inquest wasn't going to accuse him of driving his mistress's husband to self-murder. They'd have found for divine intervention if they could."

"The march of justice," Crozier murmured. "Go on."

"Well, my father married Mrs. Clayton five months later. They should both still have been in blacks, but they held a full wedding, not even privately, but with all possible pomp and ceremony."

"Attended by the great and the good, I suppose?"

"Fewer than you'd think, actually," Alec said. "It was less than a year after Mother's death, and a lot of people wanted nothing to do with the business. The Duke of Ilvar, and nobody from the Royal Family attended his wedding. The Duchess was furious. I remember her shouting."

"Mmm. And how was she as a mother, afterwards?"

Alec laughed. There was nothing to do but laugh. "Oh, she loathed us. There was George—Earl of Hartington, you know—Cara, me, and Annabel, and she didn't want four children. She was twenty-five when she married Father, and George was fifteen. A stepson only ten years younger? No, she hated us, and she made sure we all knew it. George because he was outspoken about the insult to Mother's memory; Cara because she was sickly. The Duchess can't bear sickliness, you know, it revolts her. I'm not worth her notice, and Annabel—one might have thought she'd want Annabel. She was so young; she could easily have come to love a new mother who cared for her at all. But the Duchess wanted her own children."

"I don't recall they have any?"

"No. She was expecting a couple of times. I used to lie awake at night wondering what would happen if she had a son, with George and me ahead of him in the line of inheritance. What she might do. Just childish fears, you know," he added hastily. "In any case, it never came about."

"I don't suppose that made her fonder of her stepchildren," Crozier said. "It all sounds very unpleasant. I understand the Ilvars are not popular outside the home either."

"In Society? No, not at all. My father isn't the sort of man who's liked, if you know what I mean. He's invited for his title, not himself. And of course he's entitled to pride because of his position, but once he started demanding, not just courtesy but humble deference to the mistress he married—well, the sort of people who like dukes don't much like that. And she's every bit as proud of her place as he is. She ranks above everyone but the Royal Family now, so she never tried to win friends, or good opinion. I don't know if she thought she'd gain them by right or if she just doesn't care."

"One could almost respect that, you know. Like a medieval queen."

"She is medieval. She runs Castle Speight 'sacked if seen', so if any servant who isn't meant to be there dares to intrude on her view, they are dismissed at once. If she catches a housemaid doing her job or sees a footman in the wrong place or a groom not in the stables, that's their lot. God help anyone who is meant to be there but doesn't bow with sufficient deference, come to that. The locals call it Castle Spite."

"They must have quite the changing roster of staff. Interesting. So she wasn't much of a stepmother to you. Your father didn't seek to improve relations?"

Alec rested his head on his arm. He hadn't spoken about this in years. Family wasn't a subject he discussed with anyone but his siblings, who already knew. "No, not at all. He took her side in the arguments—there were a lot of arguments—and he always made it clear that if it came to a choice between his wife or his children, he'd choose his wife. Eight years ago it did, and he did."

"Leaving you where?"

"In an attic," Alec said. "George has a small income as Hartington—well, a very good one for a young man, which is what it's meant to be, but he's had Cara and Annabel, our sisters, to support since the break, and a family of his own now, and a wife who didn't expect to penny-pinch when she married an earl. He's had to shoulder all the family obligations because Father won't. He's never even met his grandchildren, do you know that? George has two sons, one of whom will be the Duke of Ilvar eventually, and Father doesn't give a damn. He won't acknowledge any of us unless we bow the knee to him and grovel to his wife."

"And you won't."

"We oughtn't have to. I don't say the Duchess should have loved us, but the fact is, Annabel was four years old when they married, and I was eight, and we didn't deserve to be punished because we wept for our mother. George oughtn't have to be de facto head of the family, with all the burdens and none of the benefits. Cara—" He broke off, glaring through the glass at nothing.

"No," Crozier said. "Some might say that nobody at all has a right to the kind of obscene wealth possessed by your family, but I quite see that if you're born to it, it would be exasperating not to have it."

"I'm well aware George's income could support all the families in this street, if he lived like the families in this street," Alec said testily. "But he's a duke's heir. He's got to keep up appearances, to keep them up for his wife and children. You said yesterday, one ought to reach for what one wants and not miss opportunities. Well, George and his wife and his children and Annabel have the opportunity to be part of the highest society. And if George gets a job as a clerk, say, or Annabel becomes a governess, they and their children will suffer for it. You must know that."

"They'd prefer aristocratic poverty to joining the middle classes?"

"Yes," Alec said. "They would. Because George *will* be a duke one day, when Father dies and if he and his children have become an object of pity and contempt to their peers, well, that's not fair on them. And Annabel is the Duke of Ilvar's daughter. It's not unreasonable that her intended's family should want her to bring something to the marriage, but Father won't give her a penny for a wedding portion. And if she could marry and George didn't have to worry about her any more, that would take a strain off him too. She and his wife don't get on awfully well—nobody's fault, but it would be better for everyone if they didn't share a house. If I could give her a sum to marry on—"

"Is that it?" Crozier asked. "Are you funding Lady Annabel's dowry with the Duchess's jewels?"

"Henry, with whom she has an understanding, is a gentleman," Alec said. "Which means he needs to marry money rather than making it himself." That came out slightly more sarcastically than he'd intended, and he heard the ghost of a chuckle from behind him. "I don't mean to be rude. He's pleasant enough, but not the most energetic fellow, or terribly bright. He's a drone, not a worker bee."

"And as a worker bee yourself, you disapprove."

"Not really. I'd have liked an idle life of luxury as much as anyone."

"Would you?" Crozier said. "This room seems to me a hive, as it were, of industry. It suggests a man who puts importance on his work."

It didn't lack markers of his profession, Alec was aware: he had pictures pinned haphazardly to the walls, pots of drawing materials, piles of images for reference. It was a working space more than anything and he did feel a certain satisfaction in his Bohemian existence, at least when the commissions came thick and fast. Not to mention that artists and journalists tended to have better conversation than sons of gentlemen, to be rather less demanding in matters of dress, and considerably more open in their pleasures.

"I have a knack for drawing," he said. "And as it happens I like it, and the society it's brought me into, well enough. Naturally I'd rather have more money; I dare say we all would."

"I dare say." Crozier sounded rather dry.

"If Father had given me an income to live on, I don't suppose I'd ever have taken up drawing seriously, and I'd have missed out on a lot of things. But he didn't cut me off to teach me to live a useful life. It wasn't a lesson; he just doesn't care. So even if I don't feel I've been wronged as George and Annabel have, it's still not right." He took a deep breath. "And then there was Cara."

"Yes," Crozier said. "Tell me about Lady Cara."

"He wouldn't pay for her." Alec stared out of the skylight. There was a cat on the roof opposite, a brindled one, basking in the sun. He fixed his eyes on it, because sometimes, if one fixed one's eyes on a thing, one didn't cry. "She was never strong, always short of breath. The Duchess called her sickly. She ought to have been in the country, with clean air, but instead she lived with George. He did try to send her to the seaside when he could, but with all the expenses—he couldn't afford to keep up two households, and I needed to be in London to get work, and she didn't want to go to a sanatorium on her own. And then last autumn the fog was so dreadful that I wrote to Father. I begged him to invite Cara to Castle Speight. I told him she was unwell, that she needed to be out of London, and please would he help. And his secretary wrote back and said His Grace could not countenance my request unless Cara wrote to make a personal apology for her intolerable insolence. His *secretary*."

Crozier was silent. The brindled cat blurred in Alec's vision. He blinked the tears away. "She caught a cold. It would have been a mere chill for anyone else, George's boys constantly have them, but it came at the same time as that bad week's fog in early December, and she died. Her weak chest, you see. It was very sudden. We'd been worried, but we didn't expect her to die."

"I'm sorry," Crozier said softly.

"So am I. And Father refused to pay for the funeral. He said the expense was not convenient."

There was a slight pause. "That's quite a statement from one of the richest men in England."

"Yes. He said he had an obligation to his Duchess which took priority. That was the diamond parure. As if he couldn't have afforded to pay for the funeral too, as if his own daughter's funeral shouldn't have been more to him than another set of jewels. George had to pay, and we didn't have flowers. Cara loved flowers but in December—hothouse lilies are awfully expensive— There was holly. One of the vases was knocked over and berries rolled everywhere, on the floor. People trod on them." He remembered the red drops splashed like blood against the stone and the sharp smell.

"Yes," Crozier said, as though he were agreeing with something, instead of listening to Alec ramble about holly. "I see. It's the insult of indifference."

Alec swung round at that. Crozier was only a couple of feet away. Alec hadn't heard him move. "That's exactly what it is. He has no right to be indifferent. No right to treat us as though we don't exist. No right not to come to Cara's funeral, not to care."

"I'm surprised he wasn't concerned with public opinion."

"We didn't want people to know. George says it would make things worse if everyone was talking about us as hard done by, and he's probably right. And in any case, I don't think Father would care what people say. He's so entrenched in his outrage at people's failure to pay suitable homage to the Duchess that he doesn't see anything else. It's the only matter of right or wrong in his world. And Cara would rather have died than apologise. She *did*."

Crozier's brows angled down. "An extreme stance even in a family dispute."

Alec had no intention of going into her reasons. "Well. Is that what you wanted? Enough of my family misery to be getting on with?"

"It's a start." Crozier seemed unconcerned by the belligerence of his tone. "The obvious question: Given the situation you've described, how do you propose to claim your place at the anniversary dinner?"

Alec put his chin up. "I'm going to apologise. I'm going to reconcile with my father and bow to the Duchess. He'll want that: it will prove he was right all along."

"And what have your brother and sister to say to that?"

Alec's stomach clenched. "I haven't spoken to them yet."

"What are you going to say?" Crozier pressed.

"Well, I'm not going to tell them I've hired thieves," Alec snapped. "I don't know. That I'm tired of the fighting, that I'm giving in to Father in order to wring money out of him for Annabel. What else can I say?"

"That you need the money yourself. It's very heroic to sacrifice yourself for your sister, but firstly she might refuse the offer, and secondly, if you announce that you'll do anything to get money for her and then the jewels go missing, your siblings would be fools not to link the two things. Whereas if you admit to a minor villainy now, they will believe they know what you're up to, and there won't be an outstanding mystery to which the theft will, in due course, be a solution."

"Oh. I see, I think. So I should say I want his money, and I don't care about what he's done?"

"Not that you don't care, but that you can no longer keep to those principles. Let's say you have accrued gambling debts. You've fallen back into expensive society—that's me—and need to hold your own. You're tired of scribbling for pennies. You'd prefer to have lilies at your funeral."

Alec couldn't help wincing. Crozier held his gaze, giving a deliberate shrug. "Forget your sensibilities. You'll need to ask your father for money, lots of it, well before we do the job. Another safeguard: why would you steal from the goose when it's started laying you golden eggs again?"

"Yes. Right. Christ." Alec made a face. "George and Annabel will despise me."

"I'd say it's considerably more likely that once one of you has thrown in the towel, the others will follow. Try not to despise them if they do."

"I don't think they will," Alec said with some understatement.

"In that case, yes, this is likely to be unpleasant for you with the people you most care about. Are you prepared for that?"

"Am I prepared to have people say cruel things to me?" Alec asked, almost incredulously. "Yes, probably I am. I went to school with everyone quite sure my father had married his mistress after driving her husband to suicide and covering it up. I grew up in the Duchess's power. I think I can tolerate my brother and sister's poor opinion for a couple of months. I don't much want to, but I can."

"Good, because you'll have to. If your father is to believe in your submission, you can hardly be on good terms with the offspring who defy him, can you?"

Alec hadn't quite thought of that. "I suppose not."

"Three months," Crozier said. "Two to prepare, the job, and then at least another month of good behaviour before you arrange to be cast into the outer darkness once more and can rebuild bridges with your siblings. This is what we call playing the long game, and it has a price. Don't imagine any of this comes free and easy."

Alec tried an eyebrow lift. "You look free and easy enough."

Crozier's lips curved responsively. "I already told you. I'm never sorry."

He was two feet away, very close in a room which seemed suddenly rather smaller than usual. He wasn't sorry, and he didn't care about things, and he was going to guide Alec down the primrose path to villainy, and Alec wished to God he hadn't drunk so much last night because it always made him randy the next day. The last thing he needed right now was, for example, Crozier taking two steps forward, grabbing his hands, pressing him against the wall or down over the drawing table...

The second last thing he needed right now was to be sporting a hard one, and he was well on the way. He put a hand casually behind his back, in order to dig two fingernails into the sensitive ball of his thumb. "Well. I'd better get on and speak to my siblings, then."

"Before your father? Would you do that if you had no ulterior motive? What if he's not interested in your submission?"

Alec resisted the obvious, tempting, unsayable reply. *Keep your mind on the job, damn it.* "Uh... I don't know what I'd naturally do. Probably not this at all. I'd rather speak to George first."

"Or is it that you'd rather put off contacting your father a little longer?"

Alec glared at him. "I dare say you're very acute, but it doesn't make you any more likeable."

Crozier laughed aloud. "I'm sure it doesn't. Look, from what you tell me, it will be harder than I suspect you realise to do as your father wishes. You'll have to say a number of unpalatable things. Yes?"

"Yes."

"Tell them to me."

Alec didn't want to tell him anything. It stuck like brambles, all of it. He shut his eyes, which didn't help, and opened them to find Crozier a silent step closer.

"You're crossing the Rubicon," the thief said softly. "If you were doing this because you meant it, you'd be renouncing a great deal of what has guided your life to this date. As you aren't, you're taking a significant step down a path that you don't want to walk. But this is nevertheless the way to your goal, so tell me, what will you need to say?"

"That I apologise for my insolence to the Duchess." Alec's throat felt thick; he had to force the words out. "That I regret my failure to give due respect to my father and my father's wife. That I pray to be accepted back into their good graces, that I promise proper filial piety from now on and will—will do as I'm told."

Crozier nodded slowly. "Yes, that's rather a lot to swallow." He paused for a fraction of a second. "Do you not like to do as you're told?"

"It depends what I'm being told to do," Alec said. "Just as it depends what there is to swallow."

Crozier's eyes snapped wide, and Alec felt a fierce pulse of satisfaction—*wrong-footed you there, you bastard*—alongside the appalled realisation that yes, he had said that. There was silence for a few seconds. Alec's blood was pounding; he could hear Crozier's breath and his own. The air felt thick.

And then Crozier smiled, and Alec thought, *Oh shit.*

It wasn't a nice smile, or a complicit one of shared understanding, or even the sort of smile that was a precursor to being bent over a table. It was a smile that could only be called predatorial. His brows were slanted in a truly satanic way, and Alec's ribcage was suddenly rather too tight for comfort.

"That's very true," Crozier said slowly. "If it's a matter of humiliating necessity, say, to which you're driven by sheer desperation...that wouldn't be good, would it?"

"Not at all." Alec's mouth was dry. He swallowed involuntarily, saw Crozier's eyes dip to track the movement of his throat.

"Desperation is a terrible thing," Crozier said. "It's amazing what a man can find himself doing once he's on his knees."

Alec tried very hard not to whimper. He wasn't sure if he'd succeeded. Crozier's smile tilted, a crooked curve. "You know, in my line of work it's useful to have a few characters. Identities, you might say, entire personalities that you can slip on or off like a garment. It's far easier than struggling to reconcile difficult realities or remembering a mass of loose facts."

"I don't understand."

"It's simple enough. Don't write your letter as Alec Pyne, degrading himself in his own eyes with lies he'd rather not tell. Write as, shall we say, 'Lord Alexander', the weakling nobleman who comes on in Act One. A man of no real strength, easily swayed by bad company, who'll do absolutely anything he's told to."

Alec blinked. "A character from the melodrama, you mean?"

"Precisely. The effete young cipher, the hapless plaything of stronger men's will. Create the part and play it. And then, you see, you'll have Lord Alexander ready and waiting whenever you need to go to your knees. For any reason."

"That's your professional advice, is it?" Alec managed.

Crozier took one more step forward, so he was far too close, mouth almost at Alec's ear, breath warm. "I'd be delighted to help you create the character."

Oh God. Alec had to lock his knees to stand straight. This was all appallingly wrong and a terrible idea and...

...it might work. The Lord Alexander that Crozier had sketched out would write the vile, humiliating letter that he needed to write. He'd do anything a strong ruthless villain like Crozier wanted. Anything at all.

"Or," Crozier said softly. "Perhaps I could let you think about it, and you could have my words at the back of your mind as you write your letter and create your character, and try it out on paper and in person. All that time you could be speculating about how far Lord Alexander can be pushed, and what he can be made to swallow. Do you think that might help your inspiration?"

"Possibly," Alec said. His voice was a trifle high.

"Give it some thought." Crozier stepped back. "I, meanwhile, am going to do a little digging. Meet me at the Cafe Royal, two days' time, eight o'clock. Have your approach to your father made and sent by then, Lord Alexander. Don't fail me."

He took up his hat and turned on his heel. Alec stared at the door long after it had closed.

In over his head didn't even begin to describe it. That conversation ought to have been a humiliating agony—Cara, the plain awfulness of what he intended to do—and instead it had become the thing it had, and now it felt almost like a game. A wicked game with stakes he didn't want to consider, but still a game, and he wanted to play. He wanted to win this round, to meet in two days' time with the letter written, to prove to Crozier that he could manage his hand. As it were.

Oh God.

Alec walked over to the door and threw the bolt. He leaned on it, bracing himself with his right hand, unbuttoned himself with the left, paused.

Crozier had clearly wanted to leave him in this squirming state of shameful arousal. He'd seemed to feel that would fuel Alec's ability to create his character. And he might even be right, because if three-quarters of Alec's mind was on his painfully tight cock, perhaps he could manage his more distasteful duties without thinking too much.

He released himself, buttoned his trousers again, and went to the table, but hesitated over a pen. He took up a pencil instead, twisting it in his fingers, thinking about Lord Alexander. A weak-willed aristocrat, a spineless clothes horse, easily bent to another's commands...he let the pencil drift over the page, creating something not his own face but not so far off as to be unrecognisable. A character that would instantly strike an experienced viewer of the melodrama as a third rank villain, never to be trusted, though liable to repent in the final act. A weak mouth, a petulant curve to the slightly open lips, a sulky, evasive look to the eyes...

He could do this. He could create a version of himself that resembled his truth as much as the sketch did his face and write the letter without staining his own soul, because it wasn't him. Lord Alexander would submit to the Duke of Ilvar's will, and grovel far more than Alec could stomach, and Alec would stand back and laugh as he did it.

And as to Crozier, and what the devil he'd been playing at talking Alec into this state of desire and humiliation and pretence...he'd just have to find out on Friday night at their assignation. He only knew that if Crozier had been acting in character, he'd been sufficiently immersed in his role to have sprung a very substantial bit of stiff. Crozier had been as caught in that moment as Alec, and if he was being toyed with, at least it was by a skilled player.

He let his mind dwell on that thought as he reached for the pen.

Chapter Three

Alec sat in the Earl of Hartington's drawing-room, knees pressed together, carefully holding his teacup. The clock ticked. He felt unwell.

"What..." George's lips moved as though he were trying out phrases, or his brain wasn't quite connecting to his mouth. "What do you mean you've written to Father?"

Alec felt a stab of guilt. George looked so worn. His cuffs had clearly been turned, his furniture was faded, his wife was swelling with her third child and obviously not enjoying the process any more than the first two because she looked pallid and drawn. Alec had made a vow not to add to George's burdens and had prided himself on achieving financial independence, about which his brother had been vocally disapproving and privately relieved. He didn't want to make things worse now. He wished Melissa and Annabel weren't here.

"Written to say what?" Annabel demanded. She was looking well in a dress that wasn't too obviously last season's and was decidedly fresher than Melissa's voluminous garment, reused from her previous interesting condition. "What do you mean, Alec?"

Alec exhaled. "I wrote to ask him for a rapprochement. To get back into his good books. That's all."

"You *wrote*? To him? After Cara? After everything, you actually *wrote*—" Annabel's voice was rising rapidly up the scale.

"You cannot be serious," George said. "Does the gross insult he offered our sister mean nothing? Do you propose to call that woman mother? Have you run mad?"

"No, I haven't. The fact is, I need rather more money than I can earn. That's all there is to it."

"You said you were doing well. You said you didn't need my help."

"I'm doing perfectly well," Alec returned without thinking. He'd made that assurance so often. "That is, I have been, but I have encountered some unexpected expenses and, well, I'm simply tired of scrimping and saving and struggling to keep my head above water."

"Don't you think we all are?" Annabel struck in. "Haven't we been for years? Do you think I enjoy appearing at the minimum possible of parties in a dress that's been refurbished for the fifth time—"

"Then maybe you should follow your brother's example if George can't keep you to your liking," Melissa said furiously. "Considering he supports you as well as his own children, all of whom go without for your adornment—"

"I wasn't complaining!" Annabel cried, going scarlet. George shut his eyes.

Alec said, loudly, "But that's the point, isn't it? That we're not keeping our heads above water. We're not managing."

"But you were," George said. "You *told* me you were."

"Well, I'm not," Alec snapped. "Or not enough. I've got some bills I can't pay and—"

"Then give them to me." George sounded exhausted. "You know very well I never wanted to turn you into a tradesman."

"Hartington," Melissa said, shooting Alec a look of startling viciousness. "May I remind you your son is to start at Eton next year, and your second son will also require an education."

"I will support my family. All of it." George spoke with determination that was as heartfelt as it was threadbare.

"How?" Melissa almost shouted. "You're already stretching every penny until it snaps! Will we turn off the cook next, or should you like me to black the grates myself to save the housemaid's wages?"

"Alec has never asked me for a penny before now and if he needs help this once—"

"It's not a case of *this once* and Melissa is quite right," Alec said. "There's no reason you should be responsible for my gambling debts."

There was a tiny silence, then George, Melissa, and Annabel all said, "Your *what?*" in a discordant chorus of fury. Alec's nausea rose; he could hardly have felt more guilty if he had indeed run up bills at baccarat. *Be Lord Alexander*, he told himself. *Play the part.*

"How can you gamble when you know damned well you can't pay?" George thundered over the two women. "What sort of irresponsible, stupid, dishonourable way to behave—?"

"Do you have *any idea* how hard George works?" Melissa was demanding. "Do you have any idea how much he already has to do for your family as well as his own?"

"How could you?" Annabel cried. "Haven't we been made enough of a disgrace already? Alec, how *could* you?"

Alec let his shoulders rise into a defensive hunch and adopted a petulant tone to match. "I'm Lord Alexander Pyne-ffoulkes. As George says, I oughtn't be a tradesman."

"You said you enjoyed it!" George protested.

"You promised you wouldn't ask George to pay your bills," Melissa added over him.

"Well, I'm not, and I don't see why you're all shouting at me as though I am. I don't have any intention of hanging off George's sleeve. I simply want to live according to my station, and I'm tired of this endless fighting with Father. Where did it get Cara?"

George's mouth dropped open. Annabel said, "Alec!"

"Well, it's true." The words came with surprising ease now, almost as though part of him believed them. "If Cara had given up fighting with Father she might be alive today, because she'd have been living by the sea instead of coughing her lungs up in London. She's dead, and we couldn't even send her off with flowers, and for what? It's not as though she persuaded anyone outside this room to take her part, or as though Father suffered in the slightest by her stand. It's all a stupid waste of time. I've only got one life and one chance to enjoy it and I'm going to take it."

"How can you?" Annabel whispered. "You know what he did."

"I know I'm a duke's son and I've spent eight years scraping a living where my peers are enjoying their youth," Alec said. "I know I'm twenty-eight and I don't have any prospect of more than a single room and drudging at the draughting table for the next thirty years and I'm embarrassed by my wardrobe when I mix with gentlemen. And I know that we'll never get the victory Cara wanted. Well, I don't propose to keep fighting a war I can't win for no gain at all. I'm sorry if you don't like it, but I don't much like living this way either."

Annabel had gone white. George was going red. Melissa looked between them, and at Alec, and he prayed with everything in him, *Don't agree with me, please, please don't agree...*

"You can't mean it," Annabel said. "You made a promise. Have you—have you been waiting for Cara to die so you can go back on your word?"

It was a dagger-stab, and Alec flinched. *Play the part*, he told himself fiercely. "Well, I do mean it, and I don't see that a promise is binding when the person one made it to is dead, and the fact it, it wasn't a fair promise in the first place. We only had Cara's word for the whole thing."

Annabel gasped shrilly. George rose. "Leave," he said, and the harried household manager sounded like a peer of the realm then.

"Get out of my house, Alec. I hope you will think again but don't come back until you do. Cara—your promise— Get out. Get out of my sight."

"There's no need to be like that," Alec said, through lips that hurt, and that was when George started shouting.

Alec was still stiff with misery the next day, filled with it so that every thought he had floated on a dark churning sea of unhappiness. He dressed for the evening with automatic movements and felt like an observer of the whole proceeding, as if he were watching himself on the stage. The Second Villain, weak and vile, cast out by his family.

He hadn't even heard back from his father. He'd cast every relationship that mattered into hazard, bet it all on a single card that wouldn't be turned over for God knew how long. If Father had his secretary write back to signal his lack of interest in his second son...

He did not want to go out with Crozier now. He wanted nothing less than to pretend friendship with the vicious devil who was escorting him down a path he should have rejected out of hand the moment it was proposed. But he was the one who'd started this, he'd thrown away the love and respect of his siblings by his own choice, and he might as well carry it through. So he dressed with no enthusiasm at all, and dragged himself wearily to the Cafe Royal.

Crozier was waiting at a table. He rose to greet Alec with a smile that turned to a look of concern in which Alec didn't believe for a minute. "I say, old fellow, are you all right?"

"Not marvellous," Alec said, sitting. "I've done that business of which we spoke when we last met. Wrote my letter. Spoke to my brother and sister."

"Have you had a reply to the letter?"

"No. It was entirely as you'd have wished," he added bitterly. "I crawled on my belly with all the unctuous phrasing at my disposal."

Crozier's brows rose. "You look like you need a drink. Waiter!" He lifted a finger. "We're in urgent need of a bottle of champagne here. Lord Alexander requires a hair of the dog that bit him before his respected father does the same. Talking of whom, is the Duke of Ilvar expected in tonight? Find out, will you?"

The waiter bowed and removed himself. Alec blinked. Crozier had suddenly become the epitome of the affable, confident, very nearly vulgar man about town, the character shift total and somewhat unnerving. "Are you serious? Is my father coming here?"

"I doubt it. I just want your presence noted. So, an unpleasant conversation with your siblings. What did you tell them?"

"That I'd decided to give in because I had gambling debts and I was tired of fighting."

Crozier nodded. "Well done."

"Is that all you have to say?" Alec demanded. He wasn't even sure what he thought Crozier should say; he simply wanted to hit back at someone in this miserable mess he'd created. "I've alienated my brother and sister, and for what?"

"In the larger sense, don't ask me," Crozier said. "From my point of view, you've taken a temporary loss to play for a very substantial gain."

"If it happens."

"Granted, but this is how you'll make it happen. It's a long game. I told you that."

The waiter reappeared with a bottle, which he uncorked with a loud pop, adding a bow to Alec and a murmured regret that His Grace of Ilvar was not in fact expected. Crozier thanked him, and slipped him a generous tip once the glasses were filled.

"Your health."

Alec made himself raise his own glass. "I've no desire to get drunk again."

"Very wise. But I'd rather you didn't look like a man on the way to his own execution. Can you cheer up, do you think?"

"I doubt it, since I've alienated the people I most care for," Alec said, low and savage. "You told me you weren't sorry for anything you've done. I'd like to know how you manage that."

"Practice helps. So does enjoying the fruits of your actions, which you won't do for a while. So, also, does reminding yourself that shame is merely society's weapon, used to keep us obedient."

"Sorry?" Alec said. "I wasn't expecting political philosophy."

"It's not complicated. I'm sure you've done things of which you'd be utterly ashamed if they were made public, while feeling perfectly content with the actions themselves. Therefore, shame isn't about what you do, just what gets found out."

"Rubbish," Alec said. "Of course we ought to be ashamed of things we do. I *am*."

"And will you withdraw your letter and tell Hartington and Lady Annabel you've changed your mind? Go back on yourself with nothing achieved?"

Alec snorted. "You sound like Macbeth. 'I am in blood stepped in so far that, should I wade no more, returning were as tedious as go o'er.' Nobody would ever repent based on that argument."

"People repent when they fail," Crozier said. "'But screw your courage to the sticking-place and we'll not fail.'"

"You know your Shakespeare. So you must know that attitude didn't go well for Macbeth."

"He was infirm of purpose. Are you?"

"I'm disgusted with myself." Alec tossed back his champagne in a gulp. Crozier reached across with the bottle to top up his glass. "If you're interested in how I feel, that's how. I feel dirtied and degraded in my own eyes—"

"I told you to create a part and act it."

"I did. But it's no good saying that my grovelling to Father was false if my brother's anger and my sister's disgust are real."

"But they aren't," Crozier said. "Or, at least, they aren't based in reality. They've formed a mistaken impression of you, admittedly because you've deliberately given them that wrong impression, but it's still wrong."

"And they still won't want to speak to me."

"How fortunate that you'll be preoccupied." Crozier's brows angled invitingly. "You've a lot of ground to make up with the Duke in a short time. I've got things in hand but you, my friend, will need a smile on your face. Tell me, what would put one there? You didn't seem a particular aficionado of the music hall. The opera? The theatre? Sporting events? No? Then what?"

As though Alec gave a damn for fashionable entertainments. "I don't care. Whatever you want."

Crozier picked up his glass and took a deliberate sip. "You're not listening. I want you looking significantly less doom-laden, so we're going to talk about things you enjoy. What are those?"

"Oh, I don't know. I like the theatre but I haven't seen anything recently, so I can hardly make conversation about that."

"Then I shall procure tickets for something. Melodrama or the nobler heights of Shakespeare?"

"Whatever you choose."

Crozier exhaled audibly. Alec hunched a shoulder. "You want to exhibit me in public as part of your 'long game'. Forgive me if I don't find that an enjoyable prospect."

Crozier's facial expression didn't change, but his eyes did. They hardened, or chilled, so that he looked quite suddenly like a man who broke the law for a living, and Alec felt a pulse of sudden alarm. He knew damned well he was behaving like a sulky boy over a fate he had brought on himself, and it seemed as though Crozier's patience with that had come to an end.

Crozier leaned forward over the table, wearing a pleasant smile that didn't touch his eyes. Alec knew an impulse to blurt an apology, if it would only head off whatever was coming.

"Lord Alexander," Crozier murmured in a confiding tone. "Apparently I need to make myself clear. The purpose of this excursion is to establish that you're charmed and delighted by your new best friend, so you will be charmed and delighted or I will fucking make you. I suggest you fix your thoughts on eleven thousand pounds' worth of shiny stones, and the chance to stick it to the Duke in a way he won't forget." He smiled with a clubman's practised warmth. "And if you still want to wallow in self-disgust and degradation, I will happily take you into a back alley and give you something to be really ashamed of. Anything to cheer you up."

Alec felt his mouth drop open. Crozier lifted his glass and tilted it as though making a toast. "I don't care how you approach your role, Lord Alexander. Willing or not, you're going to do what I want, so you might as well take it with grace. As it were."

Alec could feel, physically feel, the blood rushing to his cheeks. "That's—that's—"

"Entirely up to you," Crozier completed for him. "Notwithstanding, you seem to be struggling with all sorts of moral complexities and remorse and self-doubt, none of which I find troublesome. I could take charge of this, Lord Alexander."

"Take charge," Alec repeated.

"Make the decisions. Tell you what to say, and write, and do. I will make sure you come out of this job clean; you have my word as a dishonest man on that. Do as I tell you, and it will all be taken care of. Might it not be easier, and more pleasant, simply to do as you're told?"

Alec's toes curled in his shoes. His heart was pounding with a mixture of humiliation, anger, and desperation. *I'll fucking make you* still rang in his ears. "And how far does doing as I'm told extend?"

"Smile," Crozier said. "The waiter is coming. We're having a pleasant chat. Smile, *now.*"

Alec forced his mouth into the required shape. "I'm not hungry."

"But you're going to eat. Ah, marvellous," he added to the waiter with an instant smile. "Tell me, is Monsieur Francois offering his sweetbreads tonight? For both of us then, and a half bottle of Pouligny-Montrachet, I think. One hates to rush a good wine, but Lord Alexander has an engagement. Thank you."

"Do I have an engagement?" Alec asked when the waiter had gone.

Crozier divided the last of the champagne between their glasses. "Do you want one?"

"I don't know what you're asking." Alec felt a little flown by drink, very tired, exceedingly on edge. "I don't understand any of this. I don't know what to do. I had the most awful row with George and Annabel and I'm terrified my father won't write back and it will all have been in vain. I don't know what you want from me, and I'm tired of trying to make decisions when I'm not even sure I should be doing this at all."

"Then let me make them. It seems to me you've enough to do being Alec Pyne, illustrator. Why don't you put Lord Alexander under my direction?"

Alec could have wept. It was a momentary impulse, but so strong he had to shut his eyes briefly to regain control. He moistened his lips. Crozier's eyes flicked to his mouth as he did it, and he saw one brow tilt. "As long as—as long as you understand the difference."

"Well, I think I do," Crozier said. "Do you? It seems to me that Alec is a courageous, talented, dedicated artist making a success of himself on his own terms, with admirable determination for one brought up to be an idle waste of air."

"Oh." Alec felt himself going pink with shock and, undeniably, a twinge of pride.

"Whereas," Crozier continued, "and do correct me if I'm wrong, Lord Alexander might *be* that very idle waste of air. Lacking in all determination, all too ready to bend to the whim of a stronger will. Positively wanting to be given orders—or even not to be given a choice?—in a way that Alec's pride couldn't possibly condone."

"You make me sound like Dr. Jekyll and Mr. Hyde."

"Dr. Jekyll's hidden urges were monstrous ones, if I recall. Selfish cruelties and callousness. I think your secret vices are an entirely different matter."

"What about you?" Alec demanded. "Do you have a Mr. Hyde, or am I talking to him now?"

Crozier threw his head back and laughed. "Ha! No, the good doctor's potion wouldn't do much for me. I fear there's no virtuous do-gooder lurking within."

"You don't have a secret life as a vicar?"

"No, I'm straightforwardly disgraceful." Crozier grinned at him. "And you're changing the subject."

"So would you, if you were me."

"My friend, if I were you, I'd have gone out and taken what I wanted years ago. Or, rather, given it. May I make a proposal?"

"What?" Alex said, with some trepidation.

"We'll eat. Discuss work and theatre and light subjects. And then we'll go somewhere private and you will tell me, quite honestly, what, let us say, Lord Alexander wants, without shame or prevarication or fear of being overheard. The truth. Have you ever told anyone the truth?"

"More often than you, I'd bet!"

Crozier grinned crookedly. "On this specific subject. No, I didn't think so, somehow."

"Perhaps that's because I don't want to."

"Don't you?"

Alec shifted in his chair. He wanted to keep fighting, and he wanted to surrender. He felt an urge to toss Crozier's presumption back in his face, and a stronger one to give in, to confess the shameful desires and longings and see what happened. He wondered if he'd feel this urge to confess after participating in a robbery. *Only if the policeman is particularly handsome,* he told himself, and took up his glass to stifle a nervous laugh.

The sweetbreads arrived. Alec had forgotten Crozier had ordered for him, and the thought gave him an internal squirm that was somewhere between uncomfortable and enticing. He'd never have chosen sweetbreads, left to himself. They were delicious.

"So, the Shakespeare book," Crozier said. "Have you heard anything from the publisher yet?"

Alec made some reply, was drawn to explain the commissioning process for illustrators and the likely competitors for the role, and to his own astonishment became caught up in the conversation. It felt unreal to be discussing work, and a glass of Pouligny-Montrachet on top of the champagne added to that, but he rarely had the chance to talk shop except at the Sketch, and there he was always in competition with louder, more confident men who knew they belonged. Crozier wanted to listen to him, or was astonishingly good at pretending to, and Alec was startled to discover that his plate was clear.

Crozier summoned the waiter with a crook of his finger. Alec said, "Surely I—"

"Not at all. My pleasure. Shall we go?"

Alec followed him out. Neither had brought an overcoat; the evenings were getting warm, the air thick. Alec almost wished it was colder. He felt overheated and sweaty.

They walked in what any observer might have taken for companionable silence. Alec wondered if he'd find himself pushed down an alleyway. The tension throbbed in his wrists; he flexed his hands, trying to loosen fingers that felt clumsy.

If they went down an alleyway. If Crozier told him to go to his knees. If he could just forget, let go—

He hadn't thought about his family situation in an hour. He realised that with a small shock and felt a dull throb of misery at the reminder, but Crozier was knocking on a discreet door of a very ordinary-looking house, and greeted the slab-faced man who admitted them with a murmured word. Alec followed him in, trying to look around without showing that he was doing so. The house seemed to be a hotel, with a certain amount of noise and tobacco smoke issuing from down the hall. Crozier led the way upstairs to a small room, and ushered Alec in.

He'd expected a bedroom. He'd honestly expected that, rather than a sitting room with a small card table, a chaise longue, a couple of armchairs by the empty fireplace.

Crozier gestured to one of the chairs, and locked the door, an act that didn't make Alec feel any more secure. "There's brandy in the decanter, although it's bloody awful here."

"I've had enough, I think."

"You aren't missing anything." He seated himself in the opposite chair, steepling his fingers. "Well, then. We said you'd tell me what it is you want."

"No, you said that. I don't recall agreeing."

Crozier's lips curled. "And yet you're here."

That was undeniable. Alec stared at his own hands, ink-stained, the index finger dented by use of a pen. The faint noise of male carousing rose from downstairs.

"Tell me about Lord Alexander," Crozier said softly. "You've drunk Dr. Jekyll's potion. Alec Pyne goes in like the weatherman to his house, Lord Alexander comes out. What does he want?"

"Oh, not to be responsible," Alec said. His voice was rather thin. "To have someone—someone like you—tell him what to do. Not to have to struggle for job after job, always hoping and worrying. Not to feel guilty he can't support himself and his sisters while his brother feels guilty for not supporting him. Not to be constantly aware of—of things that are wrong. Not to care they're wrong."

"No. That's you," Crozier said. "Lord Alexander *doesn't* care. Lord Alexander is the weaknesses you fight, the moments of indulgence, the truth you'd prefer wasn't true. What does he want?"

Alec wanted to say that was nonsense. But it had been so easy to argue against his siblings, to reject Cara's insistence, and the promise they'd made her, and the lifetime of miserable helpless anger. He'd felt the power of the words as he'd spoken them, because they *were* true to his feelings in a horrible shameful way that he'd been trying to run from.

He tried to run from so much.

"And what does it mean if I tell you? That all of it is real? That it's what I am deep down?"

"That it's part of you," Crozier said. "Why should it not be? Dr. Jekyll came up with his potion to separate out his worse impulses from his better precisely because he had worse impulses. Everyone does. His tragedy came about because he tried to eliminate them."

"Whereas you think I should embrace them."

"I think you should acknowledge they exist, and then spend less time making yourself miserable about the fact that you're imperfect. Really, if you think *you're* flawed, you ought to spend a day with Templeton."

"But I don't want those impulses to exist," Alec said through his teeth. "That's the point."

"But they do. *That's* the point. You can try to eliminate every trace of them like Dr Jekyll and tear yourself apart, though preferably not in such a Gothic manner. Or you can accept that your soul is as tarnished and mouse-nibbled as everyone else's and consider what to do about it. You aren't really going to give up your work and grovel to your father for income, are you? No matter how much easier and more pleasant it might make your life?"

"No."

"Because?"

"Because it would be utterly shameful of me."

"Why? Where does the shame lie? Who would it harm?"

"Me," Alec said. "I'd be revolted by myself. It wouldn't be more pleasant, it would be weak, and wrong. Utterly wrong."

"Weak," Crozier repeated, dwelling on the word. "Very well. In that intriguing conversation a couple of days ago, you told me that whether you like taking orders depends on the order. Do you remember that?"

"Yes."

"Is that another of Lord Alexander's foibles, to enjoy submission? Is that weak too?"

Crozier's eyes were intent. Alec swallowed. He didn't like this probing. It felt as though a scalpel were gently separating congested layers of thoughts that had become matted and tangled together, and it hurt to have them picked apart. He'd thought Crozier was simply going to fuck him. "I. Uh."

"You aware that there is an entire industry of houses and whores that cater to such desires, because so many people share them?"

"Are you talking about flagellation and that sort of thing? Because I don't want that. At all," Alec added, to avoid doubt.

"Don't want to want it, or actually don't want it?"

"The latter. I've no idea why anyone would enjoy being whipped."

"No accounting for taste," Crozier said. "So what is your taste, Lord Alexander? What particular orders do you want to take? What is it you'd like to be made to do?"

Alec shut his eyes. He heard the soft sound of Crozier rising from his chair, sensed movement, felt a hand close gently on his chin.

"I asked you a question," Crozier said. "Answer me. Do you want to be told what to do—in the right circumstances?"

Alec's breathing rasped in his own ears. He wanted to say something, something clever or defiant, to push Crozier's hand away and tell him he was entirely wrong. It would be so much easier if he was wrong.

"I think Lord Alexander is looking to surrender himself," Crozier said softly. "That can go bad easily." Alec wasn't aware he'd reacted to that, but he felt Crozier's fingers tighten slightly all the same. "And, I suspect, did. What are you thinking of?"

"There was a man." Alec didn't open his eyes. The room was warm; Crozier's fingers were firm but not tight. He'd never told anyone this; there was nobody he could tell for the shame of it. Nobody except this stranger-friend, this openly dishonest man who demanded the truth, and now the words came with surprising ease. "I wanted—oh, just to have him do it. Up against a wall. I didn't need him to care for what I wanted; I just wanted him to have his way, you see. And I said that, and when he was done he, uh, he pulled me round and spat in my face. So when you ask what I want—"

"I see," Crozier said. "Christ. Good Lord, there are some cunts in this world."

Alec's eyes snapped open. Crozier released his face and propped his backside on the arm of the chair. "Do you know this fellow's name?"

Alec shook his head. "He was just a man. Someone I met in a public house. I suppose I—"

"Don't finish that sentence," Crozier warned him. "Unless you were going to say 'shouldn't have kicked him in the balls till he passed out', and even then I'd disagree. Well. That sounds a very discouraging experience."

Alec attempted a smile. "You might say so."

"Extraordinary. Here I am, entirely consumed by thoughts of pushing you up against a wall myself, biting your lovely neck and hearing you gasp as I have my way with that delectable arse, and you tell me about this mannerless tosspot. I'm offended."

Alec stared up, speechless. Crozier brushed a strand of hair over his ear, a touch so gentle that Alec shivered. "If you want to be used, Lord Alexander, you have no idea how I should enjoy using you. And I don't spoil my tools."

Oh God. Alec's throat was closing, and the blood was rushing away from his head. Crozier's smile crooked at his silence. "I did say *if.*" He was so close Alec could feel his heat. They hadn't kissed; they hadn't even touched. "Explain it to me. The heart of it, the thing you need. Not to be hurt, I grasp that, and not to be treated with contempt. So what is it that's making your breath short and your eyes so deliciously dark at this moment? What is it you want?"

"I don't know. I can't say."

"Lord Alexander?" Crozier took his chin again, fingers a little harder this time. "I want you to explain. I don't care how little you want to. You *will* tell me."

Alec swallowed. The room felt unbearably hot and close. "Not to—not to have a choice, I suppose."

Crozier gave a slow nod. "To say no and be overruled, powerless in a ravisher's hands? Is that your pleasure?"

"No. No, that's not—I don't—"

"Spit it out," Crozier said softly. "And don't shut your eyes. Look at me."

Alec clenched his hands, making himself get the words out. "It's not that I want to be forced to anything. I just want someone else in charge. That's all."

"Ah." It was a breath. "Not someone cruel, or careless. Just someone to take the burden of choice and responsibility and decision from you."

"Yes. Yes, that's it." It sounded extraordinarily simple, put that way, or extraordinarily foolish. "I dare say that's contemptible."

"You say wrong," Crozier told him. "A pliable, obedient young nobleman doing my bidding is the best idea I've heard in months. If you *wanted* to pant and beg and spend at my command, of course."

"Oh God."

Crozier's fingers released Alec's chin, skimmed down his throat. "You understand that I'm not a good man, don't you?"

"Yes."

"And yet you'd put yourself in my hands anyway." It wasn't exactly a question; it wasn't quite a statement either.

"Yes," Alec said anyway. It was what he wanted and Crozier had stripped it bare for them both.

"Entirely in my hands. Which is quite appropriate, since these hands steal jewels." He ran his fingers up Alec's neck, stroking the skin against the grain of stubble. "Such a pretty thing. Are you hard?"

Alec nodded. Crozier's fingers tightened a fraction. "I like words, Lord Alexander. If I ask you a question, I expect an answer. Are you hard?"

"Yes."

"Because?"

"You. You're making me hard."

Crozier rose, without letting go of Alec's neck, manoeuvring himself round so he leaned over the back of the chair. "Unbutton yourself."

Alec reached for his waistband. His fingers were shaking. Crozier said, "Slowly. No. Slower."

One button. A second, a third. Alec had kept his evening dress for longer than a man of wealth would; he was glad that it wasn't fashionably and tightly cut. He loosened his drawers, couldn't help inhaling as his fingers bumped his own prick.

"Take it out," Crozier said from over him. His hand encompassed Alec's throat, pushing back slightly, just enough to be not quite comfortable. "And take hold of it. Don't move."

Alec swallowed, his throat working against Crozier's fingers, his prick swollen against his own, throbbing for attention. Crozier gave a soft hiss. "Beautiful. You'll do what I tell you."

"Yes."

"Let's see you play with it. Slowly, now. Slide your fingers, up and down. Move your fingers round, I want to watch you." Alec adjusted his grip, dreamlike. "You're going to bring yourself off, very slowly, while I watch. I want to see you, and I want to hear you."

Alec groaned low, the sound vibrating in his throat and against Crozier's palm. He felt movement as Crozier leaned close.

"Rubbing yourself off in full evening dress, on the orders of a man whose face you can't see. There's a position to be in, Lord Alexander. Spread your legs wider. And slow down. I'm going to take my time."

"Are you—" Alec began, and clamped his lips shut.

"I said I want to hear you. Do you want to know if I'm bringing myself off while I watch you?"

"Well. Yes."

"No." Crozier sounded amused. "Tempting though it is. No, I think, when I next spend, it will be with you splayed before me and crying my name."

"Oh God."

"If you prefer, but Jerry will do."

Alec almost laughed, breath hiccupping. Crozier's hand was moving now, an undulating pressure on his throat, pulsing in time with the strokes of his own hand. "Yes, I'm looking forward to making use of you. Pressing you up against a wall or pushing you down onto a bed. Both, possibly. You don't like to talk when you fuck, do you?"

Alec shook his head, a tiny movement.

"I'll wager you moan, though. I'm quite sure you moan and whimper and writhe while a man has his way with you. Christ, I want to use your body till I'm sated and you're sobbing. Faster, now. I want you to spend knowing I'm going to fuck you, and how hard, and to think about spreading your legs when I tell you to—"

"Jesus!" Alec said, and then he was coming, prick pulsing in his fingers, Crozier's hand pushing brutally hard against his throat so that his head was held back as his hips jerked helplessly. Imprisoned, and coming for his gaoler. He gasped and spasmed, shuddering in relief, and Crozier's grip relaxed.

"Christ," he said, sounding almost a little shaky. "Well."

Alec licked his lips. He'd managed not to spend on his black trousers, thank heavens, but his hand was sticky. Crozier's arm came over the chair, holding out a handkerchief.

"Thanks," Alec managed.

"My pleasure. In every possible sense. Did I gauge that correctly?"

Alec nodded, concentrating on cleaning himself up, not sure he could look round. "Yes. Very much."

"Good. Excellent," Crozier said. "In that case, I will see you in, shall we say two days?"

Alec jerked round in the chair. Crozier was still leaning on the high back. He wore his usual mildly amused expression, except that his pupils were wide, his lips reddened and slightly parted. "But— Aren't you going to—"

Crozier extended one arm and touched his finger to Alec's lips, as a nursemaid would a child who needed silencing. "Who gives the orders here, Lord Alexander?"

It sent a shudder through him. "You," he said, against the pressure of the finger.

"If I want to fuck you, I'll tell you so. Or I'll just do it. Push you up against the wall without a word, shove your trousers down and have you in silence, without troubling to discuss the matter. I wonder if you'd come harder that way."

"I don't know," Alec whispered, feeling the pressure against his lips. *Please do that. Please.*

Crozier held his gaze for a moment longer, then stepped away. "We may find out, sooner or later. So we both know where we stand, I'm not going to seek permission, but I will take refusal." Alec nodded, but apparently that wasn't enough, because Crozier's eyes narrowed. "I'm not sure you're listening, Lord Alexander. If something is not to your liking you *will* say so. I don't take pleasure in inflicting unwanted suffering. Unlike wanted suffering, which I can do all day. Got it?"

"Yes. I'll say."

"Good. After all, I can be *so* much worse if I can push to the edges of your pleasures."

Alec gave him a look. "Is that intended to be an inducement?"

Crozier grinned evilly. "You tell me. Very well. I shall seek theatre tickets."

"You'll what?"

"Theatre. We discussed it at dinner, remember? I'm tempted to suggest the touring production of *Jekyll and Hyde*. It's well done, and seems somehow appropriate. I'd be happy to see that again."

"I've heard it's very good." Apparently they really weren't fucking any more. Alec got up, straightening his clothing, legs a little uncertain under him. "I'd like to see it."

"You'll receive instructions. If you haven't heard from your father by then, we will consult on next steps."

"Right. Yes."

"You look blank."

"I'm finding it quite hard to keep track," Alec said, with some understatement. "You know, being Second Villain to a jewel thief, and trying to manage my family situation, and having you do, er, what you just did, and then back to jewel theft. It's a bit confusing."

"I see no reason the duties of Second Villain shouldn't include being First Villain's helpless sexual plaything. It would make the melodramas a great deal more entertaining. Follow my lead, do as directed, and leave the rest to me."

Alec could almost feel the weight slipping from his shoulders. It was an appalling temptation. Crozier was a bad man; he'd made a point of that himself. Bad, highly competent, very evidently someone who liked to be in charge of every possible element. And all Alec had to do was give up and let him take over.

"Good Lord, you look exhausted," Crozier said. "Let's get you a growler."

"I don't have the funds. And you can't keep paying for me."

"Oh, the Duke of Ilvar will be paying eventually. Don't worry about that. In fact, don't worry at all about any of it." He ran a finger gently down Alec's face, slid it under his jaw. "Everything is entirely under control."

Chapter Four

Alec did his best the next day. He tried to work. He tried not to listen for every knock at the door in case it was the postman bearing a letter from his father. He tried not to think of what would happen if his father rejected his overtures and he'd alienated his siblings in vain, and he tried particularly hard not to think about Crozier's promises to take care of it.

Everything is entirely under control. It was so tempting to believe him.

Alec had been seven when his mother died, quite old enough to be aware of the world fracturing around him. He'd been left in no doubt of the relative importance his father placed on his second wife and his offspring; he'd also been very thoroughly taught at school that the sins of the father were visited upon the children. Alec had been a pariah for years, the other boys gleefully repeating the things their parents said about the Duke of Ilvar and his new Duchess. If only they'd known.

Growing to manhood and carving out his own career hadn't brought any more certainty. It should have—and, Alec had sometimes thought in rebellious moments, it would have, if he'd cut himself off from his brother and sisters. If he was permitted to be plain Alec Pyne who earned his own living and mixed with journalists and artists and was of no interest to anyone... But he wasn't, because he was Lord Alexander and his behaviour reflected on his brother and sisters, clinging onto gentility by their fingertips.

Cara had once suggested Annabel might train as a copyist, a perfectly respectable occupation for a woman. Alec still winced at the memory of that argument, and George and Melissa's fury. They were the heirs to Ilvar; sooner or later Father would die, and George would be duke, and assuming Father hadn't ploughed every bit of his capital into jewels for the Duchess by then, they'd be able to take their place in society. But not, as George had pointed out, if his sister were a type-writer and his brother a newspaper drudge. They had to hold to their stations in life or they would be nothing. What sort of man would marry Lady Annabel Pyne-ffoulkes, with no portion to speak of, if he had to pluck her from an office?

Alec's descent to the industrious classes didn't reflect nearly so badly on the family as Annabel's would, but George had still been disappointed that Alec was working at all, and that, since he was working, he wasn't doing so in a bank or a stockbrokers' firm. That would have been a respectable occupation, where he could actually bring in enough money to make a difference or, even better, strike a bargain with a banker's daughter who would pay to become Lady Alexander. If only Alec had had the capacity.

It had added up to a wearyingly familiar sense of isolation even before his estrangement from his siblings. Cara had known him, but she was dead; George tried his best, but he'd never understand. Work had brought friendships as far as they went with people constantly scrabbling for the same jobs, but little else. It had come out very quickly that he was titled—one could hardly mix with people who worked on the papers and expect to keep that sort of secret—and his colleagues had generally lost interest in him when he'd refused to spill secrets of Society that he mostly didn't have. And his private life was, frankly, a blank. He'd had plenty of encounters, thanks to boyish good looks—he had a feeling that wouldn't be the case much longer, given his blond hair had started to grey and his wide blue eyes were acquiring crow's feet—but nothing that had lasted. Men didn't tend to seek him out twice; he was silent and passive to a fault in the bedroom and the kind of men who liked that in a partner had not so far proved to be men he wanted anything to do with.

The fact was, he reflected as he sketched the next day, sunlight streaming through the skylight and hot on his hand, he was lonely. He was neither fish nor fowl socially, he disappointed his family whatever he did, and though he had plenty of acquaintances, he had very few real friends. He'd never had those, because how could you make friends when you couldn't tell people the truth?

He'd told the truth—one truth—to Jerry Crozier and he wasn't quite sure why, except that he'd already put himself in the man's power so he could scarcely make matters worse. That, and there was something about Crozier's shameless confidence, the casual authority, that Alec wanted in his own soul. Wanted to have, wanted to be had by: he wasn't sure which.

He wished to God he could talk to someone about this, but there was nobody, and he wasn't sure what he'd say anyway. *This fellow told me to stroke myself off while he watched. No, that was all. No, he didn't touch me, except for his hand on my throat. Not like that, I could breathe, just holding me still. Yes, best fuck of my life. No, I can't name him. He'd be angry if I spoke about him in any way, and he frightens me a little bit.*

It was an uncomfortable thought. Crozier could be a charming companion and an intelligent listener, and he'd teased out precisely what Alec wanted so carefully and given—no, *offered*—it to him. And yet he was frightening; he took what he wanted and wasn't sorry, and when Alec had tried his patience too much, the look in his eyes had been genuinely alarming.

Alec had put himself in this dangerous man's hands anyway, and been promised that everything was under control, and the dreadful thing was, he believed it.

He didn't get a great deal done that day. The next day brought a rejection on the Shakespeare job, which was a blow, an acknowledgement of his submitted artwork for the fairytale book, and a stiff note from George requesting he reconsider his foolish actions and offering fifty pounds to meet his immediate obligations. Alec doubted Melissa would be happy if she heard about that, sent his brother an appreciative thought, and penned a brief, sulky note of refusal. There was no letter from his father.

What would, what *could* Crozier do if the Duke chose not to reply?

He'd find out soon, he decided, because the second post brought a ticket for *The Strange Case of Dr. Jekyll and Mr. Hyde* plus a scribbled note on Army and Navy Club notepaper:

Evening dress not required.
Call me Jerry.

The former was a relief, since he'd sent his one shirt for laundry; he wasn't entirely sure what to make of the latter. Jerry. It seemed uncomfortably intimate, but intimacy was the impression they were trying to give in public, and if one could toss oneself off at a man's command, one could surely use his first name.

He put on his better suit and the green waistcoat, spent too long prodding at his hair, and went out with a jangling combination of nerves and excitement, and a little pot of petroleum jelly in his pocket because one never knew.

Jerry was lounging outside the theatre when Alec arrived, chatting with the doorman. He straightened as Alec approached. He looked rather more clubbable today, in a smart check, like an ordinary sort of man about town. "And here he is. Good evening, Lord Alexander."

"Jerry, old fellow." Alec found he was smiling. "I hope I'm not late?"

"Not at all. Thanks for your advice, Drummond." He tipped the doorman, raised his hat in jovial manner, and led the way in.